# Branch Swung His Long, Muscular Legs Over the Side of the Mattress . . .

He came closer and closer, his intense gaze probing beneath her wrapper, claiming what she would not give without a struggle.

"I want you, Amanda," he said with dark flames of desire glowing in his eyes. "Bad enough to marry you . . ."

"You don't want me. You want the oil," she cried anxiously.

"You underestimate yourself," Branch negated softly . . .

Reaching out, he unfastened the sash at her waist, then slowly drew the wrapper down her trembling shoulders. His fingertips trailing lightly up her arms and the low words he spoke while combing his fingers through her unbound silken tresses lulled her into a kind of stupor. Soon she couldn't think of any reason to stop him . . .

Dear Reader,

We, the editors of Tapestry Romances, are committed to bringing you two outstanding original romantic historical novels each and every month.

From Kentucky in the 1850s to the court of Louis XIII, from the deck of a pirate ship within sight of Gibraltar to a mining camp high in the Sierra Nevadas, our heroines experience life and love, romance and adventure.

Our aim is to give you the kind of historical romances that you want to read. We would enjoy hearing your thoughts about this book and all future Tapestry Romances. Please write to us at the address below.

The Editors
Tapestry Romances
POCKET BOOKS
1230 Avenue of the Americas
Box TAP
New York, N.Y. 10020

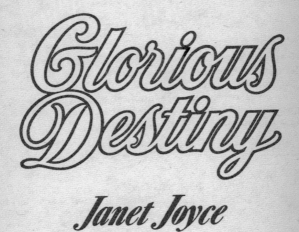

# Glorious Destiny

## Janet Joyce

**A TAPESTRY BOOK**
PUBLISHED BY POCKET BOOKS NEW YORK

**Books by Janet Joyce**

Fields of Promise
Glorious Destiny
Libertine Lady
Secrets of the Heart

Published by TAPESTRY BOOKS

An *Original* publication of TAPESTRY BOOKS

A Tapestry Book published by
POCKET BOOKS, a division of Simon & Schuster, Inc.
1230 Avenue of the Americas, New York, N.Y. 10020

ISBN: 0-671-52628-6

First Tapestry Books printing September, 1985

10 9 8 7 6 5 4 3 2 1

POCKET and colophon are registered trademarks of Simon & Schuster, Inc.

TAPESTRY is a registered trademark of Simon & Schuster, Inc.

Printed in the U.S.A.

*Dedicated to Linda Lael Miller,*
*a special friend who keeps us on our toes*
*and knows when to laugh*
*and when to cry.*

# Glorious Destiny

# Chapter One

*Texas 1903*

THE ROAD STRETCHED LIKE A DIRTY RIBBON across the rolling plains. Knotted clumps of scraggly grass and an occasional wildflower attested to the thoroughfare's lack of heavy use. The rutted track jolted the occupant of the Oldsmobile runabout as the merciless Texas heat blew against her veiled face.

Ignoring the blazing sun glinting off the shiny brass head lanterns, Amanda Hamilton gripped the steering tiller with both hands. All of her concentration was centered on controlling the chugging monster she drove with far more bravado than experience. Her blue eyes searched the horizon for some landmark that would tell her she was nearing her destination, but the grassy landscape was broken up only by thin lines of barbed wire that criss-crossed over the hills and the stark metal windmill standing off in the distance against the broad sky.

Bouncing down the next hill far faster than

1

good judgment dictated, Amanda spotted the wooden gate across the track ahead and let go of the tiller. "Oh no!" she shouted, bracing her feet against the curved dash as she reached for the brake. With her eyes squeezed tightly shut, she pulled with all her might, praying she wouldn't hear the sound of splintering wood.

The vehicle protested with a loud bang and a cough before dying with an agonized wheeze. Amanda opened her eyes. The front wheels of the runabout rested against the gate. The sun-bleached wood was in one piece, though it was rattling violently from the impact. Scooting her hat back into place, Amanda hopped down to the ground and approached the obstacle barring her way.

"Leave a gate open or shut, exactly as you find it." The stationmaster in Barrysville had shouted those last words of advice to her when she'd driven out of town. The man had been astounded to the point of speechlessness when he'd learned that the shiny, vapor-powered buggy that had been rolled off the train was going to be driven by the petite blond woman who stepped forward to pay for its freight. Recalling the man's gape-mouthed expression, Amanda couldn't suppress a grin.

Since he'd doubted that she did indeed know how to operate the "tomfool machine," as he'd called it, she'd been determined to prove herself. She'd directed the lashing of her trunk behind the single seat, then opened her remaining valise to extract the garments she would wear while she motored to her destination.

Pretending to ignore the curious stares of the

stationmaster and the small crowd that had gathered to watch, she had pulled on an ankle-length linen duster over her smart cream-colored suit and dropped a protective motoring veil over her stylish hat. Once she had secured the waist-length silk to the hat with several pins, she had pulled on the long leather gauntlets that would protect her small hands, walked calmly to the back of the automobile, and turned the crank. The nine-horsepower engine had sputtered to life immediately, much to Amanda's gratification and the stationmaster's surprise.

Still, the man couldn't have made his disapproval more plain if he'd come right out and told her that no mere female should attempt to motor any distance without a man along to assist her. If he had known anything at all about Amanda, he might not have made his feelings so blatant, for they only increased her desire to prove him wrong. With a serene expression of confidence on her face, Amanda had calmly tossed the valise to the floor of the automobile, climbed onto the seat, and put the vehicle into forward gear.

She'd kept her head erect as she drove away from the station, despite the loud eruptions from the motor and the clouds of black smoke that had followed her. The small crowd that had watched her small, straight-backed figure accelerate the vehicle to its top speed of twenty miles an hour had no idea that Amanda had been fervently praying that the automobile would at least continue running until she was out of their sight.

The vehicle had stalled only three times be-

tween the train depot and this gate, and
Amanda had gradually gained more confidence
in her driving ability. Facing the gate, she assumed her luck would hold and that the barrier
would swing open easily, allowing her to continue on her journey without any further difficulty.
However, the tight loop of rusty wire that kept
the gate firmly shut wouldn't budge. Removing
her gloves in hopes of getting a better grip on the
stiff wire, she pushed and tugged with her fingertips, but the wire wouldn't slide either up or
down the rough fencepost.

Amanda stepped back and lifted the veil away
from her face, hoping that a clear view of the
gate would help her find a solution. When, after
several moments of careful scrutiny, the problem remained, she stood back and frowned
through narrowed blue eyes, as if by sheer will
she might make the gate magically open. It
didn't. Hot and frustrated, she made a decision
she wouldn't otherwise have contemplated.

Although it was supposedly cow country, she
hadn't seen a sign of any animals and therefore
couldn't find much harm in breaking through
the gate that blocked her passage. She'd been
told that the dirt track was the only road leading
to the Box H ranch, and she wasn't about to turn
back when by her calculations she'd almost
reached her destination. She had come thou-
sands of miles to meet her aunt, Eleanora Hamilton, and she wasn't going to let a stubborn gate
stop her. The lady would just have to understand
why her niece had felt justified in breaking an
unwritten Texas law. After all, she'd only be
making a small hole in a barbed wire fence that

seemed miles long, disappearing over the hills without a break.

After turning the starting crank several times, Amanda was rewarded when the engine coughed back to life. She climbed back into the wheezing little car. Replacing her gloves, she released the hand brake and, as cautiously as possible, opened the throttle. A black cloud of oil rose up behind her, but that was all. The gears stubbornly refused to shift into forward. Furious, Amanda hit the control stick with her fist.

Like a battering ram through a fortress wall, the small automobile bolted through the splintering sections of wood, gave a loud choked cough, and then died. Amanda sat in shocked immobility until she regained enough composure to look behind her and survey the extent of the damage she'd just caused. The wooden gate had been divided completely in two, and the jagged slats were now lying in the dirt, a pile of splintered wood and rusty wire. Nervously, she scanned one side of the road and then the other, sighing with relief when there was still no sign of a single wandering animal that might charge through the large gap she'd just made.

Making up her mind to inform her aunt of the damage she'd done as quickly as possible, Amanda hopped down from the car and walked around to the boot. "I'm getting to be an expert at this," she muttered as she bent down to grasp the heavy metal crank that would restart the stalled engine.

"What in Sam Hill do you think you're doin', lady?" a deep-timbred voice roared angrily from behind her.

Startled, Amanda froze with her hand on the crank. She whirled around, backing up against the rear of the runabout as her frightened blue eyes took in the sight of a huge chestnut stallion prancing sideways in front of her. Tiny whirlwinds of dust churned up around the animal's white-stockinged legs as it sidled closer.

"Whoa, boy," its rider ordered, his low-pitched voice immediately calming the restless horse.

"I—I'm attempting to get my machine started," Amanda replied shakily, shading her eyes from the sun so she could get a better look at this rider who had come out of nowhere to catch her at the scene of her crime.

Sitting straight-backed and regal in the saddle, the man had one gloved hand on the horn, the other over the ivory handle of a gun protruding from a worn leather holster. Tall, long-limbed, and broad-shouldered, he was dressed in faded blue denim pants, sweat-dampened muslin shirt, and tan leather boots. A bright red bandanna was tied at a rakish angle around his neck. The strings of his dusty hat were fastened at the back of his head. He glared down at her from beneath the broad-brimmed hat as if he were some kind of feudal lord and she, an erring vassal.

"You bust that fence?" he demanded in a low, ominous tone that sent shivers down her spine. He pushed his hat up, and she encountered the full force of his gaze.

She'd never seen a more handsome man. His lean face was tanned by the harsh Texas sun. He had a straight, patrician nose, and there was a cleft in his otherwise square chin. But there was no hint of humor in his hard black eyes or the tight line of his full lips.

"Well—ah—I . . ." Flustered under the intense force of his autocratic gaze, Amanda searched for the words to rationalize her deed.

"If you knew how to control that silly-lookin' buggy, you wouldn't have made this mess." A long arm made a meaningful sweep to include the cut wire and broken wood of the ruined gate and the dangerous sag in the barbed wire for yards on either side.

"I had no other choice if I wanted to proceed. I believe this land is owned by my aunt—"

"There's where you're wrong, honey." The man rudely cut her off, taking off his hat and wiping his brow with the back of his gloved hand. The sun glinted off his black hair. "This is Colson land."

With a fluid grace, he swung one long leg over the back of his horse and dismounted, striding toward her with an angrily determined air that didn't suggest an understanding nature. It took all of Amanda's willpower to hold her ground at the approach of this imposing giant, but she did her best, lifting her small chin and taking a deep calming breath. "Then I'll be glad to make immediate restitution."

While over six feet of aggressive virility towered over her, she edged her way around to the side of the automobile, feeling very much like a frightened weasel slithering away from a snarling dog. "Let me get my purse."

Turning away from him, Amanda rose up on her toes and reached across the leather-upholstered seat. Her fingers were shaking as she fumbled for her purse. Keeping her back to him, she pulled off her gloves, tucked them under her arm, and nervously loosened the ties of her beaded bag. She felt the man's glittering black eyes on her every movement and quickly found her money, pulling out several bills.

Clutching them in her hand, she whirled around, the encompassing veil billowing and swirling about her slight body. "I—I don't know what it will cost to repair the damage, but I'll take your word for it," she managed stiffly, holding the bills out at arm's length.

More than anything, she wanted to be rid of the arrogant man, and her dismissive expression emphasized her feeling. When he made no move to reach for the money, she urged impatiently, "I would appreciate it if we could conclude this business in an expeditious manner."

"Expeditious manner?"

"That means quickly, sir, quickly." She waved the money in her hand and issued a firm order, assuming he was a ranch hand and was used to taking them. "Kindly accept this and be on your way."

"Whew!" An indefinable glint appeared for a moment in his eyes, then disappeared as he shook his head in disgust. "You sure are 'bout the greenist passle of sweet curves I've run across in quite a spell."

"I—I beg your pardon?"

His lazily slurred words were difficult for her to understand, much different from the sharp Eastern pronunciation she was used to. Nor did they seem quite natural to him. It was almost as if he were deliberately forcing the colorful dialect out from between his strong white teeth.

"If you haven't noticed, ma'am," he drawled, glancing over his shoulder, then pointing to her purse, "the two of us are all alone out here. What's to stop me from takin' every cent you've got in that frilly little doo-dad?"

Amanda's blue eyes went wide with astonishment, then immediately narrowed with suspicion. She hadn't lived twenty-two years without knowing a few things about men, and this one, although he appeared to be a bit slow-witted, didn't come across as a thief. "Scruples, sir. I'm sure you wouldn't stoop low enough to take advantage of a defenseless woman."

One slashing black brow arched in question. "Interestin' speculation to make on such short acquaintance. Besides, as far as I can tell, you may be smaller than a skittery bedbug, but you're not exactly what I'd call defenseless. A defenseless woman would've waited for a man to come along and open that fence for her, not mow it down with her fancy new machine."

Amanda supposed she should be grateful that he was acknowledging that the broken gate was not due to any lack of driving ability on her part, but even so his remarks were anything but complimentary. While she tried to decide if she should let his comparison of her to an obnoxious form of vermin go without comment, he rounded the car.

Leaning back against the engine casing, he folded his arms across his chest. He stretched his long legs out in front of him and began contemplating his boots. "'Course, money don't hardly mean a thing when it comes to mendin' fences. It'll take a body hours to fix a break like that."

A teasing lilt crept into his low voice, and a sparkle of amusement shone in his dark eyes as he broke off the intense study of his boots and looked straight at her. "'Pears to me, since you broke it, you oughta be the one to fix it."

"Don't be ridiculous!" Amanda flared, infuriated by his steady gaze. She was feeling miserable enough already, and in her several layers of clothing she was growing more uncomfortable by the minute. She didn't want to waste any more time arguing with this boorish man. To control at least one of the long list of irritants that were presently assailing her, she grasped the veiling that had been continually brushing across her face and tied it securely beneath her chin.

Taking up an aggressive stance, she arched one well-defined brow as she glared up at him. "'Pears to me," she mimicked his slow drawl, "we're both wasting time better spent elsewhere. My Aunt Eleanora is expecting me." She spoke firmly, though the remark was not entirely true. She had notified her aunt that she would be coming but had not given a specific date. "I don't want her to start worrying."

Amanda again offered the money, giving the man a look that reflected her opinion that his intelligence was doubtful. "Don't cowboys get paid for looking after cows or something? Let's settle this right now so you can get back to your job and I can go about my business."

"You're not referring to Ellie Hamilton, are you?" he asked, pointedly ignoring the proffered money held inches from his face. His elocution was less drawled, his dark brows were raised in disbelief, and his stare was intimidating. Amanda was far too annoyed to notice this slight change in his speech pattern.

She dropped her outstretched arm but remained steadfast in her determination to settle this incident as quickly as possible. Unfortunately, the obtuse man leaning so indolently against her newly purchased Oldsmobile seemed more inclined to discuss her aunt.

"You're not kin to ol' guts and vinegar?"

"Eleanora Hamilton is my aunt, yes," Amanda admitted, annoyed by his colorful sobriquet for her elderly relative. Of course, she'd never met the lady but couldn't imagine that her father's sister, a woman nearly seventy years of age, deserved such an offensive label. "And I'll thank you not to vilify her in my presence," she informed him tartly.

The cowboy's loud chuckle split the morning silence as he heaved his tall body away from the car. He rose to his full height and looked down at her, amusement sparkling in his dark eyes. "Shoot, ma'am, you wouldn't be sayin' that if you'd ever met up with that fire-breathin' dragon. Besides, I wasn't castin' no *as-per-sions* on old Ellie. She's a mighty fine woman in her own way. We've been friends, of sorts, for years."

With an audacity that rendered her speechless, he pushed her hat off her head until it dangled behind her neck from the knotted veil. She was too startled to do anything when he

11

placed a gloved hand under her chin and forced her face up. As he insolently assessed her large blue eyes, pert up-tilted nose, and soft, generous mouth, his amusement increased. A dancing light flickered in his dark eyes. "Yep, could be some family resemblance."

"Well, of course there is!" Amanda exclaimed heatedly, attempting to pull her chin from his grasp. Her action was to no avail. His fingers tightened like a clamp. Stiffening her stance, she glared up into his face and announced, "She is my father's sister."

To her dismay, her emphatic words and plucky demeanor only widened his grin. "Let go of me at once," she commanded irately, but all he did was chuckle.

"In due time, honey," he drawled through flashing white teeth. "All in due time."

Slowly, keeping her trapped beneath the mesmerizing intensity of his hot obsidian eyes, he lifted a shiny silken strand of her pale blond hair. Tucking it behind one delicate, shell-like ear, he judged softly, "On closer inspection, you're not like Ellie at all. Nope. You're all peaches and cream, and she's gone a mite crusty. Why, she could eat you up and spit you back out without swallowing twice.

"If I were you, I'd high-tail it right back where you came from, honey. There's nothin' out here to interest a refined, citified lady like yourself, but I see plenty to interest a poor ol' cowpoke like me."

Amanda had been keeping her temper in check, but his arrogant perusal was too much. Without considering the consequences, she swung her arm and connected a stinging slap against his lean, beard-shadowed jaw, knocking his hand away from her chin in the process. "Let go of me, you big, dumb galoot!"

Instead of stepping away, he moved closer. One hand snaked out to grasp her about the waist. Since the top of her head barely reached his shoulder, she was given an unwanted close-up of his broad chest as he drew her toward him.

His soft, cream-colored shirt was stretched tightly, and Amanda could readily discern the dark configuration of chest hair covering the well-developed muscles that rippled with his every move. The heat of his body radiated from him in waves and seemed to surround her along with the heady mixture of scents that clung to him. Leather, tobacco, soap, and male sweat mingled together but entranced rather than repelled her.

At first, she was more terrified by the confusing sensations coursing through her body than by his reprisal. She squirmed against the steel grip that held her, but it had little effect. He promptly brought his free arm behind her back to join the first. "Wh—what are you going to do?" she breathed.

"I'm not so dumb I'd let a little hellcat like you get away without samplin' a bit of her fire." One gloved hand slid up her back and into her hair, roughly pulling her head back as he stared down into her pale face. "You can pay up for the fence and for hittin' me, honey, but it won't be with cash. I prefer a much more pleasurable swap."

His disturbing gaze lingered on her trembling mouth, then moved on to study the delicate line of her jaw, the graceful curve of her slender neck. Retracing the same visual path, his eyes came to a halt at her lips. "My, but you're a purty little thing."

Amanda's heart was pounding as strongly as an Indian war drum. "Don't . . . please," she begged, unsure if the plea was from fear of what he might do or fear of the insidious throbbing that was welling up inside her. His gaze was as possessive as the physical attack she knew would soon follow.

"You owe me, Peaches," he murmured in a velvety smooth voice, husky with male hunger.

With the swiftness of a striking rattler, his dark head claimed the petal-soft lips that had parted to voice another protest. He extracted payment in a way that seemed to drain every emotion in her. As his mouth moved over hers, he pulled her even closer, and Amanda felt the strength of his loins, the power in his arms and legs. His mouth branded, yet the burn did not cause pain but a flaming excitement.

Her struggles were useless, for he would not be denied until he was satisfied that he had taken all that was coming to him. The kiss was deep, soul-shattering, leaving her without any means of denying the instinctive response it inspired within her. His tongue fought for entrance into her vulnerable mouth, then conquered it with an expert demand that robbed her of all thoughts but of him. A black vortex appeared at the edges of her vision, and her legs went weak as she sagged against him. A soft moan rose from her throat just before he ended the searing kiss.

Male triumph was reflected in the deep grooves beside his mouth as he swung her off her feet and into his arms. "Let me help you, lil' lady," he drawled, his dark eyes glittering with the knowledge that he had made her respond and that she was aware of it. "You overpaid, and I'm purely grateful."

Audaciously, he reached over her shoulder for her hat and plopped it back on her head. "Can't have the sun burnin' holes in your purty skin."

As if she weighed nothing, he lifted her higher and plopped her into the open automobile. She landed ignominiously on the tufted leather seat. Her skirts and petticoats fluttered about her in frothy confusion, giving him a scandalous view of her silk-stockinged legs. Aware of his appreciative gaze, Amanda pushed at her skirts and scrambled for an upright position, humiliation bringing scarlet spots to both cheeks. Her embarrassment increased when she heard his rumbling laughter.

She stared straight ahead until the faint jingling of his spurs told her he had moved away. When she finally dared to glance over her shoulder, she was surprised to see him striding around to the boot of the vehicle. With a few effortless turns of one hard-muscled arm, he cranked the car's engine back to life. Still incapable of speech, Amanda watched as he whistled between his teeth and the huge chestnut came to his call.

In a quicksilver motion, he mounted the horse and then slapped his hat across one thigh before positioning the shading headgear over his thick black hair. "A little mite like you shouldn't be operatin' such a powerful machine, but you're almost to the Box H, Peaches, so I'll let you finish the trip by yourself."

His deep voice had no trouble carrying over the rumbling engine. Mocking black eyes laughed at her flustered efforts to gain control of the vibrating vehicle. Several loud explosions were emitted from the back, accompanied by the acrid scent of gasoline fumes and a large puff of black smoke. The spirited chestnut danced excitedly and reared up on its hind legs, pawing the air. Effortlessly, the man kept his seat in the saddle, and once the animal was calmed he tipped his hat to Amanda.

The runabout's engine settled down to a low chugging as the man drawled politely, "Be seein' you, ma'am." Drawing the leather reins through his hands, he turned his horse toward the hills, then loped away at a leisurely pace across the grassy plain.

"Not if I can help it!" Amanda called after him, but her furious cry was lost on the wind and buffeted back in her face.

Amanda jerked the runabout into its highest gear. With one hand on the throttle and one on the tiller, she accelerated until she was sure she was out of visual range of the dark-haired rider. Only then did she slow down.

Praying there would be no further mishaps, she continued on her journey. A strange sensation enveloped her when she drove through the final gate, one with a dangling sign declaring the property as the Box H—Hamilton land. She'd never been here before, but she felt as if she were coming home. Her lungs pulled in the clean, dry air, invigorating her body with each breath. Her eyes surveyed the endless, rolling landscape, loving the sensation of freedom it gave her, the beauty of green hills under a vast blue sky.

Here she would pursue her dreams unhampered by any restrictions. Here she would be taken seriously. She was a woman, but she would never be content to let a man take care of her, no matter what society dictated.

Fortunately, like his daughter, Benjamin Hamilton had believed that a woman was capable of achieving as much as any man. He'd taught his only child to love learning and to be independent, and he had fostered her determination to go after what she wanted no matter how high the obstacle. With his encouragement, she'd attended Cornell University and had graduated near the top of the class of 1902 with a degree in geology.

She'd managed to tackle successfully every mathematical problem and scientific experiment that was presented during her years in college. Refuting the opinions of many of her male counterparts, as well as the majority of her instructors who believed such complex pursuits were too much for the "weaker female brain," she had not lost her wits or gone insane. How they would laugh, however, if they knew that it had taken only one kiss from an insolent cowboy to render her completely mindless.

She could still feel the imprint of his hard muscles on her body, the steely strength in the arm he'd wrapped around her waist. Her lips still throbbed from his kiss. Furthermore, there was an ache in her lower regions that had nothing at all to do with the hours she'd spent bouncing on the automobile's seat.

"Beast," she labeled the man who'd aroused these heretofore unknown feelings. Yet he was the most exquisite example of manhood she'd ever encountered.

Primitive, arrogant, ill-mannered, and disrespectful—he was all those things and more, but *forgettable* was one adjective she could not honestly apply. As she completed the final leg of her journey, a dark-eyed, bronzed, lean face continually superimposed itself on the passing landscape.

# Chapter Two

"YOU TURN THAT MACHINE RIGHT 'ROUND, YOUNG woman, and go back where's you came from! I'd just as soon shoot you as look at you. You're trespassin'!"

Amanda stared wide-eyed at the figure holding a double-barreled shotgun. "Ah—I'm looking for Miss Eleanora Hamilton. I—I'm her niece, Amanda."

"Maybe so, maybe not," was the skeptical reply, but the shotgun was lowered fractionally as its owner stepped out from the shadows of the sagging veranda.

Amanda's accoster was dressed in clothing far too large for the frail figure beneath, but the voice was strong as it boomed across the patch of weed-choked grass that separated the porch from the dirt road. A wide-brimmed sombrero that had seen better days kept the person's face hidden from view. A faded blue jacket, rumpled and dusty, hung from straight but spare shoulders. Voluminous trousers of indistinct color and fabric were held up by a wide, very worn belt and tucked into dusty boots.

"You could be her, but a body cain't be too careful these days." The gun-toting figure came a little closer but retained a firm grip on the weapon. "You got any way of provin' you are who you claim?"

Amanda still couldn't see the face of her challenger, but she could almost feel the wary scrutiny she was under. Uncertain whether she was going to be believed, Amanda kept one hand on the tiller of her automobile and the other ready to throw the gears into reverse. "Please," she found herself begging for the second time that day. "That gun isn't necessary. I have a letter from Miss Hamilton. It's in my purse. If you care to see it, I'll find it for you."

Amanda started to reach for her purse but froze when she heard, "Keep your hands where they are so's I can see 'em."

"I—I was only going to get the letter. I'm sure once you read it you'll believe I'm Amanda Hamilton, Eleanora Hamilton's niece. My aunt didn't know I'd be coming today, as I was unable to apprise her of my exact date of arrival, but she is expecting me. If you would be so kind as to inform her that I'm here, I feel certain she will confirm my identity."

In her nervousness, Amanda was speaking far more rapidly than normal. She knew it, but she couldn't stop her babbling or the trembling in her hands and knees. In the space of one short hour, she'd been threatened twice. At least the arrogant cowboy had only wanted a kiss, a very small price compared to what she was presently facing.

The gun barrel lowered a notch. The sound of the safety catch clicking into place offered Amanda some assurance that she wasn't going to be shot immediately. "Might I show you the letter?" she ventured once more.

"Don't need to show me the letter. Just tell me what's in it and how you come to have it."

"My father, Benjamin Hamilton, was Miss Hamilton's brother." Amanda waited to see if this explanation was enough but received only a brief nod, which she interpreted as a sign that she should elaborate further. "Her letter is a response to the wire I sent informing her of my father's death along with a request that I might visit her. I've come all the way from New York City to meet her." All the while Amanda was talking, the gun-wielding person was advancing on the Oldsmobile. "I . . . really am her."

"It really *is* you, ain't it? Land sakes, child. You're a Hamilton, all right. Ain't no mistake about that. A body'd have to be blind not to recognize that yeller hair." The voice was no longer cold and threatening but the exact opposite as the person peered at her from beneath the concealment of the wide-brimmed hat.

"Don't that beat all? You're a regular lady, ain'tcha?" The shotgun was now directed straight down, dangling loosely within the grasp of a gnarled hand.

Feeling considerably more comfortable, Amanda loosened her grip on the gears but kept her hand in place on the tiller. It appeared that a fast getaway might no longer be necessary, but in light of all that had transpired since she'd arrived in Texas, Amanda was still unwilling to negate the possibility. Forcing herself to relax against the back of the seat, she returned her challenger's scrutiny.

Though the atmosphere between them was far less hostile, Amanda remained uneasy. "Is Miss Hamilton at home?" she asked tentatively.

"Sure is. Git down offen that blamed machine so's I can git a gander atcha. I'm the one you're lookin' for. I 'spect that makes me your Aunt Ellie."

The huge hat was swept away to reveal a lined, weather-beaten face. The elderly woman's white hair was piled haphazardly on top of her head, a bun of sorts leaning slightly off to one side with numerous wisps falling free from the pins. "So you're Ben's gal."

*Ol' guts and vinegar.* That was how the cowboy had described her aunt, and at the moment Amanda had to admit that his choice of words was probably more apt than any she might have used.

From Amanda's vantage point, she estimated the woman to be several inches taller than herself. Like her brother Benjamin, Eleanora Hamilton was an imposing figure, even when dressed in the voluminous garments that fit her about as well as those draped on a scarecrow. The woman had the same sparkling blue eyes that Benjamin Hamilton had had before illness and pain had dulled them.

Remembering the tall cowboy she'd encountered on the road, Amanda wondered if all Texans were alike—tall, lean, and tough as leather.

Her father had been like that, even though there had been such gentleness inside him.

Amanda turned off her sputtering engine and secured the brake before alighting from the vehicle. *Say something, you ninny*, she chastised herself as her feet touched the ground. Gaining time by slowly lifting the motoring veil away from her face, Amanda searched for the proper words to greet her only living relative. Then, not knowing what else to do, she nervously extended her hand. "Hello, Aunt Eleanora."

Her hand was ignored. Instead, the gun was dropped to the ground and Amanda was enveloped in a bear hug that threatened to crack her bones. Choking as much from lack of air as from her emotional reaction to the elderly woman's effusive greeting, Amanda tried to regain her breath. After the terse letter she'd received and the years of estrangement that had separated her father from his sister, she certainly hadn't expected this kind of welcome. "I . . . it's so good to be here and finally meet you."

The woman released her, wiped at her eyes with her shirt sleeve, then took a step back. "Honey, forgive me for such a mean greetin'. I sure didn't figger you'd be arrivin' so soon, and I never expected you to drive up in one of them newfangled machines. If I'da knowed you'd be here today, I wouldn't have met you with a gun, that's for sure. Gittin' jumpy and suspicious of everybody these days." She shook her head and clucked her tongue in self-derision.

"You must be wonderin' what the world's comin' to when your own kin greets you with a gun," she offered by way of apology, then abruptly changed the subject. "Not more'n a mite, are you? And here I was thinkin' you could be connected to them blamed Colsons. Don't that beat all?"

Slipping a thin arm around Amanda's waist, she started pulling her toward the house. "Ain't had visitors for so long, I'm forgettin' my manners. You come on in and get out of this gall-durned sun, and I'll get you somethin' to drink. A body could just dry up and blow away on a day like this."

A thoroughly perplexed Amanda was led up onto the shaky-looking veranda and into the large house as Eleanora Hamilton kept up a nonstop litany. It was as if the woman had been saving up words for months, possibly years. She asked questions and saw no need to wait for answers. Benjamin Hamilton had been such a quiet man; Amanda had mistakenly expected his sister to be the same. The loquacious woman had temporarily thrown her off-kilter. She was nothing like the reserved, refined woman Amanda had expected.

"You're Ben's gal, all right," Ellie rambled on. "Look just like Ida, God rest her soul. Did your pa tell you about our little sister, too? She weren't more'n 'bout ten when your pa left. You got that same yeller hair like she had and a sweet little face, too. You drive that crazy machine? Land sakes, you're a tiny little thing. Must take after your ma, but then Ida was on the small side, too, like our ma, your Grandma Hamilton."

Without pause, the woman continued, seemingly oblivious to Amanda's stuttered attempts

to respond. "Have any trouble finding this
spread? The dust must be coatin' yer insides as
well as the out, by the looks of you. Take off that
coat and hat before you swelter, and set yourself
down."

The last directive was accompanied by a firm
shove into a room that was probably the front
parlor. Then, without further ado, Amanda was
left to her own devices. With coat tails flapping,
Eleanora strode rapidly down the center hall.
Amanda could hear the heavy thumping of the
woman's boots as she headed somewhere toward the back of the house.

"Yes, I did drive, and no, I had no trouble,"
Amanda said to the empty room. Shaking her
befuddled head, she thought, *That is, if I don't
count breaking a fence, being kissed by a swag-
gering cowboy, and staring down the wrong
end of a shotgun barrel as trouble.* This meeting had been the oddest one she'd ever had, but
Amanda decided that her aunt must have her
reasons for being so leery of strangers.

After all, the ranch was isolated, and apparently there was no one else around. If her aunt
did employ some men to work the ranch, they
were probably far away from the house at this
time of day. A lone woman, up in years, might
seem like easy prey to all sorts of hoodlums. It
was the twentieth century, but from what
Amanda had seen of Texas thus far, the state
didn't seem all that civilized. Surely Indians
were no longer a problem, but perhaps there
were roving bands of thieves.

Amanda put those disturbing thoughts aside
as she reached for her hat and looked about for a

place to put it down. The room was so cluttered that she couldn't locate a single space that seemed able to hold one more object. Curiously, Amanda studied the scattered contents around her. So this was the house where her father had been born. She was anxious to investigate the rest of it, hoping to learn more about her father's childhood.

Remembering the line of coats she'd seen hanging in the hallway, Amanda retraced her steps and hung her hat on the only empty peg. As she unbuttoned her travel-stained duster, she could hear the clatter of glassware coming from what she surmised was the kitchen. Spying a cracked mirror, Amanda peered into the hazy glass in order to determine how disheveled she might be.

Unable to see herself, she was tempted to take out her handkerchief and wipe away some of the gathered grime on the mirror but then thought better of it. That surely would be an insult to her aunt's housekeeping, and she didn't want to do anything that might mar this first meeting. Far more than establishing a relationship with the woman was at stake here. Amanda wanted to do nothing that would diminish her chances of pursuing her main purpose in coming to Texas.

She contented herself with running a hand over her hair, checking for loose tendrils, and pinning them back into place. Returning to the parlor, she hesitated. Where was she supposed to "set herself down"? Every one of the chairs, as well as the long empire-styled divan, was littered with books, periodicals, and old newspapers.

Finally, she chose a dainty, carved mahogany chair and carefully cleared off the few books it held, placing them on the divan. She was perched precariously on the edge of the worn needlepoint seat when her aunt returned, bearing a wooden tray holding an earthenware pitcher and two heavy glass tumblers.

Seemingly oblivious to the unsteady surface, Eleanora set the tray down on an uneven stack of books that littered the top of a table. "My, my, my. Ben's little gal," she murmured as she poured some amber-colored beverage into the glasses and then handed one to Amanda. Unconcerned, she swept off a spot on the divan to make room for herself.

Amanda kept her distaste hidden as she took the filmy glass, wondering just when it had last been washed. She was indeed thirsty and tentatively took a sip of the liquid, discovering that it was heavily sweetened cold tea. "This is just what I needed," she pronounced politely, all the while wishing she could have a glass of pure water to weaken the cloying sweetness and better quench her thirst.

"Thought so," her aunt announced with a satisfied nod. A wide smile split across her tanned face. "Iced tea washes down the dust. Knowed you was a lady from the looks of you. I had to be crazy to think you was hooked up with them no-account Colsons."

Before Amanda could ask what her aunt had against her neighbors, Eleanora rambled on. "Smart, too. I could tell that from the fine letter you sent me a while back. 'Course, my brother wouldn't have raised up no molasses brain." She drained her glass of tea and immediately poured herself another.

"You here to stay, aren't you, gal?" Eleanora's abrupt changes of subject continually threw Amanda off-balance.

"Ah . . . ," she stammered, unwilling to reveal immediately that her reason for coming had not been solely to establish familial contact and possibly mend the breach that had existed between her late father and his sister since The War Between the States. "I don't have any definite plans, Aunt Eleanora."

"Call me Ellie. Everybody else does," the woman directed tartly. "Been so long, almost forget what my given name is. Prob'ly wouldn't answer to it no more. This is your place, too, gal, and with your pa gone and me gettin' on, it'll all be yours afore too long."

Ellie paused in her ramblings, a wistful look coming into her lined features and a hint of tears making her blue eyes appear unnaturally bright. "I cain't tell you, gal, how sorry I was to hear that your pa up and died without us seein' each other again. Ben and me let too many years of stubbornness keep us apart. The war's been over long enough. Ain't right for families to keep on fightin' betwixt theyselves.

"I blame myself for that. Cut him off, that's what I did, just 'cuz he fought with them Yankees. It's a sorrowful thing when a body's got to die to bring relations together. Didn't know what had happened to him 'til I got your letter. I fretted on that. Not knowin' 'bout your kin is a mighty bad thing."

Swiftly brightening, Ellie smiled and patted

Amanda's knee. "But what's done is done. The important thing is we finally found out about each other, and you're just where's you oughter be. Right here with your only kin. Ain't such a bad place to have. No, a body could be in lot worse straights than to have a spread like this to call home."

Amanda was feeling more and more guilty about her reasons for coming. Her aunt seemed so genuinely delighted to see her, as if her being here could somehow erase the years of lonely, bitter estrangement. Feeling an instant affection for the elderly woman, Amanda decided that other topics of conversation could wait until later. It would be cruel to discuss her plans now, but it seemed equally cruel to give her aunt the false hope that she intended to stay on permanently.

"Ah, Aunt Ellie, I wouldn't want to impose on you. I'm not quite sure of the future, and—"

"Ain't no imposition. This here's your home as much as it's mine," Ellie proclaimed loudly. "Didn't Ben tell you this place was still part his? Once Ida went to her reward, it belonged to your pa and me. Share in it equally. That's what our folks wanted, and now Ben's share's passed on to you. He must've wanted you to have it since he finally told you about me and the Box H afore he died. I 'spect Ben wanted you to come make your home with me iffen they's nobody else."

"Ah . . . yes. He did want me to come here, Aunt Ellie," Amanda agreed uncomfortably. Her father *had* wanted her to come. He'd wanted her to meet his sister, but he'd also encouraged her to come to Texas for another reason. He'd told her about the pools of smelly black sludge that were common to the Box H and had suggested that she drill for the oil that lay beneath the surface of the earth.

"'Bout time the next generation of Hamiltons took over. I've just been holdin' on to it, hopin' there'd be one that'd really care about this place, and now here you are. 'Sides, where else you goin' to go? Ain't got no other kin, has you?"

"Well, no, but I'm not without some means," Amanda insisted, thinking of the inheritance her father had bequeathed to her, more than enough to satisfy her every whim. However, the life of a dilettante was not for her, and her father had known it; hence his deathbed insistence that she put her education to good use at the Box H. "Papa made sure I was well educated. He believed that was the best legacy he could leave me."

"Educated, you say? Well, we already got a schoolmarm, and by the looks of her she'll be one 'til she dies," Ellie deemed staunchly. "No man'd want a stick like her. Got some idea where you might use all your larnin'?"

It was a struggle to keep up with the woman, but Amanda did her best even if her reply was evasive. "Some, but after Papa got sick I set my vocation aside for a while."

Amanda was reluctant to reveal that she wouldn't have had a position to go to even if she had wanted to leave her father's bedside during his long illness. For the first few months after her graduation, she'd been unable to persuade any of the oil companies back East to employ her. However, when she had realized that her father's condition was hopeless, she'd been thankful she hadn't obtained a position and had therefore been able to share every day of his last months.

The conversation continued to center on Amanda's future, with Ellie insisting that she make "this here spread" her home. Amanda didn't disagree, but she didn't agree either, thinking it was no time to argue that her "larnin' " would be wasted out here on a Texas ranch unless she tried to drill for oil. She doubted that a degree in geology would be of any use in overseeing the workings of a cattle ranch, though she might use some of the engineering basics she'd learned to shore up the house and outbuildings. From what she'd seen when she'd driven up, the first strong wind could topple every one of the rickety structures.

Just before her attention had been diverted by a shotgun, she'd caught a glimpse of charred rubble that had probably once been a barn. After that, she'd had but a few seconds to take in the details of the other buildings before her aunt had hustled her inside the house.

The sprawling, two-story family dwelling with the wide gallery encircling the second floor was in sore need of repair. It had probably been a sparkling white, gracious home, much in the style of a Southern plantation house, at one time. Now, however, the siding was silvered by years of weathering without the protection of paint, the wood was warped, several window panes were missing, and the empty spaces were covered by a variety of makeshift materials.

Amanda was neither an architect nor a carpenter, but she began making a mental list of the things she thought needed to be done. If it turned out that the oil on the land was not sufficient to warrant drilling, at least she'd leave the ranch in better condition than she had found it. It was the least she could do for her aunt, who she feared was growing a bit senile.

Amanda's inheritance was considerable, and she could well afford to subsidize a few repairs. At the war's end, Benjamin Hamilton had been nearly penniless, but he had chosen to remain in the North. By holding down three jobs, he had managed to gather enough money together to become a member of the first class to enter Cornell when the new university had opened its doors in 1869. Through hard work and a natural ability for accounting and investments, he'd eventually become one of New York's most prominent bankers and had accumulated a fortune.

He'd left his daughter a large block of shares in his bank, and the dividends she received quarterly were exceedingly more than her needs required. They were also more than adequate to cover initial drilling operations.

Listening with only part of her mind as her aunt rattled on about the merits of the Box H, Amanda temporarily put aside her thoughts about oil and took inventory of her immediate surroundings. Beneath the clutter and thick accumulation of dust were many fine pieces of furniture. A good cleaning and polishing would do wonders for the room. Housekeeping wasn't one of Amanda's favorite pastimes, nor was she particularly skilled at it, but she felt a need to put the house in some kind of order. She was trying to think of an inoffensive way to volunteer her services when her aunt asked something that put Amanda on full alert.

"Can you handle a gun?"

"What?"

"I asked if you could handle a gun. When them rotten Colsons realize they ain't scared me off yet, they'll probably come a-shootin'. I don't have many men left here, so's we'll need every gun we can muster." Ellie's gregarious tone changed, the twinkling good humor replaced by bitter determination. "Now that I've got you to take this place over, they's even more reason to fight it out with 'em."

"Aunt Ellie," Amanda inserted a bit desperately. "What are you talking about? What's going on? Why do you think these Colsons would start shooting at us?"

Amanda hadn't intended to include herself in the fight, but Ellie assumed she had, and a smile of satisfaction settled across her lined face. "Knowed I could count on you, gal. You're a Hamilton, all right, and we'll see this thing through together."

"Well, of course, Aunt Ellie, but—"

"They thought they got me when they set the barn on fire with me in it, but I fooled 'em. I got out the back door and got the horses out too. Them cowards didn't stick around long enough to make sure they done the job right. Wouldn't have done 'em any good to have killed me anyhow. They'd still have you to contend with.

"No sir. As long as there's one of us left, them Colsons won't get this land for a good long time, maybe never." Ellie looked across the littered space toward her niece. The twinkle returned to her blue eyes. "You come just in time, gal, and I'm purely grateful to the Almighty for bringin' you."

Amanda had the sudden feeling that she might have been better off not to have made the trip at all. However, whether it was out of family pride or stubbornness, she was determined to stand by her aunt if the woman truly was in some kind of danger. Benjamin Hamilton had raised his daughter to be a lady but not a coward.

Along with that, he'd instilled another philosophy, a philosophy of thoughtful caution. Gather all the facts, study them carefully, make a decision, and then stand by it. Her father had lived his life that way, and so did his daughter.

"Start from the beginning, Aunt Ellie. Why do you think the Colsons want your land? From what I saw on my trip from Barrysville, they have quite enough of their own. I want to know what's going on."

Draining her glass, Ellie studied her niece. "You sound just like your pa, and his afore him." She gazed off as if remembering something from the past.

"They was always ones to think before they leaped," she remarked, more to herself than to Amanda. "Glad to see that finally comin' out in a Hamilton woman. Yes sir, mighty glad. If I'd been more like you . . ."

Ellie's dreamy expression faded, and her sharp gaze returned. She reached across to Amanda's hands and patted them. "It's a long story, honey. Goes back to my father, your grandpa, and that scalawag Hamish Colson, Big John Colson's grandpa. It's Big John what owns the Circle C, now, and a meaner critter you're never likely to meet."

Ellie got to her feet and hitched up the belt that was wound around her thin waist. "Ain't no use goin' into it right now. Leastwise, nothin' more's likely to happen for a few days. I'll tell you all about the feud over supper. It'd be a waste of daylight to get started on it now. I'd best be gittin' outside and see that my men been doin' what they's been told."

She strode briskly toward the hallway, her quick, sure step belying her years. "I'll send one of 'em up to the house to carry in that trunk I seen strapped to your machine. You can have any room 'cept the one at the back on the ground floor. That one's mine. The whole upstairs is left. Take any room you like."

# Chapter Three

"AUNT ELLIE? WHAT PROOF DO YOU HAVE THAT it was a Colson who set your barn on fire or had anything whatsoever to do with all the other things that have happened?" Amanda's trembling hand lowered her cup, and it clattered against its saucer. Her aunt had resumed their earlier conversation during dinner, and by meal's end Amanda was thoroughly shaken by what she'd learned. According to Ellie, after years of feuding over the boundary of their connecting lands, years of ill feeling, the fight between the Hamiltons and the Colsons had recently escalated into violence.

"Saw one of 'em, that's how. As sure as I'm settin' here, it was one of those two young Colson pups," Ellie confirmed with a set look. "Couldn't've been Graham. He's the onliest one of Ida's boys that ever took to schoolin' and got some sense. Prob'ly the onliest one who'll ever amount to somethin'. He's a lawyer, and some folks say he's goin' to be a state senator or maybe even governor one day.

"Yep, fine gentleman is that Graham. Don't live on the Circle C like his no-account brothers. Got an office in Barrysville and had a house of his own built. You prob'ly seen it when you drove out of town. It's that big white one stuck up on a little hill. Got all kinds of fancy geegaws hangin' on the outside."

Amanda nodded, remembering the three-story Victorian house that had seemed so out of place at the edge of the small town.

"He still comes by to see me now and again. 'Course, his pa don't know it, and I doubt he brags on it to his snooty wife Opal. Don't know why he married that gal, but I don't have to live with her, and he seems happy enough." She set her thin mouth in a tight line as if to prevent herself from saying more.

Then, in an abrupt change of subject, Ellie went on. "Yep, had to be Reese or maybe Billy who tried to do me in. Those two are always in some kind of trouble. Have been ever since they was old enough to sit a horse by theyselves. Spend too much of their time drinkin' and chasin' women. Saw the straw-colored hair peepin' out from under the varmint's hat, I did."

Ellie filled Amanda's cup with strong coffee, not bothering to ask her niece if she wanted more of the thick black brew. "Ain't nobody else 'round these parts got hair like that. Only Hamiltons, God help us, and that's about all the two youngest boys inherited from my dear sister. Too young when she died to get the good lessons Ida would've taught 'em."

37

"But they're your nephews. They're my—"

"Don't matter none to the likes of them," Ellie went on in the same acerbic vein she'd adopted as soon as the subject of the Colsons had been brought up. "They's too much like their pa to pay any mind to the Hamilton blood flowin' in their veins.

"That John Colson took advantage of my sweet little Ida just hoping to git his hands on her share of the Box H," she said with a small break in her otherwise forceful tone. "But I fixed him. I bought Ida's share fair and square. Ida wanted the money to buy pretty clothes and such. Don't know what she did with all the rest, but it makes no never mind. Big John didn't get nary an inch of good Hamilton soil to call his own."

Turning her back on Amanda, Ellie placed the heavy coffee pot down on the stovetop. Shoulders slumped, she focused her gaze on the sooty wall behind the cookstove. In a voice so quiet that Amanda could barely hear her, she remarked, "Big John killed her just as sure as if he'd put a bullet in her. She wasn't strong enough for a man like him. I tried to tell her, but she was set on marryin' him. He didn't really love her, but he still wouldn't leave her alone. Broke her heart and then bred her right into the grave."

"Aunt Ellie?" Amanda asked gently after a moment's recovery from the shock of hearing such a bitter and painful story. "You said there were four Colson sons. What about your other nephew? Do you think he's in on this too?"

Ellie didn't answer immediately. Instead, she

started clearing the table, dropping the dishes on the washtable. Still not answering, she proceeded to dip water from a bucket into a large kettle. After she'd placed it on the stovetop, she returned to the soiled dishes and started scraping them. Just as Amanda was about to repeat her inquiry, Ellie spoke.

"That'd be Branch." Ellie paused, gave Amanda an intense look, and added, "He ain't no relation."

Her voice held none of the bitterness it had when she'd spoken of Reese and Billy. In its place was a kind of sadness, or was it resignation? Amanda wasn't sure, but she waited, sensing that Ellie was struggling with some strong and painful emotion as she scraped at a bar of brown soap with a knife.

"He's the oldest, older'n Graham by nigh on a year. Must make him close to thirty. Ida wasn't the only pretty young thing Big John took advantage of, but Ida was the only one that had someone to stand by her and force him to marry her. Branch's mama was all alone. Lord knows how many of Big John's bastards are probably spread around these parts, but Branch is the only one I know about for sure."

A low hum came from the kettle, and Amanda rose to lift it from the burner. Carrying it to the washtable, she poured hot water over the soap shavings Ellie had produced while she'd been talking. Ellie seemed not to notice that Amanda had taken over the dishwashing. She continued staring out of the window, her gaze fixed somewhere beyond the rolling hills.

Again, Amanda waited for her aunt to continue, concerned by the change that had come over her. The woman had been very forthcoming until mention of the fourth Colson son. Then each word had seemed to be forced.

"I always liked that boy, even when he started hounding me 'bout them mineral rights. He never took to his pa, and that was just fine by me. Caint see how he coulda done this, but looks like he's a party to the doin's since things started happenin' after I told him I didn't want no holes dug in my grazin' land. Guess he's got an eye out for hisself just like the others. 'Spect that's the Colson in him. Had to come out one day."

"He and his father don't get along?" Amanda asked, uneasy with Ellie's attitude toward drilling and the unsettling news that she was not the only person interested in obtaining mineral rights. If Ellie had already turned down this Branch Colson, for whom she had some affection, just how would Amanda, a heretofore unknown relative, fare when making the same request? Though half of the Box H might rightfully belong to Amanda, the mineral rights were held jointly, and she couldn't begin operations without Ellie's approval. Still, even if Ellie felt drilling would ruin the land, considering the apparent poor state of the Box H, the wealth to be gained should convince her aunt that it was a worthwhile endeavor.

"Why, Big John didn't even know about Branch 'til the boy was half-growed," Ellie relayed. "He was down in Mexico all that time with his mama. I heared he laid into John something terrible when he was brung back

40

here to live. That little feller was almost half-starved, but he tried to kill Big John with his own knife. Woulda liked to seen that, that's for sure."

Her gaze swung back to Amanda, life returning to her eyes as she reached for a piece of cloth hanging on a nail and started wiping the dishes. A little smile played around the corners of her mouth.

"His ma was Nita Villanueva," Ellie announced. Her smile grew wider, adding light to her blue eyes. "Her people lived in these parts longer'n 'bout anybody, 'cept maybe the Injuns. If they'd known Big John had his eyes set on Nita, they'd have taken a gun to him. They was nice folks, decent people. Lost most of their land after Texas won her independence from Mexico, but they was real aristocrats way back. Little Nita was the sweetest little gal you ever did see. There's a lot of her in Branch."

With a return of her previous harshness, Ellie continued in a condemning tone, "Big John ruined her too. Poor little thing run off to old Mexico, she was so ashamed. Nobody 'round here knew what happened to her 'til Big John come riding up one day with that boy in tow. Never said how Nita went to her maker, but for once in his life John did right. He gave the boy his name and raised him along with the other boys. It sure was a blessing that Ida didn't live to have that shame brought down on her." Ellie set her mouth in a tight line, stacked the plates in a cupboard, and hung up her drying cloth.

"Branch is—" Ellie stopped midsentence and

shook her head. "He's nothin' like the others. He's just Branch, even if Big John makes him call hisself a Colson."

She paused consideringly, then revised, "Never thought I'd see the day, but it 'pears like he's finally revertin' to his pa's blood."

Amanda's head was spinning with all the information her aunt had imparted. She had three cousins, sons of a man her aunt despised, but they were her relatives all the same. Maybe, and it was a big maybe, her generation could come to some understanding, bring an end to the old feud, and avert a new one. She was not totally convinced that Ellie's condemnation of Reese or Billy was entirely fair. And then there was the other brother, Graham. Surely an educated man, an attorney, would be able to help her put an end to this feud—that is, if it really existed outside her aunt's vivid imagination.

As she stepped to the edge of the back porch to throw out the wash water, Amanda's mind was reeling. There had to be more to this entire affair than what she was hearing from Ellie. Her aunt had mentioned the mineral rights. Was Branch Colson trying to pressure Ellie into selling so he could buy up those rights? Or worse, was one of Ida's sons so impatient to inherit a share of the Box H that he was willing to kill for it?

"There's plenty more hot water for washing up if you've got a mind," Ellie directed as she disappeared down the hall. "Time for this old body to get itself to bed. You can do as you please, but I'll be servin' up some breakfast afore daylight. Night, Amanda, honey." A door clicked behind her, leaving a bewildered Amanda in the middle of the kitchen holding a metal washpan.

"Er . . . goodnight, Aunt Ellie," Amanda called down the hall. "That was certainly abrupt," she said softly to herself as she hung the pan on a hook beside the washtable. "I hadn't even started asking all the questions I want to have answered."

She thought longingly of the deep bathtub with hot and cold running water in the bathroom of the fashionable brownstone townhouse where she'd grown up. How nice it would be to have those facilities available to her now. She'd accumulated a layer of dust and grime from the top of her head to the tip of her toes during the course of the day. First had been the hours of driving down a dusty road and then the hours she'd spent cleaning the bedroom she'd selected for her own use.

It was a large, attractive room at the front of the house, with French doors opening onto the second-floor balcony, but it hadn't been occupied in years, according to one of the men who'd carried in her trunk. The closed shutters and stuffiness of the air had attested to the room's long disuse, but she hadn't cared. As far as she was concerned, it was one of the loveliest rooms to be had anywhere, even with the layer of dust that had covered the furnishings before Amanda had set to work.

As she stripped off her blouse and prepared to make do with a sponge bath, Amanda thought back on the afternoon with a smile. Not long after her aunt had left her alone in the house, a light tapping had sounded from the vicinity of the front door. Wearily, Amanda had risen from her chair and left the parlor to investigate. Just beyond the threshold were two stooped, elderly black men, shifting their feet in obvious unease.

"Miz Ellie said me an' Sam should tote your trunk whars you wants it."

Amanda thanked them, then proceeded down the porch steps and toward the Oldsmobile. After unstrapping her trunk and picking up her valise from behind the dash, she realized the men hadn't followed her. They remained on the porch, eyeing her vehicle with open suspicion.

Automobiles were certainly not a new invention, but Amanda had heard there were few to be had in the whole state of Texas. In fact, horse-drawn vehicles were still the most common form of conveyance throughout the entire country. She guessed the two men were frightened and feeling uncertain about what to do. Not wanting to offend their dignity, she behaved as if she hadn't noticed their hesitation.

"This is the trunk I'll be needing," she said breezily, patting the leather top as she passed by.

The men still hadn't moved by the time she reentered the house. Assuming the stairs were at the end of the long center hall, Amanda proceeded in that direction, pausing at each doorway she passed to peer into the rooms.

She found a large dining room, another small-er parlor, a library-study, a spacious kitchen, and a bedroom, each one as cluttered as the front parlor. By the looks of things, it was apparent that Aunt Ellie never threw anything away. If all the books stacked about the house were any indication, it also appeared she was quite a reader. That was at least one thing they had in common, Amanda thought as she mounted the stairs.

Halfway up the creaking steps, she heard the sound of footfalls crossing the veranda and smiled to herself. The men had evidently overcome their distrust of the automobile. Despite her weariness, Amanda giggled aloud as she continued up the wooden stairs. What would they have done if she'd driven one of the more powerful front-engine European models rather than the small Oldsmobile, which was more buggy than automobile?

The laugh would most certainly have been on her if they'd known just how hesitant she'd been the first time she'd taken control of her machine. One day, when she knew them better, she planned to confess her fears to them. She had taught herself to drive by memorizing all the information in the pamphlet that accompanied the Oldsmobile and then got her practical experience on the way out to the ranch.

She looked on the gasoline-powered machine as a symbol of the new century. Technology had exploded as the nineteenth century gave way to the twentieth, and as a modern woman she wanted to be a part of it. Driving an automobile was only the first in a long list of things she planned to try. Armed with the latest scientific information, Amanda enthusiastically embraced the new era, which she predicted would eventually change everyone's lives.

That was why she'd spent the past few years poring over books and spending hours in the laboratories of Cornell University. Fully coeducational since 1872, Cornell had provided her with the opportunity to study geology, a predominantly male field. She planned to pursue a career that would allow her, a woman, to do the same things men had been doing for generations, and her college education was going to make that possible.

Ezra Cornell, the founder of the Western Union Telegraph Company and a guiding force in the establishment of the university bearing his name, had been committed to the scheme of education that would allow anyone to study anything, and Amanda Hamilton had proved an excellent example of the soundness of his theory. Though, as the daughter of a prominent New York banker, it would have been more likely for her to attend a finishing school or one of the fine women's colleges like Smith, Vassar, or Mt. Holyoke, Amanda had enrolled at Cornell because of its tradition of emphasis on the applied sciences.

She'd raised more than one society matron's brow with that decision, but she'd remained steadfast. Besides having been one of Cornell's first graduates, her father had given her his full support. Neither one of them was the type to worry about what others thought. The only way to succeed was to follow one's heart.

Following her heart was why she chose the front bedroom, but she questioned the decision when she couldn't open the French doors. She asked the man called Sam for assistance, but he simply scratched his head after fumbling with the latches. "Stuck all right. Don' knows when Miz Ellie las' open 'em."

He stepped back and studied the problem with his soft brown eyes. "Don't know 'bout this. It's been a long time since they's been used. Prob'ly the las' time was when Miz Ida was still alive."

The other man had already opened one of the shuttered windows and was struggling with a second. "Shut yo'r mouth, Sam. Miz Amanda don't mind to know when they was las' open. She jist needs 'em open now." Turning to face Amanda, he nodded his head deferentially. "Sorry, Miz Amanda. Sometime ol' Sam's mind wanders. We'll get them doors open fer you somehow. Never you worry."

"Thank you, ah . . ." Amanda faltered, hoping the man would offer his name.

"Thurman, Missy. I'm powerful pleased you come, and if I can do anythin' else fer you, you jist holler out. Miz Ellie been needin' her kin fer a long time." Thurman cast a small smile toward Amanda, but his tone and fathomless brown eyes gave Amanda the impression he meant more by his words than that her aunt was lonely.

Nearly finished with her bath, Amanda now wished she had asked Thurman about this supposed feud with the Colsons. She'd almost done so, but at the last minute she had decided she should hear Ellie's side of the story first. Also, she'd been in a hurry to get settled in her new room.

After carefully drawing the sheets off the furniture, Amanda had been delighted to find a beautifully carved walnut bed, matching dresser, and washstand. A return to the kitchen and a long search had finally yielded the necessary bucket for water, the cleaning rags, and the mop she'd need to put the room in order. She'd left the large wardrobe that stood majestically against one wall of the room until last, fully expecting some creature to scurry out when she opened the door. None had, only the faint scent of camphor escaped.

Recalling the ribbon-tied bundles of letters and the small, intricately inlaid box that had rested in the bottom of the wardrobe, Amanda frowned, feeling a twinge of guilt. Curiosity had overcome her sense of propriety, and she'd withdrawn one of the bundles. The papers were yellowed and crisp with age, but she'd recognized her father's handwriting. Pushing aside any guilt she felt for invading her aunt's privacy, she'd slipped off the faded old ribbon and read the letter her father had sent his sisters more than forty years earlier.

It had been short, written just before Benjamin had gone into battle for the first time. He hadn't given his location but merely told his sisters that he loved them deeply and mourned their estrangement. He had hoped they would at least pray for his safety during the war. Tears had burned in Amanda's eyes as she read his parting words:

The image of your sweet faces and the memories of the love we have shared will give me the courage I need as I take up my weapon against men I do not know and for whom I truly bear no rancor. I continually pray to the Almighty that you will understand my need to fight for the preservation of the Union. Your loving brother, Benjamin.

Amanda wiped away the fresh tears that fell as she recalled the letter, then poured herself a glass of water. As the cool liquid trickled down her tightened throat, she thought how little her father had changed in the years since that letter had been written. He had been the most gentle of men, rarely speaking against anyone, and he had the well-deserved reputation of being honest and steadfast in both his business and personal dealings. Fiercely loyal to his convictions, Benjamin Hamilton had been tolerant of and patient with those of others, only expressing displeasure if a man's differing creed incorporated dishonesty.

Quickly draining the glass, Amanda refilled it and carried it with her as she made her way through the shadowed hallway toward the front of the house.

As she stepped out on the veranda, the most breathtaking sunset she'd ever seen was spreading its glory before her. The horizon was unbroken by anything but an occasional low tree and the gently rolling hills that lay like a smoky mauve carpet beneath the vibrant streaks of gold, red, and salmon from the setting sun. Treading carefully across the shaky boards, Amanda came to a stop at the edge of the porch and leaned against one of the pillars.

The fiery sun dipping slowly in the west seemed to take some of the day's heat with it. The wind had lessened to a gentle breeze as dusk settled over the land. Sounds were muffled. An occasional bawl from the cattle settling down for the night drifted over the hills. Crickets set up their chirping in the grasses, and fireflies flitted here and there in the gathering shadows beyond the ranch house.

The bunkhouse lights were still on, and Amanda could hear the sounds of men's voices, an occasional hearty laugh. The scent of woodsmoke mingling with that of seared meat drifted from the small summer cookhouse a few yards away from the men's sleeping quarters. Thurman served as the cook and had evidently prepared a meal for the hands at about the same time as Ellie had prepared one in the main house. Besides Sam and Thurman, three other men lived on the Box H full time, while a "drifter or two" stayed on a few months at a time. Amanda hadn't met them yet, but Ellie had told her about them.

There was Bob, who, like Sam and Thurman, had been on the ranch for years. He served as foreman. The two others, Jock and Banny, were general ranch hands. According to Ellie, they were the new men, but after a little bit of querying Amanda had learned that Jock and Banny had worked at the Box H for more than two decades. The "drifter or two" turned out to be two men, Smith and Frank, who showed up regularly year after year during branding time, when extra hands were needed. They were here now, and Amanda felt some security knowing that within shouting distance were seven men who must feel some sort of loyalty toward her aunt if they'd stayed on with her for so long.

Amanda had discovered that Ellie's sense of time could be divided into three eras: the days before Ida left the Box H, the ten years of her marriage, and the time since her death. It would seem that weeks, months, even years made little difference. Nothing changed at the Box H, at least nothing that made any difference to Ellie—until recently, that is, when a string of accidents and misfortunes had befallen the ranch and its crusty owner.

Amanda shuddered as she looked toward the pile of charred rubble that had once been the stable. The burning of the barn had been the latest "accident," one that had nearly cost Ellie her life. Ellie claimed that she had smelled kerosene and surmised that the structure had been surrounded by the volatile liquid before a lighted lantern was thrown in to ignite the blaze.

"The whole thing went up too fast," Ellie had said. "A building don't burn on all sides at once."

At first, Amanda had tried to come up with a feasible reason for the barn to have burned so quickly. She hadn't wanted to believe that the fire was deliberate. But too many other things had happened for it to be coincidental.

The first suspicious incident had involved a broken fence. A large number of cattle had either scattered themselves or been run off. That had been unfortunate and had resulted in a lot of wasted manhours to round them up. When they were found, several had consumed something Ellie called loco weed and had been crazed for days. This hadn't aroused any suspicion until Jock went out to repair the fence. The barbed wire hadn't rusted through as they had supposed. Jock swore that the wire had been cut.

Next came a poisoned watering hole. That couldn't be explained away at all. "No water that's been runnin' sweet for as long as there's been a Box H suddenly turns up sour," Ellie had declared as she pounded her gnarled fist against the table. "Tryin' to ruin me or run me off, that's all."

Luckily, the watering hole had been spring fed, and after the small pond had been thoroughly drained and a few weeks had gone by, the water had once again been safe. Unfortunately, before it had been discovered and fenced off, more than a dozen head of cattle had fallen dead around it. "Saw them buzzards circlin' one day, so ol' Bob went out to investigate. Figgered he'd find a stray calf or maybe a sick cow. Never seen the like, he said." The lopsided topknot of white hair on Ellie's head had slipped another inch as she shook her head, grimly recounting the details.

In response to Amanda's question about

whether the so-called accidents had been reported, Ellie had sighed resignedly. "T'weren't worth the trouble. They don't listen to an old woman like me. Prob'ly think I'm gettin' a mite tetched, that my brain's turned to cotton like my hair. More'n that, Big John's got the local law eatin' out of his pocket."

Amanda contemplated the implications of that statement as she sipped the rest of her water. What could be done about the situation if John Colson was free to operate above the law?

Amanda sat down on the edge of the porch. Propping her elbows on her knees, she studied the magnificent sunset with her eyes while her mind examined everything Ellie had relayed. Amanda was determined to drive into town and report the incidents to the authorities even though her aunt had declared, "Won't do no good. Sheriff Boyles will just smile and tip his hat, all polite like. Alst the while he'll be thinkin' how a purty little thing like you ought'n to put her mind on such things."

Again and again, Amanda replayed the evening's conversation in her mind. Overwhelmed both emotionally and physically by all the complex ramifications, she leaned her head against the rough pillar. She sat without moving for a long time.

The sunset was a faded memory, the horizon nearly pitch black, only a faint glow remaining from the sun. Stars were twinkling brightly in the cloudless black sky. Night was closing in, and it felt as dark and ominous as the sense of foreboding that settled over her. What would the next "accident" be? And when?

Realizing that soon there would be no light and that no lamps had been left on in the house, Amanda rose. Once inside, she fumbled around in the darkness until she nearly knocked a small lamp off a hall table. Fortunately, a box of sulphur matches was sitting beside the lamp, and Amanda was able to light the wick and replace the globe without mishap.

Her diminutive figure cast long shadows on the dusky walls as she crept quietly up the stairs toward her room. The bare floorboards creaked and groaned with each step, adding to the eerie atmosphere of the quiet old house. Amanda found her normally logical mind imagining that the house was talking to her, welcoming another generation to its sheltering bosom but also warning her of the future.

As she undressed by the light of the single lamp, she watched the play of her shadow against the wall. The black image was amazingly tall and stretched to the ceiling. It seemed to dominate the room. Would her presence here be able to exert as much influence? Would she be any more likely to get help from the sheriff than her crusty aunt? Without that kind of help, what could she do to prevent further harm from befalling the Box H and its owners?

She struck a threatening pose, watching the wall as her shadow loomed like a giant over the bed. She lifted both hands and shaped them into claws, giggling as her shadow became an attacking creature of the night. It was so realistic that a tremor of fear prickled the hairs on her neck.

*You're really tired if you can frighten your-*

*self with your own shadow,* Amanda admonished herself as she slipped a lace-edged cambric nightgown over her head. The cool sheets felt heavenly as she climbed into bed and relaxed in the softness of the mattress. *I'll gather more facts tomorrow, then take action,* was her last conscious thought.

# Chapter Four

"How long you expect this fool's errand to take you?" John Colson shouted down the length of the polished oak table as he reached for his cup of coffee.

Branch calmly took another bite of the thick slab of steak on his plate before answering. If the sarcastic question had been asked of him a few years ago, he would have taken instant offense, but ever since the riding accident that had broken his father's back and confined him to a wheelchair, he'd tempered his urge to retaliate in kind. "I imagine a week or two."

"Hmmph," was the disgruntled reply. "Don't take that long to get to Austin and back if you know what you're doin'."

Big John waited in vain for an explosion from the man who sat at the opposite end of the table. When it didn't come, he vented his frustration on his two youngest sons. "You two scallywags think you can run this ranch while Branch is gone, or you going to high-tail it into town every chance you get?"

He shoveled another bite of his breakfast into his mouth as he waited for an answer. When none came, he demanded, "Well, Billy? Reese? Here's your chance to prove me wrong, prove you're worth more than stud service for every female in the county."

Before they could answer, Branch replied for them. "They can handle the work. It'll give them a reason to stay out of trouble." Over the brim of his coffee cup, he fixed the two young men with a steady black stare. "Isn't that right, boys?"

Meeting Branch's gaze head-on with a green-eyed one of his own, Reese nodded his head in agreement, "Can't speak for little brother here," he drawled caustically. "But I think I can manage to keep the place standin' 'til you get back."

"Just tell us what needs lookin' after, and we'll see to it," Billy added, anxious to please his father and half-brother. "We can handle it."

Ignoring Big John's dubious frown, Branch decreed, "Then you'd best get on out there, boys. You know what needs to be done."

After Reese and Billy had left, there was no further conversation in the huge dining room of the Circle C's main house. Finally, Branch pushed his chair back, tossed a crumpled napkin onto the table, and favored the housekeeper who hovered nearby with a smile. "As delicious as ever, Lucía," he complimented her. "I'll miss your cookin' while I'm gone."

"Get on with you, Señor Branch," Lucía Montez replied, a smile breaking across her smooth face.

Lucía's round eyes were as dark as Branch's. Her hair, worn in a single braid coiled at her nape, was as shiny and black as it had been twenty years ago when she'd first come to work in the big stone house shortly after John's wife's death. At sixteen, she'd been hired to help care for the motherless Colson boys, but as they had grown beyond their need of her she'd gradually taken over the position of housekeeper.

"I packed some food for you. It's waiting in the kitchen next to your saddlebags," she explained as she refilled Big John's coffee cup from the gleaming silver pot that had been resting on the heavily carved sideboard.

Peering around her, John shouted to Branch's retreating figure. "You're wastin' your time, boy. A survey ain't gonna show enough oil to bother with, and even if it does no piece of paper is gonna make Ellie Hamilton change her mind. You know as well as I that she won't let a Colson touch that particular section of land. She's been fighting to keep us on this side of the Runyon River all her life and will look on this as one more attempt on our part to encroach on the boundary between our two places."

"She's got the deed, Big John, and she owns the rights," Branch replied heavily. "The woman may be stubborn, but she's not a fool. The Box H is losing more money every year. This could very well be her chance to keep the ranch going."

"Hmmph." John dismissed Branch's words with a wave of his hand. "Well, you'll not get any money from me to buy equipment. I'll not be a party to anything like what happened down in Beaumont. That's one thing me and Ellie see eye to eye on. I won't have half the country traipsing willy-nilly over my property. This is cattle country, and that's all it's ever going to be."

Branch's shoulders stiffened slightly, but his booted feet continued in the same rhythm as they carried him across the tiled floor.

Lucía waited until Branch was out of hearing before placing her hands on her comely hips and glaring down at Big John. "Why do you always make things so hard for him? You push him too hard and he'll leave you again. When you fell off that horse, he came back from the oil fields, but if he leaves here again he'll never come back."

John spat out, "He doesn't have the guts to leave again. He knows I'll cut him off without a cent."

"That's just self-pity talking, and we both know it," Lucía retorted.

Big John's expression softened as he looked up at her. "You and the boy are the only ones not afraid of me, aren't you?"

"Branch is not a boy, Señor John," Lucía reiterated firmly, not relaxing her pose. "And no, I'm not afraid of you, and neither is that one. He is a man of courage like his father."

Big John grinned, pleased by the compliment. His green eyes sparkled as he complained, "I should either fire you or marry you. Why haven't I?"

Lucía's dark eyes smouldered, but her answer to that oft-repeated question was always the same. "We both know why. You carry the love for another in your heart and always will."

Swiftly returning to the original subject of their conversation, she repeated, "Why do you treat such a one as Branch so badly?"

"I've had to be tough on him, Lucía," John said quietly, a granite hardness to his strong jaw. "I will not tolerate his pity. I must stay strong in his eyes. That is what has made him what he is and what he has to be." He pushed away from the table, the chair's wheels rolling just inches past Lucía's feet. "God knows, the rest of them are a sorry lot."

Taking up her position behind the wheelchair, Lucía pushed it out of the room and down the hall. "Señor Graham is a respected man. You should be proud of him," she reminded him gently.

"Hmmph," John snorted. "It's that wife of his that's got the ambition." He looked over his shoulder at Lucía and taunted her, "You tryin' to think of something good to say about Reese and Billy?"

Lucía's fathomless dark eyes never wavered as she met his gaze. "They are young," she commented. "Give them time. You never tried with them, and because of Branch they have never been given a chance to show what they can do."

"Branch was more of a man when I found him than those other ones'll ever be no matter how long I wait," John growled. "He might be carried away for a time with this foolish nonsense about oil, but he cares for this land in a way that can't be learned. He tries to deny it, but my blood runs hot in his veins and marks him as the one who will carry on here when I'm gone."

"Then why do you not tell him?" Lucía berated him gently. "Why do you only talk about what he does wrong?"

"I should fire you, Lucía." John repeated the old threat once more, but there was no anger in it. "A man shouldn't have to put up with all your lectures."

Lucía laughed softly. "You will not fire me. You need me, Señor. Just as you need your son."

Branch sat comfortably in the saddle though his spirited mount shook its head nervously, anxious to be moving on. "Ho, boy," Branch soothed the animal softly as he patted its sleek neck and ran his fingers through the long silky mane. The animal quieted after one more scornful shake and a low whicker.

From his vantage point on a high ridge, Branch could see the Box H buildings. His black brows knitted together in a frown when his gaze fell on the blackened rectangle where the barn had once been. "Cristos!" The sharp expletive was emitted through his teeth in a violent whisper. The chestnut stallion pranced sideways, then raised its forelegs into the air. Once again, Branch quieted the horse with a softly spoken command and a slight pull on the reins.

His dark eyes made a quick survey of the rest of the ranch's headquarters. Everything else seemed to be in order. All was the same except for the presence of the shiny new automobile parked in front of the house. The bright rays of the morning sun sparkled on the brass lamps attached to the front of the curved dash. A glimmer of humor sparkled in his black eyes as Branch studied the little runabout and remembered his encounter with its diminutive blond driver.

He had no doubt that she was a lady, a fine educated lady, but he'd run across enough so-called ladies in his life to know that their refined manner was only surface dressing. The woman he'd so blatantly taken advantage of might be all pink and soft on the outside, but there was a lot of fire on the inside. He was certain of it. Just before he'd released her from his arms, he'd felt it. She's got the Hamilton spunk, he thought, and the spirit of a blooded filly.

With a slight pull on one rein, he directed his horse down the narrow trail toward the house. He was going to find out what had happened to the barn. He also wanted to let Ellie know where he was going in case she wanted him to bring her something from the city. At least that's what he told himself. He didn't want to think about the possibility that the arrival of Ellie's new-found relative might create more problems for him.

Nor did this visit have anything to do with catching another look at her. She was not the kind of woman he was attracted to. She was too prissy, full of highfalutin airs, even if she did burn hot beneath that cool surface. A man would have to pretend to court her at least for a while in order to get anyplace, and that was far too much trouble when there were others who were always willing and eager to share his bed.

Studying the rubble where the stable had stood, he frowned again. He supposed there could have been some kind of accident, a stray spark from one of the men's smokes, an over-turned lantern, even lightning. Somehow he didn't think any of those were the cause. The structure was burned too thoroughly. Besides, there had been too many things happening at the Box H recently for him not to worry.

Skirting around the Oldsmobile, he chuckled as he remembered how the dainty blonde had sputtered when he'd dumped her back on the seat. He could almost see her booted feet and shapely legs waving amidst the sea of ruffled petticoats. The smile died when he saw Ellie step down the veranda steps.

"You ain't welcome here no more, Branch," she bellowed fiercely, waggling an old shotgun at him.

Branch remained on his horse. "What in Sam Hill happened to your barn?"

"Burned down, as any fool can see," Ellie replied, a disdainful crackle in her voice. "Shouldn't be no surprise to you, seein' as one of your brothers did it. I'da thought you'd have more sense than to show up here."

Branch hooked one long leg over the saddle horn and leaned back casually. "Got any proof? That's a pretty serious accusation, Miz Ellie."

"Saw the varmint. Had to be Reese or Billy."

Ellie took another step across the small yard. "Don't wanta have to shoot you, Branch, but I will if you don't skeedaddle off my property."

Seemingly unconcerned by the threat, Branch pushed his hat back from his face. "Those boys can get in a peck of trouble, that's for sure, but they don't go around destroyin' people's property."

"I tell ya, I seen 'em!" Ellie shouted, and she raised the butt of the gun to her shoulder. "Now, are you goin' to turn that fancy horse around, or do I have to put a hole in you?"

"You don't want to shoot me, Miz Ellie," Branch argued gently, his deep voice tinged with conciliation. A lazy smile widened his mouth. "Folks'll say you did it 'cause you didn't want to pay up all the money you owe me from losing at poker."

The barrel of the gun wavered, and Ellie lowered it from her shoulder. "Taught you too good, I guess," she remarked with a voice full of disgust. "Don't matter now. This ain't no game of cards, and your bluffs ain't goin' to work no more. You can sweet talk me 'til the cows come home, but I know what you're after. If I don't sign those papers over to you, you and your kin will get at 'em another way. Over my dead body!"

"Judas Priest, Ellie! That's a damned—"

"I taught you your manners, and just look how you talk to me! Cussin' and a-swearin'. You talk decent. You ain't too big for me to take a strap to you."

Branch drew in a long-suffering breath. "I just

stopped by to tell you I was riding to Austin. I'll be back with a geological surveyor, and then I can show you where we want to start drilling."

"You can lay out maps from now to Christmas and I'll say the same thing. It's a passle of nonsense, and it won't prove nothing 'cept what you Colsons want it to. No way will I turn any part of my property over to you. Not above or below ground. The lowlands of the river stay mine and mine alone. Now you git, Branch Colson, before I forget we was ever friends!"

A rustle from the shadows of the porch drew Branch's attention. A slow smile came over his face, and his dark eyes sparkled with humor as he lifted his hat. "Howdy, Peaches. See you made it all right."

The petite blonde moved down the steps to stand beside her aunt. In sharp contrast with Ellie's rough attire, her slender figure was dressed in a white, lace-trimmed lawn dress. She was an image of soft femininity that aroused all Branch's senses. However, she did not return his friendly greeting but gave her full attention to the gun in her aunt's hands.

Several minutes ago, Amanda had been completely startled when, midsentence, Ellie had grabbed up the gun resting in a corner of the kitchen and raced to the front of the house, dropping shells into the magazine as she went. Amanda had heard the sound of a horse's hooves but had assumed it was one of the hands. Her aunt's voice raised in anger had brought her to her feet and to the doorway, where she had hesitated for a moment, caution warning her to stay in the background until she was certain of what was going on.

It was the sight of the flashy chestnut stallion and the low, deep drawl of the man seated on it that had brought her off the porch. Indignation had straightened her spine when she'd heard Ellie call him Branch. The miserable lout who'd accosted her the day before had been none other than Branch Colson! No wonder he'd been so arrogant about the broken gate.

"Aunt Ellie, you can't take the law into your own hands," Amanda said firmly. She had her own reasons for disliking the tall, black-eyed cowboy sitting so smugly on his horse, but it wasn't enough to warrant shooting him. He might be arrogant, but she didn't believe he'd stoop to the attempted murder of an elderly woman.

"Please, put down the gun," she asked in a low, breathless voice as she placed a hand on her aunt's shoulder. "We'll let the proper authorities look into this matter."

"This ain't no Eastern city, child. We handle things different 'round here," Ellie snapped. She was no longer aiming the gun directly at Branch, but her bony finger was still curled around the trigger. Keeping her eyes fixed on Branch, Ellie asked, "How come he called you Peaches? You two meet up already?"

"Not exactly," Amanda hedged. As far as she was concerned, the incident on the road was better forgotten.

"You might say we ran into each other," Branch interposed, the grooves in his cheeks growing deeper. "Your niece had a little trouble with one of our gates."

Amanda felt the color rise from her neck to her cheeks as she shifted her feet self-consciously. She glared up at the handsome face smiling so audaciously, daring him to explain what else she'd run into besides his gate.

"It's as good as new now, Peaches," he remarked, his ebony eyes glinting with humor.

The richness of his drawling voice wafted around Amanda, making her remember every detail of their last meeting. While she struggled to keep the emotion out of her expression, his penetrating gaze centered on her mouth.

"I fixed it myself this morning, seein' how I'm the one that got paid. Right handsomely too."

Amanda tightened her fists at her side, wanting nothing more than to wipe the grin off his face. If she were a man . . . Her lips tingled with the remembered touch of his, and the sensation made her all the more angry. But she wasn't a man, she was a woman. Branch was a man, and each time he spoke, moved, or looked at her she was acutely aware of their contrasting genders.

"I certainly hope you fixed it properly so that the next traveler won't have to go to so much trouble to open it," she berated him, wishing some glib retort would spring to mind, but unfortunately it did not. All she could do was pretend she had been completely unaffected by his embrace. "If someone had done their job correctly the first time, it would have saved us both a lot of grief."

Branch touched the brim of his hat in a brief

salute. "Like I told you yesterday, there is a family resemblance."

A puzzled Ellie frowned at them both, then planted her feet more firmly and hefted the gun back to her shoulder. "Don't know what that's all about, but don't matter. You better git, Branch Colson. Sorry it's gotta be this way, boy, but I'm takin' no chances, not even with you. Amanda, see that bell over yonder on the post?" She nodded her head toward the corner of the yard. "Go ring it. The men'll come straightaways when they hear it and escort this Colson pup off Hamilton property."

The humor left Branch's eyes, and his mouth straightened into a grim line. Unhooking his leg from the saddle horn, he placed his booted foot back into the stirrup. "It'd take more than those old men you got workin' for you to throw me off if I don't want to go, Ellie."

His tone was smooth as silk, but Amanda heard the implied threat and fully believed he might not leave just to prove his point. She didn't move, comparing him to Ellie's hired hands and knowing what would happen if any one of them tried to force Branch off the ranch. "I don't think that will be necessary, Aunt Ellie. Mr. Colson is leaving."

"Am I now?"

The stubborn look that came over his face reminded Amanda of her aunt. And he said *she* was the one who resembled Ellie! "Yes, you are," she insisted stoutly. "There's been enough trouble."

"Go ring that there bell like I told you,

Amanda," Ellie said sharply, the harsh crackle returning to her voice. "I'll give you trouble, Branch Colson. More trouble than you've ever seen."

Amanda started toward the bell. From the sound of Ellie's voice, she was dangerously close to doing something rash, and maybe the hired hands could help defuse the situation. Branch's voice followed her, softly pleading his own defense as Amanda hurried across the yard.

"Aw, Miz Ellie, don't make such a fuss. I came by to see how you are and find out if you need anything before I left. I know you've taken some fool notion into your head that I'm tryin' to hornswoggle you, but you're all riled up over nothin'. Who're you goin' to get to play cards with you if you run me off? I'm your friend, Ellie. Say the word, and I'll bring you back some of that Frenchie perfume I got you last time I went to the capital. I know how you like it."

"Save your sweet-talkin' ways fer somebody who'd appreciate 'em," Ellie expounded, refusing to bend even a little. "I don't hold no truck with none of your clan. You're nothin' but a low-down snake, and I'm tellin' you for the last time to git!"

Amanda heard the jingle of spurs and bridle as she reached for the bell rope. She paused, assuming the summons would no longer be necessary. Ellie's last remark must have hit its mark, and Branch was going to leave without further incident.

A shot rang out. Amanda turned back in hor-

ror to see the startled expression on Branch's
face as he looked down at Ellie. His dark eyes
were wide, and his mouth gaped open. A second
later, he had no expression at all as he slumped
forward in the saddle, then slid off his horse to
the ground.

# Chapter Five

"OH NO!" AMANDA GASPED, TOO STUNNED TO move from her position by the bell. "Aunt Ellie, what have you done?"

"Ain't done nothin'," Ellie declared as she dropped the shotgun. "Confound it, gal! Don't just stand there. Git over here and help me."

Having delivered the terse directive, Ellie went down on her knees beside the fallen man. "Branch?" She slapped him lightly on the cheek. "You dead, boy?"

A strong sense of foreboding spread through Amanda's stomach, but she finally managed to spring into motion and race across the yard. "My God," she murmured fervently. "Oh my God! What are we going to do?"

"We're going to get him in the house, that's what," Ellie declared in a no-nonsense tone. "And we'd best be quick about it too. He's bleedin' like a stuck hog."

"He's not . . . he's not . . ."

Ellie shot an impatient look over her shoulder. "He's not dead yet, but if you just stand there like a consarned ninny, he soon will be."

A low groan from Branch confirmed Ellie's judgment and was the impetus Amanda needed to regain her equilibrium. She knelt down beside her aunt, ignoring the nervous prancing hooves of the chestnut stallion standing next to its fallen master. "We'll never lift him. I'll call for the men."

"I sent 'em all out this mornin'," Ellie said quickly. "Got tired of them hangin' 'round me all day. Sent 'em out to the north range."

Amanda's blue eyes widened. Ellie had known all along there was no assistance forthcoming from the ranch hands, even if Amanda had rung the bell. Is that why she'd shot Branch? Had he made some kind of threatening move that had frightened her aunt into taking such rash action?

"Put your mind at ease, gal," Ellie demanded sharply. She pulled off her shirt, revealing an amazingly frilly chemise. "Like I told you afore, I didn't do nothin'." Using her teeth, she ripped her shirt in two. "My gun ain't the one that done this. I would've only peppered him some with that ol' shotgun. By the looks of that hole, he's been hit with a rifle bullet. Back shot by some yellow-bellied bushwacker! Bullet went clean through him, thank the Lord."

With a strength that belied her years, she swiftly tore open the front of Branch's shirt. She folded a piece of her own torn shirt and placed it over his wound, then lifted his head. Pulling out on his collar, she crammed another piece of material down his back to where the bullet had entered.

"This ain't no time to ponder the wherefores," she said as she lowered Branch's head back to the ground, then tucked his shirt tails more tightly inside the waistband of his pants to secure the additional padding. "You take holta one arm, and I'll take the other. Betwixt us we'll drag him into the house."

Amanda's brain was reeling, but she immediately complied with Ellie's command. Even with Ellie's attempt to staunch the flow of blood, a fresh stain was already showing through the material of Branch's shirt, and it grew larger with each passing second. Beneath the bronzed skin, his face was drained of all color. His lips were white, his jaw slack.

Imitating her aunt's movements, Amanda positioned herself behind Branch's prone body. Working together, they pushed and shoved at his shoulders until they got him into a seated position. He was dead weight, and it took all of their strength to drag him a few feet. A harsh guttural moan ripped from his throat, chilling Amanda with the agony it conveyed. The pain they were inflicting by attempting to move him had brought him back to consciousness as well as increasing the bleeding.

"Hurts," he groaned.

Ellie let out a whoop that could only have been prompted by delight. She slapped the back of Branch's hand, not once but twice.

"Git on your feet, Branch Colson," Ellie prompted him fiercely, lowering his arm and going back to her knees beside him. "Or

Amanda here will think you're nothing but a spineless pantywaist. In these parts, a grown man that cain't handle a single bullet ain't worth a hoot nor a holler. Now you stand up and show her what you're made of."

For a moment, Amanda was certain that her aunt had gone insane. Only a madwoman would take pleasure in taunting a totally helpless man, but then she saw the deep concern in the woman's expression, the telltale moisture that shimmered in her eyes. Ellie shot Amanda an urgent look, then nodded her head at Branch. He struggled to move but promptly gave up the effort.

Hating the cruelty but seeing no other alternative, Amanda jibed scornfully, "He's not nearly as tough as he looks, Aunt Ellie." She went back down on her knees but kept hold of his arm. "I could tell that the first time I met him. He's nothing but talk. We'll just have to carry him ourselves."

Avoiding his wound, she pressed her hand below his shoulder blade, biting her lip as she felt the instantaneous constriction of his taut muscles. "Poor boy," she crooned softly.

A foul expletive was emitted from between his clenched teeth, but neither woman said a word as Branch fought to get to his feet. They did offer their assistance, however, trying to take most of his weight on themselves as they helped him to rise. When he was standing, they grabbed for his arms, draped them over their shoulders, and became his human crutches.

The next few minutes went by in a blur as the threesome stumbled toward the house. It seemed like forever, but they finally staggered up the veranda steps and pushed through the door. Off-balance, they lurched into the front hall. "My bedroom," Ellie wheezed, leaning forward to propel Branch's wobbly legs in the right direction.

Like three bumbling drunkards, they weaved down the hall. Reaching the doorway, they stumbled into the room just as Branch's strength gave out. He fell heavily but fortunately with enough momentum to carry him to the large four-poster. He landed face down, his upper body draped over the mattress, his lower legs and feet on the floor.

His arms were sprawled listlessly on each side of his head, and Amanda quickly ran to the other side of the bed. She grabbed hold of his wrists before his body could slither back off the mattress. Working together, she and Ellie tugged and pushed until they got him positioned fully on the bed, still face down.

Breathing hard, the two women stared at the motionless man, then back up into each other's eyes. "Like I said, the bullet went clean through," Ellie pronounced gruffly. "That's in his favor if it didn't hit any of his vitals or break any bones."

"How do we stop the bleeding?" Amanda asked, panic rapidly overtaking her. She hated not knowing what to do, hated feeling so helpless. She'd never seen so much blood. "We have to get a doctor."

"No time," Ellie pronounced once again. "It's up to us."

"But I don't know the first thing about treating a wound like that. He needs a surgeon,"

Amanda argued, even knowing that her aunt was right. In order to save Branch's life, they'd have to treat him themselves. The closest town was Barrysville, and that was almost fifty miles away. He'd die before they could get him there or bring back help.

Ellie rounded the bed and took hold of Amanda's hands. "You were raised in the city, gal, but out here women learn to do things for ourselves. I've doctored everything from snake bite to the grippe. I know what's called for here, but I'll need your help. I'm not askin' nothing from you I didn't ask of myself. Citified or no, you're a Hamilton, and now's your chance to prove you deserve to carry the name. Can you do it?"

"What do you want me to do?" Amanda asked, taking a deep fortifying breath.

"Help me roll him over."

Once that task was completed, both women were panting, but they still had much to do. "You don't know where anythin's kept, so I'll have to gather up what we need," Ellie declared breathlessly. "You get him out of that shirt whilst I'm gone. The wound won't be purty, but if you faint he's done for. I cain't handle him all by myself."

"I'm not the kind to faint, Aunt Ellie."

After a brief approving squeeze of Amanda's fingers, Ellie let go of her hands to dig into her back pockets. She pulled out a pocket knife. "Cut his shirt off with this."

As soon as Amanda had the blade in her hand, Ellie unbuckled the gunbelt at Branch's hips. After untying the leather strings at his thigh, she pulled the holster free and draped it over her shoulder. "I'll take his gun outta here in case he gets a mind to draw on me once he comes to."

At the door, she turned back and said, "Get goin', gal. We cain't waste any time."

Time—they were in for a fight against time. Anguish seared through Amanda as she leaned down and pulled Branch's blood-soaked shirt out of his pants. How much more blood could he lose before there was none left?

Her fingers shook as she opened the knife. She slit the shirt up the center of his back, terrified that her shaking hand would slip and she'd cut him. He never moved, not when she brought the knife down his sleeves, not when she tugged the sodden material out from beneath him, not when she lifted the soaked remnants of Ellie's shirt away from the double-sided wound. She quickly replaced the makeshift bandage. It was soaked through but better than nothing to stanch the flow of blood.

She had assured her aunt that she wouldn't faint, but the sight of the ugly hole in his chest, oozing blood, made her want to do exactly that. For a few seconds, she swayed, nausea rising in her throat, but then another feeling built up inside her, overriding her panic, overriding everything. She was a Hamilton, and she had never let fear keep her from facing a challenge. This man wasn't going to die, not if she had anything to say about it.

She had a general background in physics but had never thought she'd have to apply one of the basic principles to a human being. Still, there was no reason it shouldn't work. She had studied the effects of forces on the bodies on which they act, and she'd never encountered a better time to make use of that knowledge. Branch's enemy was gravity. The ruthless external magnet was stealing his blood. All she had to do to counteract it was exert an equal and opposite pressure.

"The resolution of force." With triumphant emphasis, she spoke the theory out loud but wasted no more precious time on thinking. She needed something hard and spotted a flat board propped against the wall. It appeared to be one of the slats from the bed. She didn't care what it was for, it fit her requirements.

She could feel the adrenalin pumping through her veins. She lifted the bedsheet with one hand and slid the plank underneath it until the edge was inserted beneath Branch's left shoulder. Using her knee as a fulcrum and the plank as a lever, she pushed until the solid wood was beneath both of Branch's shoulders.

That done, she hefted up her dress and climbed up on the bed. Seconds later, she was straddling Branch, her knees wedged in the space below his armpits. Without hesitation, she brought palm over palm, placed them on the bullet hole in Branch's shoulder, and bore down. She could feel the warm seepage between her fingers, but she couldn't see the scarlet trickles of blood, for her eyes were squeezed shut with exertion. She pressed down harder and harder until the sweat broke out on her forehead and her upper lip beaded with moisture.

"Land sakes, Amanda!" Ellie sputtered when, minutes later, she came back into the room. "What the devil are you doin'?"

"I'm stopping the bleeding," Amanda swiveled her head to face her aunt, her blue eyes lit up with inner satisfaction. She didn't see that Branch's eyes had fluttered open or the incredulous expression on his ashen face as she decreed happily, "This is working. I'll keep on with it until you're ready, Aunt Ellie."

"Never seen the like." Ellie shook her head, but there was no disapproval in her tone. "We're a pair, ain't we? You're doin' handstands on the poor man's chest, and I'm fixin' to pour a bottle of old rotgut whiskey into his wound. If he don't die, he ain't likely to forgive neither of us for quite a spell."

Branch felt as if his whole chest was burning, but the woman sitting on him showed no mercy. Using all the pressure at her command, she continued to bear down, her palms digging cruelly into his chest. She had to be some kind of female demon, for her hands were like fire branding him. If he didn't fight her off, he would wear the mark of her cruel fingers forever.

He could barely breathe. She was pushing the last air from his lungs. A red haze blurred his vision, clouding his mind, but his fevered brain developed a picture of her even with his eyes closed.

Her blue eyes glowed with a demonic gleam, her blood-red lips painted into a sadistic smile. The demented female was trying to kill him, to finish the job her maniacal aunt had left half done. He wasn't going to let her get away with this, he wasn't going to break under her torture. He'd see the filthy witch in hell first. Unfortunately, he couldn't seem to move. There was too much pain.

*"Vete al infierno! Bruja sucia!"* Branch's ferocious whisper took both women by surprise, but neither of them paused in what they were doing except to comment on his surprising return to consciousness.

Calling on the last vestige of his depleted strength, Branch arched his spine to buck her off, but she rode him back down to the mattress with the expert ease of an accomplished rider. He felt like a spirited stallion being broken to the bit as her sharp talons clutched the black mane of his hair and hard metal was jammed between his teeth.

"No," he moaned, chocking on the bitter liquid that trickled down his throat.

"One more spoonful, Branch," Ellie coaxed. "Then you won't be feelin' another thing for a spell."

Frantic, Branch twisted his head back and forth, but the female demon leaned forward and clamped her fingers over his nose. He could feel the congealed blood on her fingers as she robbed him of breath, and he opened his mouth for air. Instead, he got a second dose of the poison.

A short time later, the man on the bed was inert, oblivious to the activities going on around him. Ellie poured whiskey into his wound. Within moments, the liquid could be seen mixed with the blood and particles of flesh soaking the sheets under his back.

"He's still going to feel this, even with the laudanum we poured down him," Ellie said as she fastened ropes to his uninjured arm and both ankles and then secured them to the bed-posts. "Let's get it over with. I'll need you to press down on his good shoulder as best you can, but if he breaks free stand back. He's liable to knock you from here to kingdom come. I don't need two patients."

"Don't worry. I will," Amanda promised, gaining more respect for her aunt with every minute. The older woman was outwardly eccentric and cantankerous, but beneath it all she was very much a woman, with a woman's tender heart and emotions. It was readily apparent just how much Ellie cared for Branch Colson. It had been there in her eyes when she'd taunted him to get him to walk into the house, and it was there now in her slumped shoulders as she walked slowly across the room and bent down to pick up something protruding from the bucket of burning coals she'd carried in.

"I ain't never been so wrong," she muttered to herself as she reached for one of the long handles. "Now he's laid low by a bullet that was meant for me. I owe him."

"He'll be fine, Aunt Ellie," Amanda insisted, biting her lip to stifle her gasp as she saw the red-hot blade. Ellie's hand was shaking as badly as hers had when she'd used the knife to cut off Branch's shirt.

*Oh God!* she prayed. *Please let me have the stomach for this.* White-faced, but as determined as Ellie to see the grim task through, Amanda held Branch in place as the glowing blade was laid against the torn flesh at his shoulder. She swallowed the bile that rose in her throat when the room was filled with the stench of burned flesh.

The pain cut through the layers of unconsciousness that enveloped Branch, and his eyes opened. He fixed his tormenters with a sightless stare, then closed his eyes against the searing pain. He fought to escape from the torture, but even though the cords in his neck and arms stood out like iron bands he didn't have the strength to break his bonds.

Without exchanging a word, not even a look, for fear they'd lose their courage before finishing their gruesome task, Amanda and Ellie undid the ropes, then rolled Branch over onto his stomach. They repeated the same process on the point of entry, and this time Branch was too far under to do more than involuntarily arch his spine. He gave a muffled cry into the pillow, then his muscles went slack as the searing brand left its mark and the wound was closed.

"I'll get fresh bedding and more bandages," Ellie stated wearily, wiping her forehead with the back of her hand. "We'll truss him up so he cain't move, then prop the pillows so the pressure's off that shoulder. He looks worse'n he is with all that blood on him."

Suffering from the same kind of exhaustion, Amanda nodded but no longer needed to be told what else there was to be done. While her aunt was out of the room, she stripped Branch of his remaining clothes. Her hands were trembling, but she set to work. With the exception of his boots, everything was soaked with blood.

Another sort of trembling began in her legs as she reached for one of the clean white cloths on the nearby table and lowered it into a large basin of warm water. Up until this point, she hadn't really looked at him, but there was no longer any choice. To prevent infection, he had to be bathed. She chided herself for the prudish gratitude she felt that he was still stretched out face down, and for a little while she could postpone actually seeing what made a man so different from a woman.

While she was quite familiar with the various body parts, having studied the lifeless sketches in textbooks, she had never seen a naked man. But seeing and touching those same parts in a real man evoked an entirely different response from what she'd experienced in anatomy class.

Completely helpless and unaware of her, Branch was still an intimidating presence. Every inch of his naked body challenged her with its inherent strength and power. As she ran the cloth over his muscled back, blood pounded in her temples, matching the heat that flushed her cheeks a bright pink.

Branch Colson was magnificent! Beneath the layer of dried blood, his skin was polished bronze and, in those places where no hair grew, both supple and smooth. It was the same rich color from the nape of his neck to his waist.

From waist to ankle, he was a lighter shade but still tanned, indicating that he had spent some time outdoors wearing nothing at all. The image that brought to her mind brought a fresh spurt of color to her cheeks.

Attempting to clear her mind, she began washing the blood from his buttocks. She jerked back her hand, gasping when the twin muscles bunched in instinctive response to the cooling water that trickled down them. She quickened her pace, exchanging red cloths for clean ones as she finished washing his bloodied back and shoulders. Gently, she dabbed at the seared edges of the purple wound, careful not to hurt him more but knowing she could leave no residue of blood to fester the burn.

She didn't know what was keeping Ellie as she finished rinsing him. It would be twice as hard to roll Branch over onto his back without any assistance. Somehow she managed, but by the time he was sprawled face up she was breathing hard. She heard him mumble something and bent over him to catch the words, but again he spoke in a language she didn't understand.

After placing her hand on his forehead, she knew that he was slipping into the first stages of delirium. His skin was hot and dry, his lean cheeks as flushed as her own. She would have to work fast in case he started thrashing, aware of the tremendous power in his long arms and legs.

"Heated up some more water," Ellie said, startling Amanda as she carried two large buckets into the room. She left but came back immediately with a large empty basin. She set it down by Amanda's feet, then picked up the one on the table. "Cain't hardly stand to look at him like this," she declared sadly. "He's not the kind to depend on others, especially women. It's goin' to pain him to let us see to all his needs."

She gave a small chuckle as she walked back to the door. "That'll have him back on his feet in no time. I'm purely grateful he ain't goin' to be aware of it for a while. He can cuss in two languages, which I 'spect he'll do when we don't let him leave here the first time he comes around. Be right back. You're doin' fine, gal. I'm right proud of you."

Deserted once more, Amanda had no other recourse but to finish the task she had started. Branch was even more imposing to look at from the front than the back. The muscles of his chest were highly developed, almost Herculean. The smooth skin was pelted with black hair that fanned between his flat nipples, then narrowed further and further until spreading once more at his loins.

Amanda couldn't avoid looking, not when her curiosity was so great. She hid her sinful interest with fast, efficient strokes of the wet cloth at his thighs, then between them, but she couldn't hide her astonishment when the impersonal touch fostered a dramatic change. The silken shaft of his manhood moved, then started to swell.

With eyes the size of saucers, Amanda continued wiping away the streaks of blood that had spilled down his body, but with every movement the transformation at his loins continued until his size made her tremble. She knew the facts of life. They, too, had been set down in books, but nothing had prepared her for the sudden impact of their meaning.

A rush of heat and a thrill of panic tingled inside her. Some day, if she chose to marry, a man would thrust his sex inside her. Surely, if he were built anything like this man, she would be torn asunder. She had never examined her most intimate parts but was positive there was no way she could accommodate such a thing. She swallowed hard, trying not to gape. Before she could erase her stunned expression, Ellie was back again, eyeing her from the opposite side of the bed.

Matter-of-factly, she glanced down at the reason for her niece's fiery blush and disturbed blue eyes. "I reckon he could make a woman glad she ain't a man, all right. Too bad there ain't more like him."

"Ellie!" Amanda gasped, taken aback by the older woman's earthy candor.

Ellie began smoothing a clean sheet beneath their patient. She smiled a sad smile, her pale blue eyes clouded with old memories. "In all my years I've only known one man, and he was as fine as Branch. But t'weren't meant to be. I've had to make do with lovin' the land, but sometimes that just ain't enough."

To Amanda's great relief, Ellie placed a clean white sheet across Branch's body. Amanda quickly tucked in the bottom and the corner nearest to her as she continued to listen to Ellie's philosophical disclosure.

"I made my choice a long time ago, gal, and there ain't nothin' worse than a body who rails over all the might've beens. I ain't complainin', just spoutin' the facts. I've had a good life, and 'spect I'll go peaceful to my reward."

Ellie made certain there was no followup to that line of conversation by firmly switching the subject. "Folks 'round here call Branch a Mex or half-breed. Some take one look at those burning black eyes of his and fear he's mainly Injun.

That's what them Mexicans are, ya' know, half Spanish, half Injun."

As if thinking of something she hadn't thought of before, she chortled. "Guess that makes Branch a quarter-breed. Big John's part English and part Scot. Got a thick head of flamin' red hair and green eyes." She jerked a thumb at Branch. "You should see the two of 'em together. Like night and day, but there's no denyin' they're daddy and son. Got the same size and build to 'em."

She kept on with the commentary as she set to work spreading a foul-smelling salve over Branch's burns and then covering them with clean bandages. "I like readin' history, and the Colson men are in them books even if they don't know it. Branch takes after them Spanish conquistadores that first come to Texas. He's got the look, and I know fer a fact that his mama's family came down from one of 'em.

"Now you take Big John. He's as much of a conqueror. Probably could claim one of them Scottish Highland chiefs as kin. Him and Branch was bound to butt heads. They got the noble blood runnin' through their veins, and it gives 'em too blamed much pride."

Even if she felt her aunt was being highly romantic, Amanda couldn't help but think there was an element of truth in her description of Branch. He did behave like a conqueror. On the road, he had been without scruples, taking what he wanted, laughing at her outrage. He had vanquished her mouth with his kiss and used the whipcord strength in his body to place hers under total subjugation.

"You and me got a passle of thinkin' to do before the men ride in." Ellie interrupted Amanda's unsettling thoughts with an equally unnerving declaration. "We still got plenty to keep us occupied in here, but then we'll have to figure how we're goin' to keep what happened just between us for a while. Shouldn't be too hard 'til Branch gets his strength back and turns ornery."

"We have to contact his family, Aunt Ellie." Amanda couldn't understand why the woman would want to keep what had happened a secret. "And the law. We need to report this to the authorities at once."

"The only one who knows Branch came here and what happened to him was the one who shot him," Ellie explained. "Branch was s'posed to be on his way to Austin. Planned to be there for a spell. If Reese or Billy come smellin' around, we'll know they's the ones who done it. I'd just as soon know I'm wrong 'bout my suspicions there before we bring in anyone from the outside. Might take a heap of talkin' to convince folks I didn't plug Branch myself. I've threatened it more times than I can think."

When Amanda still didn't appear to be convinced, Ellie elaborated. "I told you Big John owns the law in these parts, gal. He'd be right happy to git rid of me for somethin' I didn't do. Them Colsons expect to move right in and take over before I'm cold in my grave. We cain't tell a soul what's gone on 'til Branch is standin' on our side.

"Come on, gal," Ellie ordered as she picked up a pile of soiled linen. "We've got to git our own selves cleaned up and get rid of the evidence. I'll get on outside first and take Branch's horse to an old shed we don't use no more. Everybody knows that fancy stallion he rides. Won't hurt him to be hid away for a day or two whilst we gets things straightened out. Don't know 'bout you, but after all this I could eat an old buffalo cow raw. Cain't think straight on an empty stomach."

# Chapter Six

"WHAT THE HELL WENT WRONG THIS TIME?" THE man shouted angrily, pounding his fist against the cracked plaster wall of the deserted old farmhouse. "I don't pay you for excuses."

"Didn't think you'd want a third murder on your hands, Boss," Hank Turnbull explained, gratified when he saw shock replace the ill temper on his employer's face.

"Third murder? Who else was there? I thought you made sure her men had all ridden out for the day."

"I did. It was a woman. You didn't warn me someone else was staying with her," Turnbull accused. "I shot the Mex and had my sights on the old lady when this other woman walks into the picture. I rode out before anyone else showed up."

"There isn't anyone else living there. Given the distance from where you were perched, you must be mistaken. It had to be one of the men."

Turnbull lifted his hat slightly, then replaced it. Before answering, he pulled a small pouch from his pocket and began rolling a cigarette. "I know the difference between a man and a woman, even at that distance."

The other man began to pace. "I don't know who it could be. Old Ellie doesn't have any female relatives and no woman friends that would be out visiting her." He paused, looked out through a broken window pane for a few moments, then asked, "Did you kill him?"

"Don't know," Turnbull drawled. He placed the cigarette in his mouth and struck a match. His next words were followed by a stream of blue smoke that curled into his pale mustache. "Colson's backshot and he wasn't movin' when I lit out."

For the first time in their association, Turnbull saw his employer smile. However, the man's good humor didn't last long. "Either way, this creates some complex problems. We're running out of time, Turnbull. Before this, people might have believed Ellie went loco and shot Colson, but now she's got a witness who'll say otherwise. If the old lady has a lick of sense, she'll go straight to the law and tell them all about the accidents she's been having lately."

After a long pause, he stated coldly, "It will take me a few days to decide our next step. I'll have to find out if Ellie's going to take her troubles to the law. If the Mex lives, he'll stick his nose in, and we can't have that. He's smart enough to figure out what's been going on, so we'll have to lay low to keep him off the scent. If we're lucky and nothing more happens, he'll think whoever shot him got scared off once they realized who they were dealing with."

"It might be best if I high-tailed it out of here," Turnbull declared, watching his employer's face. He could almost see the man's brain working and had no doubt that he would come up with a way out of their present difficulties, but Turnbull still had a bad feeling about this job. "I've avoided a noose this long, Boss. I'd sure like to keep it that way. My men are complaining, too. I don't see why we just can't ride in and burn the whole place down. Anybody tries to escape the flames, we'll shoot 'em down." He flinched when his idea was greeted with a cold-blooded glare.

"You forget, Turnbull," the other man stated icily. "Our objective is to get control of that land through legal channels. We still can if we don't panic."

He went on in a tone that brooked no argument. "Move your men out to the old Baker place on the Racine River. I'll contact you there."

Since he'd already been paid a handsome sum of money and was greedy for more, Turnbull agreed. "I'll do that, but only if the price is right."

"You'll get your money, Turnbull, once you've done the job."

"When will you get back to me?"

"After I find out who the woman is and if you killed that bastard. If you did, something good will have come out of this day's work after all."

"Is Mr. Colson available?"

"Good afternoon, Mrs. Colson." The clerk

looked up and smiled at the stylishly dressed young woman standing before his desk. "Always a pleasure to see you, ma'am. What brings you to the office this afternoon?"

"To see my husband, as any fool might guess," Opal Colson snapped, impatiently tapping the point of her parasol on the floor. "Why else would I be in this miserable excuse for a law office? I assure you I have no desire to associate with the riffraff that my husband has chosen to represent."

Bowing his head slightly, Jerome Eakins tried to placate her. "Of course you don't. Not a fine lady like you." His tone was a bit too snide for Opal's liking, and her lips pursed in irritation. Jerome quickly instructed her in his most ingratiating manner, "Please go right in. I'm sure your husband will be delighted to see you."

With a rustle of rose taffeta skirts, Opal pushed open the small gate that separated the clerk's work area from the waiting room. Jerome looked into the grim, weather-beaten features of the man still seated by the windows. "Sorry, Mr. Deets. It will be a few more minutes before Mr. Colson can see you."

Ezra Deets nodded his understanding, but his eyes were fraught with hostility as he watched Opal Colson sweep through the opened door behind the clerk's desk. Jerome followed his gaze, open dislike gleaming for a moment in his pale blue eyes before he lowered them back to the papers on his desk.

"Graham, why didn't you tell me about your cousin?" Opal demanded without preamble or any concern that she could be overheard by those seated outside her husband's office. "She's out at your aunt's this very minute!"

Graham Colson looked up from his desk, his blue eyes placid as he encountered his wife. Calmly, he answered, "My dear, I don't know what you are talking about."

Seeing the smoldering irritation in Opal's hazel eyes, he stood up and gestured to one of the chairs beside his desk. "Won't you please sit down so we can discuss this cousin I'm alleged to have suddenly acquired?"

Coming around from behind his desk, Graham crossed the small room and closed the door behind his sputtering wife. Taking her arm very gently but firmly, he guided her to the appointed chair. "You're looking very lovely today, Opal. Is that a new hat? Charming, just charming," he complimented her as he looked down upon the feathered velvetta creation perched atop his wife's shimmering brown curls.

"Don't try to change the subject, Graham. You know as well as everyone in this town that I've owned this hat for months. If you'd taken the position in my father's firm in Boston, I would probably have a room full of new hats. As it is, we barely make ends meet. Why you insist—"

"We've been all through that, Opal. I believe in frugality, but we live very well. I enjoy my practice, and it grows larger each year. One day soon, you will have all the things you want."

"And when will that be? Your father may be a cripple, but he shows no signs of dying. And what if he does? You'll still have to share everything with those renegade brothers of yours.

Billy and Reese are nothing but common criminals, and that—that half-breed—"

"Billy and Reese may be high-spirited, Opal, but hardly criminals," Graham interrupted. "They had too much to drink last Saturday night, and Pa thought he'd teach them a lesson by letting them cool their heels in jail. Everyone will have forgotten all about the incident by next week."

"Maybe so," Opal sniffed. "But no one in town will let me forget that Branch is nothing but a—"

"Don't say it," Graham warned. "You know that no one in our family speaks of Branch in terms like that. And as far as the Circle C is concerned, I'm entitled to no more of it than he is. Indeed, considering the amount of work he puts in as Pa's foreman, I think it's only fair that he gets a bigger share than the rest of us."

"Graham! How can you say that?" Opal screeched. "Why, he isn't fit to lick your boots. I can't understand you, Graham. Really I can't. With your education, you must see how superior you are to all three of your brothers. Not one of them is capable of preserving the family fortunes. Would you have our child depleted of his rightful heritage?"

In an effort to divert his wife from rambling any further upon a subject they had been over far too many times, Graham patted her shoulder. "Now, now, Opal. Don't get yourself so worked up. It isn't good for a woman in your delicate condition."

"And a lot you care," Opal whined, dabbing at

nonexistent tears with a lace-edged handkerchief. Resigned, Graham prepared himself for the next line of complaint. "If you really cared about me and our baby, you'd provide a decent home for us."

Thinking of the house he'd had built for his new bride, Graham winced. By the standards of Barrysville and most of Texas, it was large and fine, stuffed to the brim with the best furnishings his wife could import from Boston. He had had such hopes for that house and the society debutante who had agreed to marry him. With a sigh, he settled himself back into his chair. "Why don't you tell me about this new cousin of mine?"

"I don't think that I will now," Opal pouted. "Not until you say how glad you are to see me." She dropped her lashes in a coquettish manner that to Graham seemed completely ridiculous for a wife of five years who was expecting a child.

"I'm always glad to see you, my darling. Having you visit my office brings such beauty to these surroundings. You must know that you are the greatest joy in my life." Graham mouthed the necessary words, accompanying them with his most sincere and loving smile, for he knew how difficult Opal could be when he failed to satisfy her hunger for flowery compliments.

"Well . . .," Opal stalled prettily, her pleasure evident in the softened expression she bestowed on her husband. Rearranging her heavily ruched skirt, she said, adopting a falsely nonchalant tone, "It's all over town that a young woman arrived on the train yesterday asking for directions to the Box H. The stationmaster says her name is Amanda Hamilton, from New York City. She has to be a relative. Who else would bother going out to see crazy old Ellie? Don't you know anything, Graham? If this woman is a relative of Ellie's, then she must be one of yours."

Graham tented his fingertips and leaned back farther in his comfortable, worn leather chair. "If she is a relative, she's a very distant one, unless . . ." He bit his lower lip and squeezed his eyes shut. Moments later, he muttered, "I suppose it could be. Now that would change a few things."

Splotches of red mottled Opal's cheeks as her distress grew. "Just what are you muttering about, Graham? You know who this woman is, don't you?" Getting no answer from her distracted husband, she shouted, "Graham!"

"Uh . . . what's that, my dear?" He stared at his wife blankly, as if he had forgotten she was there.

"Who is she? You know, don't you?"

"My mother and her sister had an older brother—Benjamin, I believe. Went North after the war. I suppose this woman could be his daughter."

Opal leaned forward and hissed, "You suppose? Who else could it be, or have you some other relatives you've not bothered to tell me about? How like you not to know about anyone important!"

"Opal." Graham spoke her name as if he were trying to get the attention of a petulant child. "Everyone assumed he had died. There has been no communication from him that I know about. As for a daughter? I'm as surprised as you are."

"You should have known. You're the family's legal counsel. I should think you'd make it your business. After all, when Ellie dies, weren't you expecting to inherit all or at least some of her land?"

"My dear, as I've told you before, if you think inheriting any of Ellie's land will increase my fortune, you're very much mistaken. The Box H is only fit to raise tumbleweeds and scrub cattle." He fixed her with a steady gaze, relieved when she dropped her eyes and began to fidget with her purse.

Apparently giving up on her favorite topic—prospects for future financial gain—Opal returned to what was plaguing her most about the present situation. "Why didn't you know about this woman's arrival and tell me about it? Why did I have to find out about her from the local gossips? Can you imagine what an embarrassing spot that put me in?"

"I can't think why not knowing about Ellie's niece would be embarrassing to you. You're only related to Eleanora Hamilton by marriage and have never had anything to do with her."

"Well!" Opal exclaimed as if he had insulted her. "If you had heard what Sarah Shelton had to say about the woman who got off the train, you'd know why I'm interested. She was very fashionably dressed and—and had transported her own automobile! She drove out of town in one of those fancy little Oldsmobile runabouts designed especially for ladies." Envy was obvious in Opal's hazel eyes.

"Mmmm . . .," Graham emitted thoughtfully, leaning back in his chair. "That must have been what all that commotion was about yesterday morning."

"If you would just once get your head out of those stuffy old lawbooks and notice what's going on around you, you would have known about her arrival. Everyone else in town does! I'm surprised the ever-vigilant Jerome didn't tell you. He keeps such an eye on the street!"

"Jerome was out of town yesterday morning doing some business for me and has been too busy since to bother with anything else." Graham paused, fingering his blond sideburns as he inquired, "I still wonder why it should interest you so much. I'm sure we'll—"

"Because she's obviously quality, Graham," Opal cut in, her voice rising shrilly. "Quality right here in this wasteland. Someone I can really talk to. She's the first person I've ever heard of in this godforsaken place who might possibly be my sort of people, even if she is related to that wretched old aunt of yours."

"Please, Opal, calm yourself," Graham requested, running a hand across his brow to soothe the headache that was forming. "Ellie's not a bad sort."

His wife emitted a most unladylike sound. "You get out to that ranch immediately, Graham, and invite this Amanda Hamilton to dinner before anyone else in town beats me to it."

"Do you intend to include Ellie in that invitation?"

"Certainly not!" Opal rose to her feet, her parasol landing with a clatter on the wide-planked floor. "She'd only embarrass us. She'd probably show up wearing those disreputable men's britches and boots."

"Don't you think that might seem a bit rude if this Amanda is Ellie's guest?" Graham contained the triumphant smirk he felt just as he might have done in a courtroom when he'd effectively tripped up a witness. Instead he kept a practiced look of polite expectancy on his face as he awaited his wife's answer, sincerely curious about how she might circumvent including his aunt in the invitation. If there was one thing he knew for certain about his wife, it was that she would never knowingly commit a social faux pas, at least not when someone she considered of social importance might find out and express disapproval.

Opal's gloved hands clenched into fists. "Oh!" she moaned. "You *would* say something like that. We'll just have to invite the dotty old woman and pray she doesn't come." The anger fled from Opal's narrow face to be replaced by hope. "She won't come, I'm sure of it. Hasn't she said how much she hates the Colsons and would never step foot on the Circle C? You're a Colson, surely she wouldn't want to come to our house. She's never come before."

"Perhaps that's because you've never extended an invitation. She does seem to enjoy my occasional visits to her," Graham replied, taking perverse satisfaction in disarming his wife. Seeing all the color drain from her face and seriously concerned that she might swoon, he offered, "But you're probably right. She doesn't like town and won't want to come."

He retrieved his wife's parasol, handed it to her, and started to guide her from his office. "Now, if that's all settled, I think it best if you went home. You're looking a little peaked from all this excitement, and I wouldn't want anything to happen to you. Shall I have Jerome see you home?"

"No." She negated his suggestion immediately, just as Graham knew she would. "That won't be necessary. I'm fine, really, Graham. It's kind of you to be so concerned."

She was through the doorway and approaching the low balustrade that divided the outer office before she turned. "You won't forget, dear, will you? I want an answer as quickly as possible. You know how much planning goes into an occasion like this."

She glanced at Jerome to make sure he was listening, then went on, "I refuse to have dear cousin Amanda think we're remiss in offering our hospitality. Indeed, it might be even more fitting if I hold a party in her honor. She's come all the way from New York to be with her family, and we must make her feel truly welcome."

"Yes, dear, I won't forget. I'll see to it as soon as possible." Graham kept up his smile until his wife was through the doorway and out on the boardwalk beyond. Nodding to Jerome, he asked, "Do you have the necessary papers ready for Mr. Deets's signature?"

"Yes, Mr. Colson. I have them right here." The young clerk closed the thick volume he had made an appearance of reading and reached for the papers lying at the corner of his desk.

"Very good, Jerome," Graham complimented

101

him as he checked over the documents. "You'll make a fine lawyer one day. I admire both your ambition and your efficiency."

Turning his head, Graham bestowed a broad smile on the other man in the room. "Sorry to keep you waiting, Ezra."

"The longer the better, Graham," Deets declared, his dark features set in grim lines. "I'm not sure this is the right thing to do."

"Of course it is," Graham reassured him. "Your ranch hasn't made a profit in years. I know Big John is my father, Ezra, but, as your lawyer, I believe the offer is more than fair. Twenty thousand, man! That's more money than the Lazy D has ever made for you."

"But only a drop in the bucket to Big John," Deets declared bitterly, his gray eyes reflecting hot anger. "He's runnin' me out, Graham. We both know it, so don't go tellin' me his offer is fair."

Graham's expression never changed as he showed the raw-boned rancher into his office. "We'll need you to act as a witness, Jerome," he called back over his shoulder.

"Right away, Mr. Colson." Jerome quickly vacated his chair and followed behind them.

# Chapter Seven

CHEEKS FLAMING, AMANDA RUSHED OUT OF THE bedroom. Slamming the door behind her, she shouted back through the wood, "We should have let you bleed to death, Branch Colson!"

Deep, uproarious, and totally male laughter echoed loudly through the door, making Amanda's fury rise even higher.

By the time she'd reached the kitchen, her ire had reached mammoth proportions. Plate, bowl, and cup clattered dangerously on the tray that she slammed down on the table. "That man is the most insufferable, the most miserable, the most . . .," she sputtered with indignation.

"The most man you've ever met or ever will meet." Ellie finished the sentence for her, a twinkling gleam in her blue eyes. Ignoring Amanda's angry grumbles, she continued along the same vein. "Yep, that Branch is one helluva man. Told you we'd be in for it when he started gettin' his strength back. 'Spect he's feelin' mighty ornery 'bout now. What'd he do to git you so riled up?"

Amanda halted midway across the kitchen, nearly dropping the heavy coffee pot she was carrying. "I—it doesn't bear repeating," she muttered, feeling another wave of anger build up inside her as she recalled Branch's insults. However, anger was not all she was feeling.

Inexplicable sensations of warmth spread from her center like the ever-widening circles formed by a pebble thrown into the waters of a placid pond. Even if he were pale, weak, and utterly hateful, Branch Colson had the ability to call out to everything that was woman in her and gain an overwhelming response. No matter how she tried, Amanda couldn't seem to control the ripples of excitement that came over her whenever she was near him.

During the first twenty-four hours, he had been in and out of consciousness, sometimes delirious as his body fought against fever, the loss of blood, and the trauma caused by his wound. However, once he'd regained consciousness, he'd become an increasingly more difficult and thoroughly obnoxious patient. It had been only four days since he'd been shot, but he had already taken command and was issuing orders to everybody. Amanda marveled at his astounding recuperative powers.

The only time he'd been reasonable had been when he'd believed Ellie's denial of shooting him. That had been accomplished late on the second day, when his brain was no longer so befuddled by laudanum and pain that he could not reason. It was obvious by his easy acceptance of Ellie's explanation for his wound that he hadn't wanted to believe she would shoot him in the first place.

However, once he'd accepted that he'd been shot in the back by some unknown assailant, he was "hell-bent," as Ellie would say, on getting up and going after whoever had done it. He hated being taken care of, was furious with the injury that made him too weak to get out of bed, even to feed himself. He was nothing like his brother Graham.

Graham had arrived at the Box H yesterday afternoon. He had stopped by the ranch because his wife had heard about Amanda's arrival in town and was extremely anxious to meet her. He had been in the process of informing Amanda that Opal was planning a huge party to welcome her to Texas when Branch's bellow had resounded through the halls.

Amanda had hastily explained the circumstances that had precipitated Branch's presence in the house, and together they had answered Branch's autocratic summons. Graham had been visibly shaken by the sight of his brother lying wounded from a sniper's bullet. It was only after he had the reassurance that Branch was going to recover that he agreed to follow his older brother's directives.

Branch ordered Graham to tell their father of his condition but wanted it made clear he didn't need anyone from the Circle C coming over to the Box H to look after him. He did request, however, that Graham have Reese send some Circle C hands to guard Ellie's property until they found out who was behind the series of accidents that had occurred. Whatever else they had discussed was unknown to Amanda, as Branch had summarily dismissed her from the room.

After conversing privately with his brother, Graham had sought out Amanda to see if she would be free to attend the soiree that Opal hoped could be arranged two weeks hence. By the end of his visit, Amanda had felt very close to her newfound cousin as he'd welcomed her into the family, making it sound as if her arrival was the best thing that ever could have happened to Ellie. He had thanked her for watching over their elderly aunt and also for taking such good care of his wounded brother. She could still remember his parting words: "You'll have your hands full with those two, Amanda."

She had her hands full, all right. Although she agreed with Branch's assessment that Ellie must not make herself an easy target, she nearly had to tie the recalcitrant woman up to keep her close to the house. And then there was Branch. Tonight she had taken him his supper and had been forced to leave the room before resorting to violence.

"Cristos! I'm not a baby!" Branch had bellowed at her when she started to tuck a napkin under his chin.

"But you can't feed yourself yet," Amanda had returned, and she continued spreading the napkin over his chest. "Until your shoulder's better healed, you shouldn't move it."

With his good arm, he'd reached up, grabbed the square of linen, and hurled it across the room. Amanda had taken a deep breath, reminding herself that he was probably still in a great deal of pain and therefore entitled to be belligerent. Remembering the unending patience displayed by the nurse who had taken care of her father, she'd ignored the childish action, seated herself beside the bed, and dipped a spoon into the savory beef stew. She'd even ignored the vitriolic stream of words that had spewed from his mouth, though she guessed he had been cursing her sex, her intelligence, and her looks in Spanish.

When the spoon had been scant inches from his lips, he batted it away, spattering Amanda with the contents. The shock of the rich, warm broth hitting her face and sliding down to soil her crisply starched shirtwaist had been the final straw. Her temper had broken loose from its moorings, and she'd jumped up from the chair, shouting, "You're nothing but an unruly, spoiled baby, Branch Colson!"

"I'm a man!" he'd bellowed up at her, his dark features a demonic mask. Then they'd changed as he watched her dab at the wet spots on her blouse, his gaze paying particular attention to the furious heaving of her full bosom. A leering smile had appeared just before he'd challenged, "Why don't you get rid of all those clothes, you trussed-up prude, and climb into this bed. I'd be glad to prove it to you!"

Her mouth had dropped open, and her eyes had widened in shock. "Why you . . .," she'd started, then stopped herself before using the term she thought most apt.

In his particular case, the derogatory label was accurate, but, as furious as she had been, some inner caution had stopped the word *bastard* before it had escaped past her lips. He might have deserved a good dressing down, but Amanda hadn't wanted to attack him so viciously while he was still incapacitated. It hadn't seemed fair.

"Go on, Peaches," he'd prompted. "Or aren't you woman enough to say what you're thinking?"

His mocking tone and scornful chuckle had goaded her, but she'd held on to her reason. She'd leaned over the bed, hands on hips, fury flaming from her blue eyes. "I don't need to stoop to your level," she'd informed him with as much vehemence as her small body could exude. His continued smirk had fueled her anger, and without thinking she'd blurted, "I'm more than enough woman for the likes of you!"

"Maybe, maybe not," had been his silkily drawled response. His dark eyes were sharp and assessing as his gaze moved down her figure and back up again. "Only one way to find out." He'd patted the mattress beside him and announced, "This bastard's willing to give you a chance to prove yourself."

Amanda had reached for the tray, fully intending to throw it at him, but again she'd been able to stem her more primitive impulses. She had whirled away from him and started out of the room, mustering a stiff-backed dignity. His final remark had been directed at her fleeing figure just as she'd reached the door.

"Come on back, Peaches. You deserve a reward for taking such good care of me."

"Didn't eat much, did he?" Ellie's question broke into Amanda's thoughts.

"Er . . . ah . . . no, he didn't," Amanda answered distractedly, trying to keep her fingers from shaking as she used both hands to lift her mug of coffee to her lips. She could feel Ellie's eyes on her, could sense the questions forming in her aunt's mind, but she refused to meet the woman's gaze.

How could she tell her aunt that what had really "riled" her was the feelings Branch aroused in her with little more than a glance from his long-lashed black eyes? How could she admit that every time she saw his lips move she remembered how they had felt against hers and that every night she dreamed about being in his arms again? The thought of stripping off her clothes and climbing into bed with Branch was at once exciting and frightening.

Ellie was right, Amanda thought. Branch was "one helluva man." He was nothing like the men she'd known before. She'd met a fair share of attractive ones but none who could compare to Branch Colson. None had turned her knees to water by just looking at her. The sound of his voice, even raging at her in another language, had the ability to set every nerve in her body on edge.

Amanda couldn't seem to erase the memory of his naked form from her mind. He was still naked except for the bandages at his shoulder and the sheet drawn up to his waist. His wide bronzed chest was magnificent. The sight of all that taut muscle and curling black hair spread across its breadth did absolutely incredible things to her equilibrium every time she walked into the room, and it made her experience sensations she couldn't define.

All she knew was that each night as she lay in bed, her body felt as if it were going to explode. Too many times, she awoke from a fitful sleep feeling as if she were straining toward something, yearning for something. Whatever it was, she instinctively knew Branch Colson was the cause and, frighteningly, also the cure.

"You know, Amanda honey, I've been thinkin' on your idea 'bout diggin' for oil." Again Ellie's crackling voice broke into Amanda's thoughts, bringing her sharply back from the misty unknown that plagued her more and more often.

Amanda had finally screwed up her courage the day before and gently explained her educational background, reiterating what her father had said about oil on the ranch and expressing her desire to look for it. Ellie had listened but dismissed the subject soon after as a bunch of foolishness, saying she didn't "hold with messin' up the countryside."

"Oh, I know I didn't sound like I was for your ideas when you tol' me 'bout bein' a geologist and all. But even an old woman like me kin see that this here's the twentieth century and things is a-changin'. Once this was just the Hamilton farm, had an orchard, but we mostly grew cotton. Had a few cows but nothin' like the herd we got now. I was prob'ly jest 'bout your age when we stopped farmin' altogether and turned the place into the Box H cattle ranch.

"I told you when you come that I just been

holdin' on to the place 'til there was another generation of Hamiltons to run things. Since you already own half of it, gal, you're it. Iffen you want to poke holes in the land and pump out that black gold, well, I 'spect it can be worked out."

Amanda reached across the table and squeezed her aunt's hand. "Aunt Ellie, I don't want to run the Box H. Even if I do strike oil, part of this ranch should always have cattle on it. It's far too beautiful to ruin with oil derricks everywhere. I've seen Titusville, Pennsylvania, and I've heard about what happened and is still happening in Beaumont. I don't want that to happen here."

The smile that wreathed Ellie's lined face indicated how much Amanda's assurances meant to her. "You're a Hamilton, all right. The Box H'll be in real good hands when I pass on."

"That won't be for a long time yet, Aunt Ellie. I've just found you, and I need you too much, and the Box H needs you, too." Every word was sincere. This crusty elderly woman had become very dear to Amanda in the short span of time since they'd met. She'd also come to love this rolling, grassy countryside and saw a beauty in it she had come to cherish and truly did want to preserve for future generations.

Ellie brushed her sleeve across her eyes. "Get on with you, gal. You'll have this old woman bawlin' her eyes out with much more of that kind of talk." She took a long swallow from her coffee mug and with a bright smile immediately changed the subject. "Seems to me, you and Branch oughter form some sort of partnership."

Amanda nearly choked on a swallow of her

111

own coffee. "Branch and I? A partnership? Whatever for?"

"You're both so set on gettin' in on this oil business, you might as well work together. What with all that education you got and the experience Branch got working down in Beaumont a few years back, seems to me you two oughter join forces."

"Branch worked in the oil fields?" Amanda exclaimed in surprise.

"Yep, he sure did," Ellie confirmed. "After Branch came back from fightin' with the Rough Riders down in Cuba, he had a flea in his bonnet 'bout gettin' rich on oil. Up and left Big John and started wildcattin' with one of his army buddies. Lost his shirt by the time Big John needed him back home. Spindletop came in just a few months later, and Branch never got over missin' out on it."

"I see," Amanda replied thoughtfully, her mind racing.

"Yep. Now you know why he keeps pesterin' me about them blamed mineral rights. Big John won't hear of it, but Branch knows I got a soft spot for him. He was on his way to Austin to get hisself a geologist, just hopin' the feller would convince me to let Branch start diggin'. But now, with your know-how, gal, Branch won't be needin' nobody else."

Amanda considered what Ellie had just told her. So, Branch had some experience in oil, did he? Just what had he done besides lend his considerable brawn to the physical labor involved in drilling?

Her practical, scientific side wanted to rush

into that back bedroom and ask him everything he knew, but her feminine side—that side of her predominated whenever she was around the man, and she could barely think straight. Besides, she had the definite impression that Branch Colson thought women were good for only one thing, and it had nothing to do with their brains. "I doubt Branch and I could work well together," she finally said.

"I don't rightly know how I can agree to one of you drillin' and not t'other. Don't seem fair somehow." Ellie's blue eyes grew even brighter as she studied her niece. "Cain't think why you'd be agin it. Branch knows all they is to know 'bout ranchin', too. A man like him'd be a big help for a lone woman tryin' to run a spread like this."

"I'm not a lone woman running this ranch," Amanda countered a bit desperately, becoming highly uncomfortable as Ellie continued to study her. "You run this ranch, Aunt Ellie."

"Yep, well, I won't be here forever, gal." Ellie gave a weak cough. "Been feelin' mighty poorly lately, but I could go to my reward and rest easy if you marry up with that man."

"Marry *him*?"

"Marry *her*?"

A resounding duet formed by a high-pitched soprano and a rumbling baritone refuted Ellie's outrageous suggestion. Amanda and Ellie turned startled faces to the tall man leaning against the doorframe. Branch had somehow managed to pull on a pair of pants and walk down the hall to the kitchen.

Ellie found her voice before Amanda did.

"What you doin' out of bed, Branch Colson?" she demanded as she scraped her chair back from the table.

"Couldn't stand layin' around any longer," he remarked as he pushed away from the wood and started across the room, shunning Ellie's offer of help. He made it to the chair she had just vacated, but the exertion cost him dearly. Beads of sweat broke out on his forehead, and his complexion was several shades lighter, his breathing labored as he slumped backward in the chair.

"Branch, you have no business bein' out here," Ellie admonished, hovering close beside him.

"Sounds to me like I arrived just in time," he growled. He turned accusing eyes on Amanda. "She wants to starve me to death." He turned back to Ellie, an even darker scowl on his face. "And you're planning to marry me off." He gestured with his good arm, including both women in the action. "Just what other tortures have you two been cooking up for me behind my back?"

"Torture!" Amanda came up out of her chair, bristling with indignation. "If you weren't so childish, you'd already have had your supper, and as for marrying you . . . I'd rather marry a rattlesnake."

"Probably the only critter that'd have you," Branch jeered. "They don't mind crawling around rocks and prickly things."

"Now, now, you two," Ellie interjected. "Simmer down afore one of you draws blood. I'm not a-fixin' to have no fracas in my kitchen." Turn-

114

ing to Amanda, she directed, "Bring Branch a cup of that coffee, honey, then dish him up some more of that stew."

Plopping herself down into a chair, Ellie turned her full attention to Branch. "Now listen to what I'm goin' to tell you, boy, afore ya gets yerself all riled. Amanda here's a college-educated lady. One of them geologists you're so hepped up about. Ain't that right, honey?" she swiveled around and demanded over her shoulder.

"Yes, I am," Amanda agreed, trying not to look at Branch as she set a cup of coffee down next to his good arm. If he'd managed to pull on a pair of pants from his saddlebag, then he could also have donned a shirt! The sight of his bare shoulders and massive chest played havoc with her senses, and she needed her wits about her.

Amanda had already discovered that it was next to impossible to sidetrack Ellie once she'd made up her mind about something, but this was one time the woman could talk herself hoarse and get no compliance. Amanda could be just as stubborn as Ellie. As far as she was concerned, there was no way she'd agree to marry Branch, and nothing Ellie could say would change her mind.

"So?" Branch queried, gingerly lifting the mug with his left hand. "That supposed to make her good wife material?"

"You sure are thick in the head sometimes, boy," Ellie deemed, and Amanda wanted to cheer. "She's interested in drillin' for that oil you keep sayin's on my land, just like you," Ellie went on, propping her elbows on the table, a satisfied look coming into her eyes as if those few words explained everything.

"Is she now?" Branch inquired, lifting one brow. Amanda placed his food in front of him, noticing the new expression in his dark eyes, as if he were seeing her for the first time.

"The way I see it, you two need each other." Ellie held up her hand to stay their immediate denials. "Now hold up and hear me out."

Given no choice, Amanda took a seat and listened along with Branch as Ellie prepared to outline her plan for their future. In a tone that was suddenly far weaker than normal, she began, "The grim reaper's peerin' over my shoulder." Her dramatic opening statement was followed by a fit of coughing.

Ellie had determined that their marriage would be the best solution to all of their problems. They could combine Branch's knowledge of ranching and experience in the oil fields with Amanda's inheritance of the land and her education. According to Ellie, the squabble over the boundaries of the Box H and the Circle C might be solved by joining the two families, something that had not occurred when Ida had married Big John.

At that point, she remarked craftily, "I'd be willin' to let you two have the Box H right off." When neither Amanda nor Branch jumped at the offer, her speech turned sour. "Then again, if that lowdown rascal of a father of yours thinks that will give him a share in it, he'll have a fight on his hands." She looked to her niece for confirmation. "Ain't that right, Amanda?"

Branch snorted. "Fast on the draw, are you, Peaches?"

Amanda glared at him, not bothering to dignify his question with an answer.

"'Course she is!" Ellie pounded her fist on the table. "She's a Hamilton, ain't she? And that's not all they're good fer."

Sweetening the pot further, she relayed forthrightly, "Iffen the two of you get together, you'll raise up a fine family and . . ." She paused theatrically, then played her final card. "Since you're both so good-lookin' and healthy, I 'spect they'll be a handsome brood and plenty of 'em to boot. With folks like you, they'll do us all right proud."

In no doubt of their agreement, Ellie looked expectantly at the victims of her grand scheme. Completely humiliated, Amanda wanted to dive under the table, but Branch's response showed no embarrassment.

After a hearty laugh, he made a startling disclosure. "You might have a good idea there, Ellie."

"You can't be serious," Amanda rebuked, shocked to her toes.

"Now that that's all settled, I'll just take myself off to bed," Ellie announced, beaming angelically as she got up from her chair. "You two young folks can iron out all the details."

"There aren't any details to iron out," Amanda protested, but Ellie completely ignored her.

For a woman who was supposed to be at death's door, she got out of the kitchen and down the hall with amazing speed. She called from somewhere on the stairs, "You make sure that man gets back to bed, gal."

Amanda sat speechless, appalled when Branch chuckled.

"How about it, Peaches? Are you going to take my pants off and get me into bed?" Branch's expression was as insolent as his questions. His black eyes danced with wickedness.

"You don't need any help," Amanda snapped and stood up, determined to seek the sanctuary of her own bedroom. "You got yourself out here. You can get yourself back."

However, as she passed Branch, he reached out and caught her around the waist. She was thrown off-balance, and he easily hauled her down onto his lap. "You know what I think?" he asked, keeping her imprisoned with his uninjured arm.

"I don't care what you think!" Amanda tried to push herself away from him, but he encircled his arm around her more tightly.

"Stay where you are," he ordered firmly, but there was no anger in his husky growl.

Branch looked down into her eyes. Those beautiful eyes were as blue and clear as the Texas sky, soft as the bluebonnets that colored the prairies in the spring. He hadn't been sure of what he intended until she landed so prettily on his lap and the sweet scent of her perfume filled his nostrils.

That arousing scent had been haunting him since the morning he'd kissed her by the broken gate. It had filtered through the pain and nightmares he'd suffered during the first hours after he'd been shot, soothing him but at the same time giving him strength. Now the feel of her small, soft hands against his bare flesh heightened his senses and pricked his memory. It had been her hands that had brushed across his forehead, stroked his cheeks as he'd fought against the pain, offered him such gentle comfort.

There was something about this dainty woman that Branch had never known in any other. He'd sworn at her in English as well as Spanish, calling up the foulest words and phrases he knew, but she'd withstood it all, at least in his presence. He'd teased her a few hours ago out of pure orneriness but also to test her, to push her until she exploded and dropped that civilized, oh-so-ladylike facade.

She'd come close, close enough for him to get a glimpse of the passionate woman underneath, the woman he'd guessed was there when he'd held her that first day. She was a thoroughbred, and Branch knew he didn't want to break her spirit, but gentle her to his touch. If his instincts were correct, his patience would be well rewarded. Go slowly, he cautioned himself. Make her want you. Make her come to you.

Amanda discovered she had no desire to move away. The dark magnetism of his eyes held her in place as effectively as shackles. All the reasons she knew she had for getting off his lap fled as he moved his hand to the small of her back and gathered her closer.

"You need a man to pet you," he murmured, running his fingers lightly up and down her spine. "To knock off all those prickly spikes you've built up," he explained, his voice softer, smoother, as caressing as rich velvet.

His lips brushed against hers, more gently than she could ever have predicted. "I know there's some fire in you," he said softly, holding her still with the black magic in his eyes.

Amanda's hands lay open against his chest. Her left palm had fallen upon the bandage at his shoulder, but her right was on his bare flesh. The soft, curling hair tickled her skin, but she couldn't move away from him. The heat of his body held her hand in place as if it were welded there. His heart throbbed beneath her touch, becoming steadily more rapid as he bent his head toward her.

"But I need to know how much," he said, a whisper away from her lips, his breath a warm caress.

At first his lips merely pressed against hers, then ever so gently they began to move, slowly at first, back and forth across the soft curves of her mouth, but never opening or covering hers. The tip of his tongue teased and moistened, but his lips retreated each time she was sure he would claim her mouth. Again and again, Amanda anticipated his possession, but each time she was disappointed when he pulled back, his mouth hovering a hair's breadth away.

Amanda could stand no more. Her hands slid up around his neck. She thrust her fingers into his luxurious dark hair and pulled his head down, forcing his lips to hers. The reality of his touch was too close to her dreams, and she couldn't resist giving in to the fantasy. His lips were warm, welcoming, persuasive, and his taste was all that he was—wild, exciting, and beautifully male.

Branch took what she offered, unable to restrain himself any longer. He had to fight his need to crush her against his body. She was so tiny yet all woman. He took her soft mouth, forcing her to open to him, without aggression but with the erotic rhythm of his tongue. In seconds, he knew she was an innocent, but that didn't stop her from accepting pleasure or giving it.

Amanda received his intrusion and invited more, her own tongue beginning to explore. Tentatively, she delved deeper, savoring each new and incredibly thrilling sensation. She felt the soothing touch of his fingers at her throat, caressing her collarbone, and she feared nothing until, moments later, she realized that he had unfastened her shirtwaist.

She gasped at her first experience of a man's hand stroking her breast. She tried to pull away when he tugged at the ribbons of her corset cover and pushed the fragile material aside, baring her bosom. He cupped one breast in his palm and lifted the pearly weight as he lowered his head. Her nipple swelled between his moist lips, but then it was too late, too late for her to demand that he stop when all she wanted was for him to continue giving her such pleasure.

Suddenly, he lifted his head, his dark eyes like brands as they probed her flushed face. Stunned and bereft, Amanda could do nothing but stare back at him. His features were taut, the deep grooves beside his mouth even deeper as his lips arched upward at the corners. "I'm sure we can do business together, Peaches, but we can't complete the union until I'm more physically able to take part in the negotiations."

# Chapter Eight

AMANDA COULDN'T BELIEVE HER EYES WHEN, three days later, she looked out her bedroom window and saw Thurman and Sam helping Branch into the back of a wagon that was pulled up by the paddock fence. From the first moment he'd regained consciousness, Branch had denied any need to see a doctor, so she knew he wasn't planning a trip into Barrysville to consult a physician at this late date. Then where was he going?

Skirts flying, she raced down the steps and arrived on the veranda just as Thurman was taking his place on the wagon seat. Her eyes clamped on Branch's figure sprawled back against several feedsacks. She could see the lines of strain that tightened his mouth, the gray pallor of his skin, and she was determined to stop him. She shouted across the yard as she ran. "Branch Colson! You're in absolutely no condition to travel. Now where on earth do you think you're going?"

"I tol' him, Miz Amanda. Me and Sam tried to keep him from doin' more harm to hisself, but he said I gotta drive him. Says he's gotta tell his daddy what's been happenin' to our Miz Ellie. He done ordered me, Missy."

"I'm sure Ellie has told you I own half this ranch, Thurman. Therefore, it follows that I also own half of this wagon." Ignoring the blazing black eyes burning into her set features, she went on, "I won't allow it off the property, and only I or Ellie, not Mr. Colson, can give orders to Box H hands. I say you get down from there and go back to doing whatever chores my aunt has outlined for you this morning."

Thinking she had instilled just the right amount of authority in her tone, Amanda was appalled when neither Thurman nor Sam hastened to do her bidding. Both men turned soulful brown eyes on Branch and didn't move until he pronounced, "It looks like Miss Hamilton and I have a few things to discuss, boys. See if you can help my crew with the barn raising until I call. That is what Ellie told you to do today, isn't it?"

"Shore 'nuff, Mister Branch," the men replied in unison, and they immediately complied with his directive.

Amanda stared after their retreating backs, seething with frustration. "Why does everyone around here treat you as if you were a king or something? You're just an ordinary man, Branch Colson, and a sick one at that! Everyone else might be at your beck and call, but I'm not. I say you belong in bed, and that's just where I'm taking you."

"I thought we'd settled this once before, Peaches." Branch shifted his legs across the floor of the wagon until he could lean over the side. He grinned down at her. "Last time you said if I got out of bed I wouldn't be needing your help to get back into it. To be honest, you do seem a bit on the puny side to be taking me anywhere."

"At least I'm not puny in the head," Amanda retorted as she flounced to the back of the wagon. Hands on her hips, she ordered, "Get down out of there. Graham has informed your family of exactly what's happened, and I'm sure your father has already taken the appropriate steps to see that justice is done. If he isn't behind these accidents, then I'm positive he can find out who is. According to Ellie, your father and Sheriff Boyles have a close association. If the sheriff's been brought in, there is absolutely no need for you to jeopardize your health like this. Let the proper authorities handle it."

Branch whistled through his teeth, then shook his head. "If you knew Big John, you wouldn't be thinking that he'd let Sheriff Boyles handle a damned thing that concerns our family. My old man may be crippled and tied to a wheelchair, but he still makes his own laws. I'm not only his son, Amanda, but his whip hand. Until he hears from me, he won't make a move. Besides, I've got to get over there and explain why I've tied up so many Circle C hands on the Box H."

"I'm sorry." Amanda's ire was dampened by

sudden sympathy. "I had no idea that your father . . . The way Ellie speaks of him, I thought . . ."

Branch's laugh sounded more like a rough bark. "You thought he was ten feet tall and could lift mountains." His mouth twisted, and it almost sounded as if he were speaking to himself. "Sometimes I still think of him that way myself."

After a long pause, he shrugged. "He broke his back about three years ago. A horse threw him. But there's no need for you to waste your pity on him, Amanda. He'd hate you for it if you did."

"Do you pity him, Branch?" Amanda queried gently, sensing what lay behind Branch's warning.

"I'd pity any man who couldn't do what he was cut out for. Before the accident, Big John was just like this land—cruel, proud, and free as the wind. He's still tough as leather but also as ornery as a three-legged bull."

"Ellie says you're just like him." Amanda offered a tiny smile, but it wasn't returned. Indeed, she was taken aback by his fierce scowl.

"I'm nothing like him."

The embittered statement was charged with so much feeling that Amanda was at a loss for words. Eyes wide and perplexed, she stared at Branch, confused by the anger that emanated from him like a visible force. It was almost painful to look at him. "But surely you love your father, Branch. Why else would you be his foreman? His whip hand, as you call it?"

She could see that her estimation was wrong

by the glowing fury in his eyes. "Then, if not love, at least you must share a mutual respect."

"If you and I ever do decide to form some kind of partnership, you'd better know something straight off," Branch cautioned with soft menace as he stood up and walked to the end of the wagon. One hand clutched over his bad shoulder, he jumped down to the ground beside her.

"What Big John and I share has nothing to do with love or respect for each other, but what we feel for this land. It'll come down to me through him, but I'll possess it for my mother's family, who knew and loved it first. Before the Colsons even knew this place existed, my mother's family lived on this ground. When the Villanuevas lost their Spanish grant, they were reduced to servants in their own homes, but some day I, their only living descendant, will own all that was lost."

The spasm of pain that crossed his face was quickly followed by the clenching motions of his jaw. Amanda was almost certain he had never intended to reveal so much about himself but was driven by some inner demon. She took a step back, but his good hand shot out and took hold of her arm.

"I may be a Colson by blood, but my heart and soul carry another name." He spat out the words as if they were caustic acid. "Big John got my mother pregnant, then sent her away because she wasn't good enough to be his wife. She was only seventeen. She couldn't bear the shame my birth would have brought on my grandparents, so she ran away to Mexico. We stayed there, living in a filthy hovel, until I was ten years old. I saw her sweet spirit destroyed by hunger and sickness. I watched as her beauty was ruined by men who were only too glad to make use of her body in exchange for the few pesos she needed to keep me fed and clothed. It's her I look like, not him, and every time he sees me, he must face what he did to her."

Amanda felt the tears on her cheeks but didn't dare move to brush them away. She knew from what Ellie had told her that she was the only person who had ever heard this much of the story. Branch was filled with rage, but with every word he spoke it seemed to drain from him, until, in the end, his words were no longer angry but filled with an incredible sadness.

"Sometimes, when I'm riding alone in the hills, I can hear her voice crying out to me. She sounds so tormented, just as she did the night she died in Big John's arms." His voice dropped, and again he spoke not to Amanda but to himself. "I loved her, but the last name she spoke was his. Why? Why did she call out to him and not me? Why did she say that she loved him after all he'd done?"

Amanda's heart went out to the young, grief-stricken boy who couldn't understand why the one person he loved more than anyone else had turned to another for solace in the face of death. No wonder he'd gone after Big John with a knife. No wonder he still mourned for his mother. He couldn't let go of his grief until he reconciled the hatred he felt toward Big John with the love Nita Villanueva had never relinquished even unto the grave.

"I'm so sorry, Branch. Losing your mother must have been very hard," she whispered. "She must have been a very courageous and lovely person. I know how much you must miss her."

Branch's eyes, clouded with dark memory, had difficulty focusing but then bore into Amanda's. His fingers dug into the flesh of her arms. "How can you know how I feel? Nobody knows how I feel."

"My mother died when I was a baby, so I don't remember her, but I loved my father very much." Amanda met his gaze without flinching. "I was forced to stand by and watch as the cancer ate him alive. He was strong and good, but when it was over he was only a tiny shell of himself. I had to say goodbye and let him go to a place where he could be strong again. Your mother is there, too, Branch and they're both at peace."

"My mother was a *puta*, a whore. What peace can she have?"

Seeing his glazed look of despair, Amanda felt an immediate need to alleviate his suffering. Her throat ached as her mind tried to find the words that might ease the terrible pain he'd been carrying around with him for so many years. Unconsciously, she lifted her hand to his cheek, her eyes holding his as she began speaking.

"She might have been forced to do many things to keep her child safe, but I believe her spirit was never touched," she said in a tone she hoped conveyed all the conviction she felt. "Whatever she did, she did out of love for you. I don't know about you, but I refuse to believe in a God who would sentence a person like your mother to eternal damnation for placing her child's needs above all else. I'm sure she is free now, Branch, free of all torment, and I know she wouldn't want you to waste the life she gave you with bitterness and hatred."

For a long time, they just stood there, staring wordlessly at each other. Amanda felt many things as she gazed into the unfathomable black depths of his eyes. He was still a virtual stranger to her, but she had never felt closer to another human being as she sought to heal some of his torment with her understanding. The visual messages they transmitted to one another were more powerful than any words they could have spoken and bound them together in ways neither of them could have foreseen.

Amanda knew the exact moment when he stopped drawing on her inner resources and began to call upon his own. It was almost like watching a dark cloud rising away from the sun. His eyes lost their leaden sheen and began to sparkle like polished black onyx. She knew she had helped him in some deep, indefinable way, so she wasn't expecting the sharp incredulity that replaced the anguish in his eyes.

He brought up his palm to cover the small hand that still rested on his cheek, then fastened his fingers around it. He kept her hand within his grasp as he lowered his arm, but then he abruptly released it and took a step back. "You—you're a strange kind of woman, Amanda Hamilton."

Amanda tilted her head, frowning with confusion. "Why do you say that?"

The admittance came hard, but he finally ground out, "I've never told anyone what I just told you."

He looked at her as if she were some kind of witch who had cast a mystical spell on him. "There's not another person alive besides my father who knows what really happened to my mother. I know damned well what folks around here would do with that kind of information. Is that why you wanted to know about my past? Did you make me tell you all those things so you can use it against me?"

"How could I do that?" she asked, her gaze quizzical as she tried to comprehend his sudden suspicions. "I didn't pry into your past. You didn't have to tell me anything if you didn't want to."

A minute ago, they had shared something very special, but now he was acting as if she were a cruel and devious woman who had ruthlessly invaded his privacy, exposed his vulnerabilities for her own gain. What kind of persecutions had he suffered as a child to make him so mistrustful, so willing to think the worst of people? "I don't think I like what you're implying, Branch Colson."

"You may not like it, but is it true? Are you going to spread the news that my mother was a dirty Mexican whore? Is that how you hope to persuade Ellie that you and not I should get those mineral rights?"

Amanda brought back her arm and let fly with

all the strength at her command. The force of
the open-handed blow she landed on his cheek
was enough to jerk back his head and leave the
raised impression of her fingers on his skin. She
was so angry that she didn't consider the fact
that she had just struck a man twice her own
size, a man who could easily break her in two.
Nor did she think it the least strange that he
stood perfectly still and accepted the outraged
barrage that followed.

"That's the vilest . . . the most depraved . . .
odious accusation," she sputtered furiously as
she prepared to deliver a swift kick to his shin.
"Oh! How could you think that I—? Why you—
you're despicable. You're—"

Unaware that her furious attack on him had
drawn the avid attention of the crew of men who
were rebuilding the barn, Amanda swiftly
brought her foot forward to make bruising contact with his leg. In the next second, she found
that her forward momentum didn't gain her the
satisfaction of landing another well-deserved
blow to his hateful person. Instead, she was
lifted and tossed over his good shoulder as if she
were a lightweight sack of meal. With the hearty
applause of their amused onlookers ringing in
her humiliated ears, her squirming, kicking
form was carried off toward the house.

Beside herself with embarrassment, Amanda's face burned with the force of her temper as
she listened to Branch whistling a jaunty tune
through his teeth. She was angrier than she'd
ever been in her life, and he was whistling! He
seemed to sprint as they approached the veranda, showing no signs of weakness or pain at

the exertion. She should have let him go off in that wagon, reopen his wounds, and bleed to death.

If it was the last thing she ever did, she would make him pay for this outrage! She beat on his back with clenched fists, kicked her legs furiously, but all she got for her actions was a stinging slap on her defenseless posterior and a mocking warning.

"Settle down, Peaches, or I'll flip up your skirts and show the boys the flat of my hand meeting up with the blushing cheeks of your sweet little backside."

Having no doubt that this crude, uncivilized scoundrel whose steely arms were fastened like a vise over her squirming thighs might do exactly that, Amanda immediately let herself go limp. How was she ever going to live this day down? How would she ever be able to face any of those ranch hands again after what they had just witnessed?

"I'll never forgive you for this, Branch Colson," she vowed through clenched teeth. "I tried to help you, and all I get for my trouble is this degradation. I should have known better than to offer my sympathy to a cur like you. If you develop blood poisoning and die, I will give thanks. I hope you choke to death on your colossal ego so I'll never have to look at your ugly face again."

In a million years, she wouldn't understand why, with every insult she spoke, the more vicious her threats, his good humor increased. By the time he lowered her back to her feet to stand in front of him, he was grinning from ear to ear. "You, my dear Miss Hamilton, are like a priceless diamond. Your beauty doesn't stop on the surface but goes clean through. I've met more than my share of women, admired them, desired them, but not one holds a candle to you."

He brought up his hand to cup her chin and support her gaping mouth. "I've given you every opportunity to ridicule me for being a bastard, a lowly Mexican, an uneducated country bumpkin, but you go right past all those things to the real crux of the matter, don't you? Whenever I get your dander up like this, it's because I've been behaving like a stupid ass. It doesn't have a thing to do with my tainted blood or dubious paternity, does it?"

"I . . . that's what you . . . you thought I . . . ," Amanda stammered, then closed her mouth as Branch placed a finger over her lips.

"There's no need to say it, Peaches," he soothed indulgently, a newfound but heartfelt admiration coloring each word. "I hope you can forgive me for thinking you were like other women. It's just that this is the first time I've run across a female who hasn't invited me into her bed, taken all the pleasure I can give her, and then acted as if she didn't know me the next day. I know now that when you do come to me it will be without shame, and afterward you won't pretend it never happened."

"When I come to . . . ?" Amanda choked on the lump in her throat. A blistering warmth rose up from the depth of her being and dyed every inch of her skin a beet red. "I—I can't begin to guess how what's gone on between us today has led you to the totally outlandish conclusion that I will . . . that I'd ever . . ."

She couldn't say it, refused to contemplate the very idea that she would willingly offer herself to him like a ripe peach. She stifled a mortified groan. That was exactly as he saw her! It was even the name he called her.

"Give yourself to me?" Branch provided the words she could not bring herself to speak. "But you will, Peaches, and it will be soon. You loved the feel of my hands on your naked breast. You moaned with delight when I took your pretty pink nipple into my mouth."

His low, velvety drawl was as seductive as a tender caress. It enticed her, entranced her. A shameful moisture flooded her loins, and the pulsing warmth grew more intense with every word he uttered.

"Ever since that night, you've been unable to get the pleasure I gave you out of your mind. You are an innocent, so you don't yet understand why you yearn to feel my lips on the most feminine and intimate parts of your body. You can't quite comprehend why you want me to strip those confining garments you wear away so I can gaze my fill at your smooth, white skin. And, right at this moment, you want me to ease the delicious wanting you feel in a place no man has ever touched before."

"No," she denied desperately, but her voice sounded incredibly weak, and she didn't have the strength to thrust his steadying hands away as they settled around her waist. He knew. He knew more about her body than she did herself,

knew just how to inspire these shameful, trai-
torous responses that grew more and more un-
manageable each time he came near her. If he
didn't stop saying such indecent things, she
feared she might die from the overacceleration
of her frantic heart.

"You haven't learned this yet, but I promise
you, your desire will only get stronger the harder
you try to resist. Until you take me inside you,
these feelings you have can only get worse." His
large, warm hand slid up her ribcage and closed
possessively over one breast.

Amanda gasped at the stab of acute pleasure
that radiated from the hardened nipple thrust
against his palm, throughout her quivering
breast, then downward to the incessant throbbing between her legs. It was as if the thin cotton
of her blouse had disappeared and his fingers
stroked her bare flesh. She was inundated by so
many erotic sensations all at once, she felt like
she would explode into a hundred shattered
pieces.

She shut her eyes on the dizziness that overwhelmed her but was given no respite from the
vivid mental pictures that formed immediately
behind her closed lids. She saw herself standing
before him as she was now. She was naked and
totally vulnerable to his hot gaze.

As if he knew what she was seeing, Branch
brought up his other hand. For Amanda, reality
and fantasy fused together as he swiftly bared
her to the waist. No longer aware that they were
standing in the front hallway, that anyone could
walk in the front door and see what they were

doing, she made no protest when he backed her up against the wall.

She experienced a vague surprise when her bare shoulders touched a smooth surface, but then all thought was replaced with instinctive action. She whimpered and arched her back as he drew the delicate tip of one nipple between his lips. The moist stab of his tongue was too light, a sweet and deliberate torture. Just as she was about to beg him to take more of her into his mouth, to put a stop to the piercing agony, his lips parted and completely covered the distended peak.

If not for his thighs pinning her hips, she would have fallen to the floor. If not for his hands cupping her buttocks, her quivering limbs would have given out completely. He lifted her up, then pressed her against his jutting arousal. His tortured groan enhanced the fever in her breast as he grazed her nipple with his teeth, then coiled his soothing tongue around the blissful pain.

Amanda wanted the wondrous sensations, the dazing delight to continue forever, but then a new, thrilling, yet terrifying feeling grew to mammoth proportions inside her. In the deepest recesses of her femininity, the throbbing built and built, until it took over her whole body. She clung to him with all of her strength, and he held her close as the wild, tumultuous waves welled higher and then crashed with momentous force over her head. She drowned in relentless waves of pleasure that seemed to continue endlessly, then ebbed swiftly and without warning. Still locked in Branch's arms, she trembled with the wonder of it yet felt strangely empty as the incredible feelings waned away.

While she strove to regain her breath, fought for the courage to face what had just happened, Branch manipulated her limp body as if she were a lifeless rag doll. It might have taken him a few seconds or several minutes to replace her blouse and do up her bodice. Amanda wasn't aware of the passage of time, and, for her, it didn't go forward until she was once again capable of opening her eyes.

Slowly, she lifted her lashes and allowed him to view the intense shock she was sure would be with her forever. Seeing it, he dropped both arms to his sides and stepped back. Hating him for what he'd just done to her, wanting him again for the same reason, she almost cried out in gratitude when he spoke first. "Whenever we touch, you and I ignite like dry prairie grass and burn right out of control."

Amanda was barely able to stand upright without his support, and if the wall hadn't been behind her she knew she would have lost even that small claim to dignity. He towered over her, leaving her no room to run, so she cringed as far away from him as she could, plastering herself against the wall.

"*Infierno!*" Branch swore gruffly. "I never meant to let this go so far." More than a little concerned by the deathly pallor of her skin, he quickly softened his tone. "I know you're scared now, Amanda, but if you're honest with yourself, you'll admit you're more frightened of yourself than of me."

"I don't want to talk about it," she whispered miserably. "Please. Just leave me alone."

He almost let her go but then held his ground. He had to do something, say something that would relieve the agony and self-condemnation he read in her liquid blue eyes. Nothing had happened, not really. She was a woman. He was a man. They wanted each other. He knew she hadn't been prepared for the intensity of her climax, but she looked as if she'd just committed some hideous crime.

"What you felt is nothing shameful," he insisted firmly, but the words had absolutely no effect. Perhaps he'd have better luck with a little flattery. Women thrived on compliments. "Your passion is a wild and beautiful thing. You hold nothing back, and that makes you a very special woman."

Appalled that he would remind her of the total loss of control she'd experienced at his hands, Amanda bent her head so he couldn't see her face. She had allowed, no, she had wantonly enjoyed the intimate advances of a man she had known for little more than a week. That didn't make her feel special. It made her feel tawdry and cheap.

When he spoke again, his voice sounded pained. "Damn it, Peaches. That's the natural reaction a woman . . . no, anyone has when highly aroused. If anyone's at fault here, it's me for forgetting how swiftly a virgin can go over the edge. I just wasn't thinking."

Nothing he might have said could have made her feel worse. He wasn't thinking? She must have dropped her brains on the doorstep when he carried her over the threshold and into the house. Some women might find nothing wrong in surrendering to their most bestial instincts, but she had thought herself more highly evolved than that. She was supposed to be a strong-willed, intelligent woman, but today she had proven that she was no different from the lowest form of animal.

If Branch had wanted, he could have taken her virginity without her emitting the slightest protest. Somehow, she had to make sure she never revealed such devastating weakness again. Once she'd gotten over today's humiliation, she would force herself to be coolly polite to him, even if it killed her. She would prove by her unruffled demeanor that he no longer had any effect on her at all.

Eventually, if her aunt maintained the intractable stance she'd taken on the mineral rights, she might even consider forming a business partnership with him. That might provide the perfect opportunity to demonstrate that she had more sides to her nature than the erotic one she'd shown him today. If her knowledge of the earth's surface helped him bring in a gusher, he'd admire her for her brains, not her body. She had graduated near the top of her class but had yet to achieve the respect due a professional geologist. If she and Branch did form a partnership and struck oil, she would demand that he give her that respect.

In the meantime, even if her emotional state was nowhere close to normal, she must make it clear to him what he could expect from her from now on. "You have made a serious error in judgment, Branch," she asserted as she lifted her chin and straightened her spine. "I'm exactly like all those other women who would like to pretend what just transpired between us never happened. And, I promise you, it never will again!"

When she saw the flicker of pain glint in his eyes, she couldn't bear it and quickly clarified, "I couldn't care less that you're part Mexican, nor is my decision based on your illicit birth. I would feel the same way about any man who had the unmitigated gall to think that I would sacrifice my moral principles for the dubious pleasure of his vastly overrated lovemaking. In future, you can keep your pawing hands and lewd talk to yourself."

With the last of her rapidly dwindling courage, she pushed him in the chest, demanding that he give way. To her relief, he did just that. Willing down the strong urge to run, she moved toward the stairs with a somewhat stiff but unhurried tread. From the safety of the first landing, she leaned over the rail and concluded imperiously, "If you so much as lay one finger on me ever again, Branch Colson, I'll scream so loudly every hand on the place will come running. And if I inform them of the liberties you've taken with me thus far, I trust they'd be happy to finish the job that bushwhacker started."

Since he made no attempt to follow her and offered no rebuttal, she assumed she had attained his compliance. Feeling as though she'd regained at least some of her self-respect, she turned on her heel and continued up the stairs. He need never know that as soon as she was inside her bedroom and had bolted the door behind her, she wilted like a crushed flower and cried until she had no tears left to shed.

Downstairs, Branch ambled slowly down the hall to Ellie's room. He lowered his tired, aching body onto the mattress and cursed the unknown assailant that had reduced him to this debilitated state. He was exhausted. After a highly satisfactory but shortlived interlude of passion, he felt as if he'd gone through an unending marathon of pleasure.

He closed his eyes and smiled. He couldn't wait for the day when he could give Amanda another dose of "dubious pleasure," when he had enough strength to provide her with much more of his "vastly overrated lovemaking." She might scream all right, but if anyone heard her passionate cries, they wouldn't come running.

The smile widened to a grin. He would be sure not to crush her pride, do nothing to break that defiant spirit of hers that excited him so much, but have her he would. She was the most beautiful creature he'd ever seen, and even though she wouldn't admit it, she was his woman.

It would be his great pleasure to teach her what that meant. She could rant and rave all she liked, and he was sure that she would, but the end result would be the same. Unbeknownst to her, Amanda Hamilton had carved out a place for herself in his heart, and unlike the last woman who'd earned the right to occupy that space, Amanda would benefit from all he could give her, not be made to suffer for all he took away. Amanda had breathed new life into his dying soul, and he owed her for that.

As yet, he had put no label to the space she now occupied inside him, but his feelings for her went far beyond the urgent desire he had to bed her. She had left him in no doubt that there was only one way he was going to achieve that goal. It was going to take some time and also a good deal of planning, but she had underestimated him if she thought he'd given up.

Just before he gave in to his exhaustion, he emitted a sleepy chuckle. Amanda Colson. The name had a real nice ring to it.

# Chapter Nine

"Ah don't recall the whole gist, but Reese didn't say nuthin' too important." Sam screwed up his face at the sight of Branch's scowl. "Ah 'spect he'll nose around some once he can git out from under Big John's eye. Says your daddy ain't takin' too kindly to you bein' laid up like this.

"Why, we was jawin' on the porch, and the first thing you know, Big John lit into Reese cuz some ornery steer bust a hole in that ol' fence back of da barn. 'Fore ah knowed it, he was hollerin' at me to find out if you really got plugged or if you're jest tryin' to git out of workin' 'til you find all that black gold you think's under da ground. Ah tol' him you were right poorly, ah did."

"Are you telling me Reese hasn't found out a thing?" Branch inquired shortly, bypassing the accusation from his father. "What about Billy? Has he seen or heard anything?"

"Didn't tell me ah was s'posed to ask Billy sumthin', only Reese."

Branch's lips thinned with frustration. Why hadn't he sent Bob, the Box H's elderly foreman, over to the Circle C instead of Sam? Bob might be somewhat hard of hearing, but at least he could be counted on to take some initiative. Sam followed orders to the letter but didn't have the brains to go that extra step.

Branch took a deep breath to control his impatience. "Do you recall anything else Reese said?"

Sam stroked one hand over his stubbled jaw and thought a long time. Finally, his wide mouth broke into a huge grin. "Out workin' the line, he saw some riders he don't rightly know. They was escortin' a wagon up ol' Indian Creek Road. Says one of 'em could be an hombre he saw on a wanted poster hangin' in the sheriff's office, but he weren't close enough to tell. Had yeller hair though, jes like Miz Ellie says she saw on that sidewinder that set fire to the barn. Reese's goin' to try and track 'em once he can spare the time."

Branch swore under his breath. "And in the meantime, we might all be murdered in our sleep."

"Nah," Sam said. "Word's out you've turned the Box H into a fortress. Ah hear tell the folks who don't think Ellie put a hole in you herself reckon it was them cussed rustlers that done it. Ah knowed for a fact, their kind won't come 'round here no more, now that we's got Colson protection. None of them critters ever takes from the likes o' Big John. They only raids us small spreads."

Branch would have continued interrogating Sam, but then he heard the chugging sound of an engine. "Where the hell does she think she's going?"

"Couldn't rightly say," Sam replied, shaking his head as Branch bounded down the veranda steps. Deciding Branch hadn't heard his answer, he shouted after him, "Branch, ah said ah don't rightly know."

When there was still no response from the man who was striding swiftly away across the yard, Sam complained to Thurman, who had just stepped out of the house, "He's always askin' me questions but don't wait 'round for no answer. Don't know why he asks me in the first place."

Thurman rolled his eyes in disgust, then informed Sam smugly, "Cuz he don't 'spect no answers, you ol' fool. How many time does Miz Ellie have to explain it to ya? Them kinda questions are rhe—rhetorical."

"You know ah don't take to them fancy words, Thurman Jones. So don't go using 'em 'round me no more. A man asks me a question, ah answer him, and that's all."

Caught up in their own argument, the two men went back into the house and missed hearing the heated debate taking place in the yard.

"Hold up there, Amanda!" Branch commanded. "My orders were meant to be followed."

"Not by me," Amanda flung back in a similar tone. "I don't take orders from you."

Gripping the vibrating tiller of the Oldsmobile, she glared through her motoring veil at the angry-looking man loping swiftly toward her. Ever since that morning in the hallway, Amanda had done all she could to avoid him. She'd been successful throughout each day, except at meals, which Branch now took with them at the table. To keep herself busy and out of his way, she had even decided to give the house a thorough cleaning. She hated housework, but Branch had decreed no one was to go outside the main gate without his permission, and she'd needed something to occupy the long hours she'd spent indoors. Unfortunately, she had overestimated the extent of her patience and had given up on cleaning before making more than a dent in the monumental task she'd set for herself.

For the last several days, she had made a point of not conversing with Branch, and there had been no more talk of the marriage or any reference to the humiliating moments she'd spent wantonly returning his kisses and enjoying his caresses. For that, Amanda was deeply grateful and had assumed that the episode and any question of their marriage had been relegated to the past. She realized she and Branch might one day do business together, but that was as far as their relationship was ever going to go. She didn't intend to tie herself to a man who was so peremptory and domineering, even if hardly an hour passed when she didn't think about what it would be like if he took her into his bed.

"I'm tired of feeling like a prisoner in the house, so I'm driving out to survey the land north of Indian Creek. Ellie says there are surface pools of oil around there, and I want to take a look. There have been no further incidents, so I'm quite sure it's safe. Whoever was behind them is probably well on his way by now."

She opened the throttle and shifted into forward gear while pushing the floor pedal to set the vehicle in motion. She tipped her head at Branch. "Now, if you'll excuse me, I'll be going."

"The hell you will," Branch roared above the coughing of the engine, and before Amanda had driven the automobile more than a few feet, Branch had done a one-handed vault onto the seat beside her.

Amanda was so shocked by the action that she let out the clutch far too quickly, and the little runabout abruptly died. To her utter chagrin, Branch mocked, "Still can't drive this thing, can you, Peaches?"

"Out!" Amanda screeched at the top of her lungs. "Out of my machine."

Branch made no move to vacate his seat. "I gave orders that no one was to leave this place without my permission. That goes double for you, Peaches."

That did it. Amanda had been cooped up in the house for close to a week and had long since decided that Branch's protective measures were no longer necessary. And even if they were, they certainly should not apply to her. She had no enemies out here in Texas, and no one would gain if anything happened to her.

"I will go where I want, when I want, and you have nothing to say about it," she snapped.

"Don't be a blamed little fool. I'm in charge

here, and I give the orders," he insisted. "If you're going anywhere, I'm going with you."

"You can save your orders and your insults for the men who work for you. I'm not afraid to stand up to you, and I do what I want." Angrily, Amanda rose to her feet and stood over Branch, punctuating each word by jabbing her index finger into his chest. "I've told you this before, Branch Colson. Everyone else around here might be at your beck and call, but I'm not."

With that, she plopped back down onto the seat and pointed to the veranda. "Get back to the house where you belong. You're not nearly well enough to go bouncing around the countryside with me."

Branch struggled to control his temper. If his plans were to succeed, he could not afford to antagonize Amanda, but neither could he allow her to drive off with no protection. She didn't realize it, but it followed that if anyone discovered she was part owner of the Box H, she could be as much a target as Ellie. Moreover, he had no intention of letting her begin their business venture without him.

"Calm down, Peaches," he placated her. "I didn't mean to set you off. I was only stopping you for your own good." In the same smooth tone, he gave her the reasons for his concern, ending with, "If you're so dead set on going out there, you'll have to take me along with you."

"I still think your concern is misplaced," she argued. "Besides, what could you do to protect me? You're barely out of a sickbed."

"Do you have a gun, Peaches?" he drawled, but his expression was serious. His black eyes were opaque, not a sparkle of humor breaking the intensity of his gaze. Laying one hand over the holster strapped to his thigh, he queried, "Would you know how to use one of these things even if you did?"

"Don't call me Peaches!" Amanda decreed forcefully, but he knew she had given in when she hopped down from the seat to crank the engine back to life.

Branch let out a soft sigh of relief as he leaned back against the tufted leather, glancing over his shoulder to where Amanda struggled with the engine. Watching her furious actions with the crank, he couldn't help but smile. She was dressed in what he supposed she thought was practical attire. He had to admit that the lightweight material of her middy blouse and the free-flowing bloomers might be cool, but they looked ridiculous out here on the open range.

No bows or other furbelows adorned her hat, but her entire head was covered by the dark veiling tied snugly beneath her chin. With gloves on her hands to complete the ensemble, not one patch of her delectable skin was exposed. He found himself speculating whether or not she was wearing a corset. Since the ensemble appeared to be designed for comfort and freedom of movement, he didn't think she'd spoil the effect by trussing herself up in steel wires and laces. Even if she was a cultured lady from the East, she had a strong practical streak.

The thought that her breasts might be unfettered beneath her blouse inspired an ache in him that didn't emanate from his wounded shoulder. What would she do the next time he stripped off her blouse to kiss those full breasts, to suckle at the rosy peaks he knew were concealed beneath the crisp linen? His smile grew a little wider at the thought.

Amanda said nothing when she climbed back behind the controls of the vehicle. If Branch was going to accompany her on the pretense that she needed protection, fine, but she would choose to ignore his presence. One didn't have to converse with a bodyguard, did one?

Besides, she was determined to show Branch that she could operate the Oldsmobile with expertise. She needed all her concentration to shift gears and control the direction of progress up the steep grade in the road. His presence next to her on the narrow seat was disturbing enough without the added strain of parrying words with him.

It was not until they reached the first high ridge beyond the house and passed a man leaning against a large rock, a rifle cradled across his arms, that she realized the extent of the protective measures Branch had put into play. Her frown elicited a short response from Branch as he answered the man's nod. "He would've stopped you if I hadn't."

"Am I a prisoner, then?" Amanda ventured. The trail was downhill now, and though the little automobile shook and shimmied over the rough terrain, its driver had only to concentrate on steering.

"Not exactly."

"You know, this is probably a waste of manpower. If anything else was going to happen, it would have by now. Both Ellie and I think that whoever's behind what's been going on out here got cold feet as soon as they shot you by mistake. She's sure they're well and truly gone by now. She also assures me only a fool would tangle with a Colson who's 'all riled,' as she puts it."

Branch couldn't help but chuckle at the disparaging look on her face. "You don't seem to live in fear of getting me all riled?"

Amanda pondered the remark for a moment, then announced tartly, "So far, I've been given no reason to believe that your tirades are the result of anything more than pent-up frustration. I'm not the type to be intimidated by nothing more than so much hot air."

Amanda was expecting an angry response to that and was therefore quite shocked when he merely grinned and muttered calmly, "That does wonders for my peace of mind."

In the hopes of forestalling further conversation, Amanda increased her acceleration, hiding a smile when Branch had to hold on to the seat with both hands to keep his position.

"You do know where you're going, don't you?" he asked a few minutes later, barely concealing his doubt, when Amanda sharply steered off the trail and headed toward another ridge.

"Ellie showed me a map," she admitted through gritted teeth. "I'm not an idiot. I do plan ahead."

"Sorry, Peaches. I forgot you're an educated lady," he taunted.

"Is that so hard to believe? Can't you accept that a woman can think, can have some common sense?"

"I'm countin' on it," he replied enigmatically,

then turned away, lapsing into a silence that continued until she brought the vehicle to a halt. "What are you stopping here for?" Branch inquired, puzzlement knitting his dark brows.

"I want to know what you meant by that last remark," Amanda declared.

Branch appeared to be marshalling his thoughts as he leaned back, propped his foot on the dash, and stretched his arm along the top edge of the seat. His hand brushed her shoulder, and Amanda was immediately on the defensive. "Well?" she inquired, needing to break the sudden familiar tension that had developed between them.

"Promise me you'll hear me out before you jump to any conclusions," Branch began in a controlled, businesslike tone she had not heard him use before, at least not when speaking to her.

Amanda's suspicions increased when she noted that Branch wasn't looking at her. Giving her his profile, he waited for her to agree before continuing what she now felt was a well-rehearsed speech. Amanda had to force herself to listen, since being this close to him was having the same effect on her as always. She was struck anew by his patrician features, which seemed so incongruous with his rugged body and his often crude patterns of speech. He emanated a sensual charisma so powerful that she felt he was touching her intimately even though he was not.

What would it be like if he actually made love to her? She had only a rudimentary knowledge of the act itself and before meeting Branch had thought the whole idea rather disgusting. She had resigned herself to the possibility that if she married she would have to put up with her husband's attentions in order to have children, but she had learned after that humiliating lesson in the front hall that she might actually enjoy such intimacy.

Rather than being attentive to his words, Amanda concentrated on controlling her erratic breathing until Branch said, ". . . Therefore, we'll get married as soon as possible."

"What?" Amanda squeaked, her blue eyes incredulous, appalled at the thought that he might have read her mind. "Why would you think I'd marry you? I thought I made my position clear on that days ago."

"Haven't you been listening?" Branch turned to her, exasperation plain on his face. "I've just told you we have no other choice. If you want to drill for oil, become my partner, we have to get married. It's a sound business decision, and if you really are as clear-thinking as you stated, you must agree. Ellie has already agreed to release the mineral rights to us immediately after the ceremony. Since you're in such an all-fired hurry to get started, I assume you're willing to get this marriage business over with without delay. Ellie and I have—"

"You and Ellie?" Amanda interrupted furiously. "Don't I have anything to say about this?"

Giving her a look that deemed her of questionable intelligence, Branch shot back, "I've been trying to have this talk and let you have your say for days, but you've been as approachable as a prickly pear. Ellie's house looks a mite better than usual, but that's the only clutter you've swept out of the way."

Amanda was horrified when he dropped his hand to her shoulder. Instantly, she flinched away.

"See what I mean?" He brought both hands to his lap and drawled in the mocking tone she hated, "Ever since I gave you a taste of some real lovemaking, you've been as jumpy as a horny toad on a hot rock. Afterwards, you told me it was hands off, and that was just fine with me. I've all but forgotten it happened. Now, if you were telling me the truth when you said you didn't want us getting personal, then you should do that, too. To me, it wasn't that big a deal, Peaches, and if you weren't so naive, it wouldn't be to you either."

"It's not. I just don't want you to get the idea that I've changed my mind," she informed him haughtily, covering the hurt she felt. "And my name is not Peaches!"

Unexpectedly, Branch apologized. "Sorry, Amanda, but if we're going to get married, I figure we'd best get your fears out of the way before we meet with the preacher. I haven't laid a hand on you since that day, have I? You put me in my place, and I promise to stay put. This marriage will be a business arrangement, and once we've struck oil we can go our separate ways."

For the next hour, they argued. Amanda learned that Branch refused to take no for an answer. He had a logical rebuttal for every one of Amanda's objections. Amanda fell prey to Branch's convincing argument that Ellie would never sanction his living at the house merely to protect her but would agree to it if he were Amanda's husband.

Since Amanda acknowledged that there was reason to believe Ellie's welfare was in jeopardy, she had to admit there was some merit in the arrangement Branch proposed. Moreover, knowing how stubborn Ellie could be, Amanda knew the woman would never release those mineral rights to just one of them.

"Our marriage would be a business arrangement that would only last as long as our mutual interest in oil. Is that correct?"

"Correct," Branch stated emphatically.

"All right, then, but the only reason I'm agreeing to this farce is because I believe there's more oil under the Box H than anyone's ever dreamed of."

"I've dreamed of it, Amanda." Branch reached across the seat and patted her hand. "We're doing the right thing."

Once that was settled, Amanda decided they might as well determine the most advantageous place to start drilling, but when she parked the automobile in the middle of a section of nearly flat grazing land, Branch questioned her choice of location. "What are you stopping here for? The surface pools are over the next rise."

"I know that, but this is where I want to take some readings," Amanda explained as she unlashed a wooden box and removed a small instrument. "If my guess is right, the main reservoir is under that little mound." Ignoring his doubtful expression, Amanda proceeded to explain the rudiments of geology to Branch. He had done a good job of convincing her that there was merit in their marrying, but now it was her turn to convince him that she was the expert in finding oil.

Donning a professional demeanor, she showed how, by measuring gravity, she could determine the density of rock beneath the surface of the ground. By the end of her investigation of the area, she had conclusive proof that a salt dome existed beneath a hillock half a mile from the surface pools of oil.

Even though Amanda was convinced that the most logical place to start drilling was into the side of the dome, Branch was not so sure. "That doesn't make any sense," Branch expounded in frustration. "Why would we start drilling here when we can see oil way over there?" He pointed to a distant flat section of land.

"When there is porous rock meeting impermeable rock, oil can be trapped along the line of the fault. When this happens, the earth is pushed upward by gas until it forms a small dome that is plugged by salt. Oil cannot pass through the salt, so it's trapped against the sides of the dome. The pools you see over there are merely the smaller secretions that have escaped from the reservoir beneath this hill."

Thinking the matter was closed, she packed up her equipment and got back in the Oldsmobile. "Can you manage the crank, or aren't you strong enough yet?"

Branch bent down behind the engine and reached for the crank. "I can manage," he said mildly, but his thoughts were anything but mild. He had the strength to handle not only the crank of this little machine but the little woman who drove it as well, and she was going to find that out very soon. In the meantime, until he had his ring on her finger, he was going to be very amenable.

On the drive back to the Box H, neither one of them had much to say. For Amanda's part, she was just beginning to realize how disappointed she was in the unfeeling proposal she'd accepted. Branch had made it clear he didn't desire her as a woman any longer but only as a business partner, and, unreasonably, that hurt. Evidently, the samples he had taken of her charms had been enough, and he had lost interest in her. Unfortunately, no matter how often she berated herself, those same samples had simply whetted her appetite.

She hoped they would soon discover oil and whoever was behind Ellie's accidents. If that didn't occur in the very near future, it was going to be torture being Branch's wife but yet not his wife. During his proposition, he had implied that Ellie believed they could make a successful marriage and that they would have to behave accordingly in order not to disappoint her.

Obviously, Branch was far more concerned about Ellie's feelings than he was about those of his future wife. Though Amanda realized she had given him every reason to think she expected no more from the marriage than he did, she was still dismayed by what she might do if she spent too much time in his company. What if she ended up begging him to continue where they'd left off the other day? What if she went against all she had shouted at him from the stairs?

By the time they were back at the ranch, Amanda was convinced that she could not possibly marry Branch and keep up the pretense that she felt nothing for him. For no logical reason other than the uncontrollable reaction she had whenever he touched her, she did feel something for him. She wouldn't call it love, but it was more powerful than anything else she'd ever experienced.

Ever since she'd told him to keep his hands off her, all she'd done was hope he wouldn't take her at her word. It was supremely deflating to find out that he had lost his interest while hers had only increased. To keep him from knowing what a romantic fool she'd become since meeting him, she had to get out of this rash promise she'd made. The consequences of such an arrangement would be nothing short of disastrous.

"I've been thinking, Branch," she said as they walked side by side toward the house. "There must be some other way we can get the mineral rights. Marriage seems an extreme measure to take when all we want is the oil."

Branch took hold of Amanda's elbow as they mounted the veranda steps and entered the house. "Sorry, Peaches, but you're dead wrong," he stated softly and propelled her with him into the parlor. "It's too late for second thoughts now. Believe me, I've been through it with Ellie over and over again, but there's no way out. We're stuck with each other."

Before Amanda had a chance to say anything,

she saw him nod at Ellie, who sprang up from her chair and rushed toward them. The older woman's face was wreathed in smiles as she took Amanda's hand and pulled her further into the room. "Honey, I'm as pleased as all get-out that you and Branch are makin' your vows today. Come on over and let me introduce you to Preacher Cox. He come all the way out here today to do the honors."

For the first time, Amanda noticed a tall, thin man, dressed in a dark suit with a clerical collar, seated on the divan. At her approach, he rose and extended his hand. "My best wishes, Miss Hamilton. It will be my great pleasure to officiate at this joyous ceremony."

To Branch, he was less gracious but did convey his congratulations. Peering through thick spectacles, he warned the prospective groom, "I can't say I approve of what brought this marriage about, Colson, but you're doing the right thing. Miss Ellie has told me her niece has no male relatives to look out for her welfare, and I'm glad to see you're not taking advantage of that."

Both Branch and Amanda fixed Ellie with a quizzical stare, which the woman parried with an innocent smile. "All's I told him was you two had to get married real soon."

Amanda would have liked to have disavowed the minister's erroneous assumption, but Branch whispered in her ear, "He probably won't do it if we set him straight. Nine months from now, he'll know the truth."

As if sensing Amanda's discomfiture, the Reverend Cox offered, "My dear, I assure you this matter will go no further. You are not the first," he paused and looked at the ceiling. "Nor will you be the last young woman to marry in haste. We are but weak vessels, and our heavenly Father understands that."

With a pointed stare at her unconventional dress, particularly the bloomers that billowed out from her hips, he went on, "You appear to be a very modern young lady, but marriage is an old-fashioned institution. I was told you may not have reconciled yourself to this situation as yet, so let me offer some reassurance. If you truly love Branch and base your marriage on it, the joyous days you spend together will soon dispel every one of your regrets."

"Reverend Cox, I—" Amanda stammered, not knowing what to say that wouldn't make matters even worse. "Love isn't—I don't—"

Branch gathered Amanda beneath the crook of his arm and squeezed, preventing her from completing her sentence. "You can rest easy, Pastor Cox. Amanda and I share the same feelings for each other. There will be no regrets."

"That's no more'n the truth," Ellie joined in. "I could tell these two were meant to be together as soon as they clapped eyes on each other. Now let's get on with it. I know you've got to get back to town, Preacher."

So it was that Amanda's motoring veil served as a bridal veil, and her bloomers were her wedding gown. Thurman and Sam were called in to witness the ceremony, which was brief but entirely legal. Amanda choked over each word she was asked to say, but Branch spoke his vows in a clear, resonant voice. Ellie provided Branch with a ring, a delicate gold band that had belonged to her mother. Branch slipped the ring over Amanda's finger, and it was a perfect fit. When the ceremony was over, Branch gave his bride an obligatory peck on the cheek, then promptly held out a pen for her to sign the marriage certificate.

Branch's legal name gave Amanda quite a jolt and reminded her of how little she knew about him. Juan Rafalgo Gregorio Villanueva Colson, a stranger and her husband.

Her full name, Amanda Eleanora Hamilton, prompted a low chuckle from Branch. "Another Ellie, huh?" he whispered in her ear. "Are you as much a woman as she is?"

Amanda didn't like his tone nor the suggestive gleam in his dark eyes, but she said nothing as Ellie came up to include them both in a warm embrace. Afterward, the older woman stepped back and dabbed at her eyes with her shirt tail. "Too bad Ben didn't live to see his little gal married off to such a fine man. He would've been right proud, don't you think, Amanda?"

Amanda was too numb to respond. The pastor came over to offer his congratulations, as did Thurman and Sam, but through it all Amanda heard only one voice, and it was her own. *What have I done? Oh God, what have I done?*

# Chapter Ten

"WHAT ARE YOU DOING IN HERE?" AMANDA dropped her hairbrush onto the dressing table and whirled around on the bench to confront her husband.

Branch tossed his saddlebags onto the chest at the foot of the bed. "Ellie took her room back, and I'm moving in with my wife."

"Oh no you're not," Amanda asserted as she stood up. Her long nightgown swirled around her bare feet as she went to the door, opened it, and pointed down the hall. "There are plenty of other bedrooms up here. Pick one."

"The one you picked out is fine with me." Branch patted the bed, testing the firmness of the mattress before sitting down on it. Then he began removing his boots. "This is probably the best bed up here."

He dropped the second boot to the floor before looking up at her. "Close the door, Peaches. You don't want to upset Ellie. Yelling isn't the sound she's expecting to hear from us on our wedding night."

Amanda's mouth dropped open, but she recovered quickly. "Well, that's what she's going to hear if you don't get out of this room. Our arrangement did not call for sleeping together."

Branch continued undressing in a slow, leisurely fashion that showed Amanda what little effect her words were having on him. Unfortunately, the sight of his bare chest as he removed his shirt was enough to strangle her next declaration before she could make it. Only a small bandage remained to remind her of his wound. The rest of his flesh was like smooth, burnished copper. Hard muscles rippled with his slightest move, and the configuration of his chest hair drew her eyes downward beyond his belt buckle to the bulge beneath the buttoned fly.

She gulped as, before her stunned gaze, he unfastened his belt and drew the supple leather from about his slim hips. She gasped when the faded denims dropped to the floor, and she was confronted with a man who wore nothing but a pair of short white drawers. A flash of memory came back to taunt her. She knew what was barely concealed beneath the thin cotton, and the knowledge made her tremble.

Before Branch could remove the last garment, she choked out, "Put your clothes on! Have you no modesty?"

Unaware of how ridiculous the defensive action would look to him, Amanda reached for an all-encompassing wrapper to cover her full-length cotton gown. Once she had satisfied her own sense of propriety, she turned back to him.

Upon seeing that he was now minus the drawers, she quickly faced back at the door. Her cheeks were red, and her body felt hot and tingling in reaction to the sight of her husband's overwhelming virility.

"Branch!" Amanda exclaimed desperately, her voice high and quavering. "You—you can't stay here."

"Why not?" he countered smoothly, but she didn't answer him until she heard the creak of the bed and the rustle of bedclothes indicating that his naked body was safely hidden under the covers.

"You know perfectly well why not!" she then shouted, placing her hands on her hips. "You promised that we—we—I mean, it's not proper!"

"Nothing could be more proper," Branch disagreed. "Turn down the lamp and close the door before you come to bed, Mrs. Colson. I like my privacy."

Backing away from the challenging light in his dark eyes, Amanda's hand closed over the doorknob. She did not intend to shut the door but to open it wider so she could exit. She had taken only one small step in that direction when Branch's voice stopped her.

It was not the voice of the drawling cowpoke or the logical one of the man who had proposed to her this afternoon, but the autocratic command of a monarch. "You aren't going anywhere, Peaches. Shut that door and come to bed, or I'll see that you do."

Amanda had no doubt that he meant exactly what he said, but she still couldn't believe what was happening. Surely, he didn't think . . . ? He couldn't expect her to . . . ? To hide her anxiety, she flung back, "I'll shut the door, but only because I don't want Ellie to hear what I have to say."

Once the latch was slipped into place, she side-stepped across the room, seeking refuge by one of the windows. "I agreed to marry you, Branch Colson, but it was strictly a business decision based on getting those mineral rights. Ellie signed them over to us this afternoon. Therefore, we already have what we want from the arrangement. This marriage is simply a means to an end, and I have no intention of pretending it's a real one."

"You won't have to pretend," Branch assured her, his black eyes glowing as they devoured her small, defiant figure. "I purposely let you think that you were dealing with a man who has no more sense than a flea, but tonight you're going to learn that I have plenty to teach a fine, educated lady. As a matter of fact, Peaches, I've just been biding my time, for to tell you the truth . . ." He lapsed into the slow Texas drawl he could call upon at will. "I've been hankerin' after your sweet body ever since I first laid eyes on you, and I aim to do somethin' about it right soon."

Matching action to words, Branch slowly pulled back the covers and swung his long, muscular legs over the side of the mattress. "If you recollect, that very first day I expressed my interest, and, ma'am, I pride myself on bein' a man of my word."

"A man of your word!" Amanda cried. "Not more than six hours ago you told me you'd forgotten . . . you agreed that our relationship would remain impersonal, that you wouldn't touch me."

"I said I would keep my place," he reminded her, then detailed how he'd misled her. "And since we're now married, my place is with you. Before the preacher made us man and wife, I did stick to my promise, but that was voided as soon as you said 'I do.'"

His tone changed, hardened, as he walked toward her. "When I see something I want, I go after it." He came closer and closer, his intense gaze probing beneath her wrapper, claiming what she would not give up without a struggle.

"And I want you, Peaches." He verified the dark flames of desire that glowed in his eyes. "Bad enough to marry you."

"You married me for the mineral rights," Amanda insisted, flattening herself up against the wall as she strove to keep her eyes on his face. She knew what she would see if she looked down, and she had never been more frightened in her life. A second later, she was staring helplessly at the source of her fear.

She'd been wrong this afternoon. Seeing his jutting manhood coming closer and closer, she knew she wouldn't enjoy the physical side of marriage. The size of him would rip her apart, just as she'd thought when she first looked upon his startling virility.

"You don't want me. You want the oil," she cried anxiously, frantic to keep him to their agreement. "You don't want me as a woman but as a business partner."

"You underestimate yourself," Branch negated softly, then mocked, "As you said that day on the road, I hope to conclude our business in a timely manner. Given time, I probably could have talked Ellie into parting with those rights, but that wouldn't have brought you to my bed this *expeditiously.*

"Quickly, madam, quickly," he mimicked the words she had spoken to him when they'd met but with none of the impatience she had imparted. Indeed, he looked as if he had all the time in the world to consummate this new and heretofore hidden clause in their contract. "You were making fun of what you supposed was my limited vocabulary out there on the road, but there are some places where words don't matter, and this is one of them."

He stopped right in front of her, his warm breath caressing the mass of blond curls piled on top of her head. "Perseverance is sometimes more beneficial than expedience, dear wife. You've sorely tried my patience, but now I've got everything I want all wrapped up in satin ribbons."

"If—if you're behaving like this just to get back at me for insulting you that first day, I find it highly unfair," Amanda stated stiffly, her blue eyes mutinous though her lower lip quivered with fear. "I—I have done nothing to deserve this brutal attack."

Branch's brows rose at her description of what was about to take place. Reaching out, he unfastened the sash at her waist, then slowly drew the wrapper down her trembling shoulders. "This isn't an attack, so there's no need for you to be afraid. I could never be brutal to you, sweetheart. If you think back to the times I've touched you, you already know that."

As if to emphasize his words, his fingertips trailed lightly up her arms. He bent and brushed his lips across her forehead, down her face, and along the column of her throat. "You're far too small and much too lovely to hurt," he said against the hollow above her collarbone.

"As your husband, it's my duty to protect you. I know you haven't had much experience at this, but I'll make sure it's good for you too. You know how good I can make you feel. The only difference this time is that those feelings will be even better and last a whole lot longer."

Amanda could not form a coherent word as his caressing voice soothed her shattered nerves and coaxed her into a state of paralysis. She had known all along that he was a sensual force she could not withstand, but she had foolishly believed him when he'd told her he'd forgotten all about the other times he'd touched her. The low words he spoke to her in Spanish while he pulled the pink ribbon from her hair and combed his fingers through the unbound silken tresses lulled her into a kind of stupor, and she couldn't think of anything to do that might stop him.

She felt his warm fingers on her bare skin and knew he was undressing her, but her conscious mind had become her worst enemy. It was foolishly attempting to control the wild, clamorous excitement that built up inside her with each languorous brush of his hands. When she was as naked as he, he stepped back but kept one hand on either side of her waist.

Seeing the ashen color of her face and feeling

her tremble, Branch realized he could not let go of her completely, or she would crumple into a quivering mass at his feet. *Cristos*, he swore inwardly. He had expected some resistance, but not this. Fear wasn't what he wanted to see in her beautiful blue eyes. His jaw tightened as he struggled to control his mounting excitement for her. He could tell by the taut erection of her nipples and the feverish flush of her skin that she was in the beginning stages of arousal, but her desire could just as easily turn to terror if he didn't assuage all her fears.

He paused a moment longer, watched her eyes as they took in his full measure, and was pleased that shock was not the only thing he saw on her expressive features. All he would have to do to win her trust was to go slowly, let her get used to him, and increase the fragile thread of desire that linked her to him. He knew she would respond. She had the very first time he had kissed her, and the day in the hall she'd shown him a passion few women ever allowed themselves to express.

She was exquisite, like a delicate rose, perfectly formed and ready to bloom. The knowledge that his hands were large enough to span her tiny waist was almost as exciting as the sight of her full breasts and flaring hips. He had a moment of fear that she might be too small to accommodate him, and if he found that she was, he inwardly vowed to break off their lovemaking before he hurt her. Never in his life had he felt this way about a woman—fiercely protective and totally aroused at the same time.

Taking her hand, Branch gritted his teeth to maintain his control, then placed her soft palm over his heart. "You know what my hands feel like on your skin, that they can give you pleasure. But yours can do the same for me. I need you to touch me, *querida,* more than I've ever needed anything."

The vulnerability in his tone eased some of Amanda's anxiety, and the sincerity of the appeal was such that she found herself unable to resist. Tentatively, she raised her other hand to his chest, astonished when his long thick lashes closed over his eyes and he gave a soft moan.

Was he as much a victim of desire as she? Did her touch bring the same mindlessness to him as his did to her? She had suspected as much the last time they'd been together intimately, but then she'd become too caught up in her own feelings to consider his. The thought of having such heady power over a man like Branch encouraged her to explore further, and as long as he kept his eyes closed she was able to do so without being completely overwhelmed by his nakedness and her own.

After she had investigated the triangle of dark hair between his nipples and trailed her fingers over his heavily muscled shoulders, down his forearms, and back to his chest, she had all the proof she needed that her husband was not indifferent to her. The words he had spoken a few minutes ago had been true. He had wanted her that first day, and he wanted her still, had never stopped wanting her no matter what he'd led her to believe. His breathing was strangled, and his arms fell limply away from her waist when her palm inadvertently slipped to the smooth flesh below his navel.

"*Dios,*" Branch groaned and lifted her into his arms before he became too weak to do so. No woman had ever affected him like this. "To bed, *mi esposa,*" he murmured. "Let me love you."

"Branch?" Amanda cried, again frightened by the urgency she felt in him.

"Trust me," he pleaded huskily as he laid her down on the mattress, then lowered himself beside her. He slipped one arm beneath her head and gently eased her legs apart with his thigh. Again he saw the anxious blue lights in her eyes, and he stopped, hoping to ease her fears. Making certain that very little of his weight rested on her, he brought one finger to her mouth and tenderly traced the outline of her lips.

Her breathing was rapid as he inserted his finger beneath the delicate edge of her bottom lip, then tenderly pulled the soft flesh down into a delectable pout. After one lingering look into the fathomless blue of her eyes, Branch lowered his mouth and tasted the intoxicating flavor of his bride.

Amanda felt as if Branch were seeking the very essence of her as his tongue thrust deeply into her mouth. It was strange and frightening, but exciting too. His mouth was moist as it claimed hers, delving for a response. His roaming tongue began to shoot hot sparks through her body, and her loins felt as if they were melting.

His mouth left hers, only to move down her cheek to her neck. He pressed faint kisses on her throat as he traced a path to her breast, which was tingling with warmth. Amanda was only partly aware that his mouth was slowly seeking the pink delicacies that he had tasted briefly before.

What little remained of her ability to think was centered on the feel of her lips, bruised and swollen from his kisses. She used her tongue to soothe the soreness but swiftly pulled it back inside her mouth when all she could taste was Branch. It was as if he had already taken total possession of her—her mind, her body, her very soul.

He began to play her body with his hands, stroking and caressing her breasts, tantalizing her nipples until they yearned for his mouth. When he finally drew the throbbing flesh between his lips, she was beyond caring what else he might do to her. Instinctively, she knew that all she had been straining toward in her dreams was about to be totally fulfilled by Branch.

Amanda arched her back and twisted on the bed, a moist heat developing between her legs. When Branch's searching fingers sought the throbbing wetness, she unconsciously tried to shrink back into the mattress, embarrassed that he meant to touch her there. Embarrassment was swiftly replaced by a far stronger feeling as he found her and began to explore.

"Easy, *querida,*" Branch muttered against her breast as his fingers gently teased and stroked the satiny folds between her thighs. Tenderly but deliberately, he prepared her to receive him, almost losing his control when he felt her shudder towards release. "This time I will know all of you and give you all you've only imagined before."

"Oh Branch," Amanda moaned as the heated spirals spread through her. The possession of his stroking, probing fingers created a wildfire of sensations that quickly brought her beyond anything she'd felt the last time he touched her. That day, she had exploded in passion, and it had been like this, yet nothing like this at all. Finally the tension shattered and she was floating, but then, when his body covered hers, the unbearable tide of pleasure began anew. "Branch, please," she gasped. "No more. No more."

"Together, *querida,*" Branch breathed at her ear as he positioned himself between her thighs. "This time together."

Her hips rose to receive him, but, rather than fearing the union, she now craved it. She felt a small, stinging pain as he made her one with him, but it was quickly replaced by a wave of primal desire. The knowledge that she could accommodate all of him was a source of wonder to her, thrilling her to the depths. Her arms and legs went around him, clasping him to her, and she delighted in the sound of his agonized groan. She could feel him trying to hold back, but there was no need.

Branch could wait no longer. Every muscle in his body tensed with the exertion of restraint, but the writhing woman beneath him was totally receptive to his possession. The warmth of her womanhood encased his burning shaft, and he could no longer control his blinding pleasure. His name was a chant on her lips, and he couldn't help but respond to her call. Hips churning, he thrust again and again, hurling himself toward the ever-beckoning spiral of ultimate fulfillment. He forgot his promise to be gentle and claimed all she was so sweetly willing to give.

"Amanda!" he cried out sharply, pleasured by her perfect accompaniment to the rhythm he set. At the moment of release, she was with him, and she welcomed him as he collapsed within the soft warmth of her clinging arms and slender thighs.

As soon as Branch could think at all, he rolled Amanda on top of him. Unwilling to release her, he was still concerned that his unrestrained passion had hurt her. "Are you all right?" he questioned anxiously, searching her face for signs of pain.

Still one with him, Amanda couldn't seem to think of anything else and had a difficult time forming an answer. The part of him she had yearned for yet feared most had brought her such joy, and to her dismay she could feel herself growing hot with the slightest move Branch made. She had to get away before he became aware of this wanton spirit that must have overtaken her body, making her behave like an insatiable hussy.

She tried to think logically. Surely such heights of pleasure could not be reached so often within such a short span of time without causing permanent injury to the brain. Years of hard study had not rendered her mindless, but Branch's lovemaking had once again accomplished that feat in the passing of a few glorious minutes. Her heart was beating at such a rapid rate that she feared it might burst from the strain. She was certain of it when Branch shifted his hips, and the overwhelming, soaring sensations took over again, wrenching a guttural moan from her throat.

She brought her knees up, attempting to move off him, but his hands grasped her hips and seated her astride him. "No, oh no," she cried as her new position increased the fervor of her rekindled desire, intensified the heated feel of him inside her.

"Amanda?" Branch queried worriedly as he viewed her tensed features. At first, he thought her soft moans were of pain, but then he understood. Feeling again the spasmodic strokes of her womanhood, he began to swell within her. He emitted a low chuckle when he saw her stunned expression. "Don't look so surprised. You need me again, lovely lady, and I need you. That is what making love is all about, and that's why you're so special."

He knew that she heard him as he arched his hips and lifted her up and down upon himself. He brought her over the edge once more, and she cried out his name as she stiffened and collapsed upon him. Branch felt awed and more than a little bit humbled.

Watching her strained features relax into an expression of supreme fulfillment and knowing that he was the cause, temporarily stayed his own release. She was small, so delicately made, but he knew now that what she had told him days ago was true. She was more than enough woman for the likes of him.

He closed his eyes to savor the final moment,

but a vision of her sweet body yearning for him, her beautiful face reflecting the passion he inspired, branded itself in his mind. His last conscious thought before he poured his release into her and was hurled into a pool of sweet fulfillment was that he would never be able to erase the visions of Amanda from his mind.

Amanda lay spent across Branch's chest, her legs stretched over his, one hand lying limply open on his good shoulder, the other clinging to his neck. She refused to open her eyes. She didn't know whether she was more ashamed by her seemingly insatiable appetite for passion or by the knowledge that she could no longer hide it from Branch.

He knew everything! He had watched her naked body writhe with pleasure, heard her cry out his name. How could she ever look him in the face again?

It was almost a full five minutes later before she allowed herself to think beyond what had just happened and realize what was happening now. She was lying atop him as if she had no wish to be anywhere else. He was probably thinking he had married a woman who professed one thing but practiced another. After his tender initiation, she had shown that she was more than anxious for their relationship to develop beyond a business partnership. The way her cheek was nestled against his throat, her fingers clasping the silky black hair at his nape, he might even think she was resting up for another bout of lovemaking. That couldn't have been farther from the truth . . . or could it?

Amanda shifted her body, grateful that

Branch made no attempt to stop her as she slid off him and onto the mattress. She didn't want to see the knowing smirk she knew would be on his face, but she couldn't help herself. From beneath the dubious safety of her lashes, she peeped over at him. He was asleep!

Amanda sat up and reached to the foot of the bed for the linens to cover her nakedness and his. Once she was satisfied that no part of him but his head remained in view, she clasped the sheet to her breasts and stared down at his face. His expression was one of supreme repletion, the satisfied look of a man who has been plentifully supplied with all he has craved. Even in sleep he wore a smile, and she could just imagine what he would be like when he awoke. He would be insufferable, reminding her of this evening's triumph at every opportunity.

The longer she thought about the strong possibility that Branch would now think he could take her to bed whenever he chose, the more frantic she became. How could she maintain her independence when all he would have to do is kiss her to prove how dependent she could be? How could she win any of the confrontations she knew still lay ahead of them as they began drilling operations? Somehow, she was going to have to prove that even though she enjoyed his lovemaking, she would not let it affect their business relationship.

At the sound of his contented sigh, Amanda slapped him on the chest. "This doesn't mean a thing, Branch Colson!" she exclaimed fiercely. "I must have been out of my mind."

A sleepy grunt and a powerful arm drawing

her down onto the bed was his only response. She struggled to extricate herself from his hold but gave up when he wrapped his other arm around her. Unable to move, she finally succumbed to her own exhaustion and fell asleep in her husband's possessive embrace.

# Chapter Eleven

"HOW COULD HE!" THE GRACIOUS HOSTESS SMILE disappeared from Opal Colson's lips. Her eyes wide with shock, she watched her father-in-law enter the crowded parlor with Lucía Montez walking directly behind the wheelchair. "How could he bring that woman to my house!" The words were hissed through clenched teeth only loud enough for Graham to hear, though they still carried the force of a raging storm.

Graham patted his wife's hand reassuringly. "Now, now, dearest. My father may have felt he needed Lucía at his side this evening. You know how much he's come to rely on her since the accident."

Opal's response was a strangled sound. She struggled to regain her smile as she nodded to one of the other guests. Fluttering a fan near her face, she divided her attention between John Colson's approach and the reaction of her guests to the sloe-eyed woman who hovered behind him. So far, there had been nothing but friendly greetings exchanged between Big John and those he passed, but Opal was not appeased. Her eyes darted from one matron to another, expecting to find some sign that they felt the same outrage she did.

"Needing her services as a nurse is only the excuse he uses nowadays for having her live in his house," Opal gritted out from behind a false smile. "Considering his age and condition, at least we can be assured that anything else is out of the question, even if she is occupying the adjoining bedroom. Your own mother's room!"

"Don't distress yourself, my dear. Everyone seems quite happy to see Big John and most accepting of Lucía," Graham assured her. "You're worrying over nothing. I'm sure they understand my father's present need for Lucía's services despite past rumors."

He tucked Opal's arm more securely through his and started across the room. "Come, we are the host and hostess of this soiree, and we should greet them."

Opal stiffened and pulled away, forcing Graham to turn his back on their guests to confront her. "I can't do it," she stated firmly, though her eyes darted nervously from side to side. "You go over there and tell your father that that woman is not welcome. If he must have her in attendance, she may wait in the kitchen with the other servants."

Standing before his wife, Graham was able to block her from the view of the guests. "Keep your voice down," he warned. "I understand your feelings, but it can't be helped, and I'm sure you don't want a scene." Knowing his father, Graham was sure of the older Colson's reaction if it were suggested that Lucía be treated as a servant. "Remember the purpose of this affair, Opal."

"I'm beginning to wonder if the guest of honor remembers," Opal grumbled. "You did give dear cousin Amanda the correct date and time, didn't you, Graham?" She looked nervously toward the doorway.

"Of course I did," Graham retorted, his sharp tone revealing the extent of his exasperation. "It's quite a distance between Barrysville and the Box H. I'm sure Amanda underestimated her time of travel and will no doubt be arriving shortly."

He grasped his wife's arm and forced her to accompany him across the room. "All the more reason we should be stationed by the doorway. The poor girl knows no one here, and ours should be the first faces she sees, don't you agree, darling?"

Opal's reply was drowned out by her father-in-law's booming greeting. "'Bout time you two made it over here." Big John turned his chair toward them, his eyes showing no warmth as they appraised the advancing couple. "Opal, come closer. Let's have a look at you. This son of mine"—he nodded his head toward Graham—"tells me you're carrying the next Colson, finally. That true, girl?" He stared pointedly at his red-faced daughter-in-law's belly as if looking for confirmation.

"Well . . . ah . . . yes, that's right," Opal stammered, completely mortified that Big John would openly discuss something she considered an unfit topic for mixed company. Coming from such a refined home in the East, Opal was sure she'd never get used to the blunt ways of Texans.

"Good, good," John remarked dismissingly, then turned his full attention on Graham. "Took you a while, didn't it, boy? But you're a Colson, and I figured even you'd be man enough to get the job accomplished sooner or later." His sharp green eyes challenged his son to retort, but the only response from Graham was a slight tic in his jaw. Big John opened his mouth to say more, but Lucía dropped her hand onto his shoulder.

Gaining his attention, Lucía shook her head so slightly that few in the gathering were aware of her gentle censure. "Señor Graham. Señora Opal. Congratulations to you both," she offered in her soft, melodic voice as she started to push the wheelchair away. "Come, Señor John. Your son and his wife have more guests to greet, and I believe you would enjoy a cup of punch after the long drive."

Voices at the entryway heralded the arrival of another group of guests, but to Opal's disappointment Amanda Hamilton was not among them. Billy and Reese, each with an attractive young lady on his arm, sauntered noisily in. Opal recognized the two daughters of a successful local rancher and was able to conjure up a receptive smile. "At least your brothers are showing some sense of propriety this evening. Though I wonder that the Stehlings would allow Abigail and Lorena to be escorted by those two rascals," she muttered under her breath as she crossed toward the two couples.

"Stehling may be willing to overlook my brothers' many faults if he thinks it might settle his daughters into a prosperous marriage," Graham remarked. His comment brought a sharp look from his wife, but he knew they were too close to the new arrivals for her to offer any verbal rebuke. He also knew his reprieve was only temporary, and once the soiree was over he would be subjected to a long list of his and his family's social transgressions.

Graham wondered if tonight would be a good time to let Opal know just why her father had been so eager to hand his daughter over to the son of a Texas rancher. She wouldn't be so snobbish if she knew he had saved her father, the eminent Boston attorney, from bankruptcy. No, he'd save that weapon for another time, when he could turn her shock to his advantage. For now, the knowledge that he could so humble his haughty wife was enough. He prided himself on being a very patient man, and thus far that trait had served him very well.

"Where's this cousin of ours?" Billy demanded loudly, his blue eyes searching the crowd for a stranger. "She must really be somethin' if she can keep ol' Branch—"

His words were cut off by a bruising elbow to his ribs from Reese and a warning look from his brother's green eyes. Only Reese had inherited those green eyes from their father, along with his ability to use their intensity with cutting effectiveness. "Good evenin', Opal," Reese greeted, bending his blond head slightly in deference to his sister-in-law.

Reese smoothly insinuated himself between

Billy and Opal. "You know Lorena and Abby Stehling, I'm sure. Their folks'll be along in a little while. We came on ahead to get in a little dancin'." Opal had no time to question Billy's slip about Branch before both young men had swept their ladies farther into the room and joined the couples dancing to the labored strains of a trio of fiddlers stationed in one corner.

Amanda waited in the carriage while Branch secured the reins to the hitching post. He then came around to help Ellie and herself down from the old-fashioned conveyance. The sight of his lithe, broad-shouldered form sent tingles of awareness throughout her body. The past few days had been full of surprises, beginning with their marriage, the wedding night, and especially the nights since. Those never-ending nights had awakened a sensuality within Amanda that she would never have believed existed. Her cheeks flushed with vivid color every time she thought about the hours she'd spent eagerly in her husband's arms.

However, no matter how passionately they had spent those hours after dark, the days had been strictly business. They had argued over the location of the drilling site and discussed, just as heatedly, the plans for the future of their oil company. Eventually, Amanda had come to think her husband was as changeable as a chameleon and that she'd seen every shade that made up the many facets of Branch Colson. But she was wrong. The slow-drawling cowboy, the autocratic foreman, the hard-driving wildcatter, the knowledgeable business partner, even the demanding lover—none had prepared her for the urbane-looking man who had appeared in the parlor to escort them to Opal Colson's soiree.

Seeing Ellie in a dress had been the first surprise of the evening. When Amanda had finished her toilette and gone to the parlor to await her husband, Ellie had already been there, attired in a deep rose silk gown, several years out of fashion but still very grand. Her white hair had been piled atop her head, closer to center than usual, and decorated with an elaborate ornament of feathers and silk flowers trimmed with jet beads.

"Nobody's seen me in my best bib and tucker fer such a spell, might not know it's me. But cain't let them town folks think Ellie Hamilton's forgotten how to act like a lady," Ellie had remarked when Amanda found her voice and choked out a compliment. "Look real purty, Amanda, honey." She'd returned the flattery as she'd walked around her niece, taking full measure of her carefully arranged curls and the pale blue silk gown she wore. "Branch seen you yet?" As usual, she hadn't waited for Amanda's answer but had gone on, "What'd he say?"

"He says beautiful." Branch's deep voice had rumbled from the hallway as he entered the room, lifted his wife's suddenly lifeless hand, and brushed it with his lips. "Your gown is lovely, but the woman wearing it is devastating." His gaze had settled briefly on the shadow between her breasts before rising to her face.

Amanda had stared slack-jawed at Branch, her shock not so much from his words or heated gaze as from his appearance. Dressed in a perfectly tailored dark suit, snowy white shirt, and silk neck scarf, Branch was attired as elegantly as any Eastern gentleman. Moreover, his manner matched the clothing.

With a gallantry she'd heretofore not seen in him, he'd offered an arm to each of them and escorted them outside to the waiting carriage. Her automobile had already been discarded as too small to transport the three of them comfortably over such a distance. The conversation during the long ride into town had been carried mainly by Branch and Ellie. Amanda had offered little as she'd contemplated this new facet of her husband.

"Ready, Amanda? Or are you planning on sittin' up there all night?" Branch's voice broke into her musings as his strong hands clamped around her waist. He lifted her easily from the carriage and lowered her to the ground. He didn't release her immediately but gave her waist a light squeeze and brushed his lips across her forehead. "Come on, Mrs. Colson. There's a lot of people waitin' inside to meet you, and I'm anxious to show you off."

Glancing around, Amanda noted the number of carriages and saddle horses already tied to the long hitching posts that stretched across the front of the yard. "Oh, Branch, I had no idea."

"Opal doesn't do anything in a small way." He tucked her arm into his and offered his other to Ellie. "Let's go, ladies. Everybody ought to be here by now. This'll be an entrance the county won't soon forget."

Ellie cackled merrily in response to Branch's remark, but Amanda was filled with a growing sense of unease. The purpose of the soiree had been altered without the knowledge of its hostess. From what little she knew of Opal Colson, Amanda doubted the alteration would be appreciated.

"Branch, I still think it would have been better to have sent word of our marriage to your family," she remarked as they drew closer to the front steps. She'd voiced this same argument ever since she'd discovered Branch had neglected to do so.

"It doesn't seem fair to just spring it on them in front of what appears to be the entire county. Maybe we should announce it another time, after we've told your family."

The sounds of voices and the faint background of music could be heard through the windows lining the veranda. In the shadowed light of the early evening, Amanda could clearly make out the slight tightening along her husband's jawline, a sign she'd come to recognize as irritation, which was often followed by an abrupt mood swing.

"What's the matter? Embarrassed to admit in public that you've married the bastard Colson?" Branch mocked.

Amanda stopped, stunned by his remark. Heedless of her aunt's presence, she grasped her husband's arm. "I'm getting very tired of these cruel and unwarranted accusations, Branch Colson," she lashed out at him, fury mounting color in her cheeks.

"As you very well know, I don't care one whit about your ancestry or the circumstances of your birth." The sparkling humor she saw in his dark eyes added to her rancor. "It's the man you are that counts, and if you weren't such a dimwit at times you'd remember it. You'd also realize that I simply felt that your family deserved prior notice. It would certainly have been the polite thing to do. Now, if you're through insulting me and yourself, I suggest we go on into this party. We're already far later than we should be."

"Told you she was worth her salt," Ellie remarked, beaming approval at Amanda, then frowning up at Branch.

"Just testing," Branch replied in a lilting tone, flashing a grin revealing his pleasure. Grasping Amanda's shoulders, he abruptly pulled her close and planted a brief kiss on her startled mouth. "Sorry, Peaches. I just had to make sure of where you stood before we went in there."

"Don't call me Peaches," Amanda protested softly, though she was getting used to it and liked the way he almost always made it sound like an endearment. Her protest had slipped out automatically, but this time it lacked conviction.

Amanda stood staring up into her husband's face, completely lost in the black depths of his eyes. She was hypnotized by the soft expression in them as he lowered his head. His lips brushed across hers once, twice, then settled gently over her mouth for a kiss that left Amanda speechless at the tenderness his lingering caress conveyed.

For the second time in the evening, Opal's smile disappeared and was replaced by an expression of horror. Branch's appearance, flanked by two women, caused a ripple of soft gasps and startled murmurs through the throng. The dancers stopped as everyone's attention was drawn to the doorway.

"Oh my God," Opal breathed. "Why is *he* here, Graham?" she asked weakly, closing her eyes against the vision of Branch's tall, dark figure. "Bad enough your father had to show up with his current paramour. Now the result of an earlier dalliance has—"

"That will be enough, Opal," Graham ordered. "Branch is a Colson and has a right to be here, as does any member of my family. Obviously, he offered his services to Amanda and Ellie as escort. Come, where are your society manners?" he teased lightly as he pulled his wife along with him.

"Amanda," Graham greeted, a warm smile softening the strain around his mouth. "Welcome to our home. You're looking absolutely lovely this evening." He was taken aback when Branch didn't release Amanda but covered her hand with his own, effectively keeping her at his side.

"Branch. Aunt Ellie." Graham acknowledged the other two with a slight nod. Then, as if suddenly remembering his wife, he said, "Let me introduce my wife, Opal."

"You can't know how delighted I am to finally make your acquaintance, Cousin Amanda," Opal gushed, deliberately ignoring Branch and Ellie. She placed her hand on Amanda's arm in an attempt to guide her into the room. "Come. There are so many people just dying to meet you."

"Hold on there, Opal." Ellie's voice crackled. "Afore you start introducin' Amanda to all these folks, they's an announcement I'd like to make. Iffen you'll just stop them fiddle players for a little while, I'll get on with it."

"But—I," Opal stammered, the features on her narrow face becoming pinched as she looked to her husband for some assistance. None was forthcoming from that quarter. Graham looked just as perplexed as she.

"Get on with you now," Ellie urged. "When folks hear what I've got to say, then we'll really have somethin' to celebrate." She stared so belligerently at Opal that the younger woman nodded in white-faced acquiescence.

Realizing she had no choice but to do as Ellie requested, Opal prepared to suffer the greatest humiliation of her entire life. Reluctantly, she signaled the musicians to stop playing. Since all eyes were trained on the trio of latecomers, she had no trouble gaining the crowd's attention for Ellie's announcement.

Whatever it was, Opal was sure it would confirm her suspicions that the elderly woman had gone completely daft. Opal assumed Amanda had not tried to stop her aunt because she had not been around long enough to recognize the extent of Ellie Hamilton's senility. Graham would be very sorry for including the horrid old woman in the invitation.

Ellie stepped spryly into the middle of the parlor, with Branch and Amanda following in her wake. Her lined face wore a radiant smile, her blue eyes snapping with delight. "Folks, y'all came out tonight to meet my niece, Amanda,

191

who came all the way from New York City. Might be a few of you who remember my brother Ben. This purty little gal on Branch Colson's arm is Ben's daughter."

Ellie paused and looked about the room, her smile widening when she recognized a few of the faces. The smile slipped slightly when she spied John Colson but then brightened with triumph when she noticed the puzzled look on Big John's face as he stared at his eldest son. "I ain't much for fancy words, so's I'll just come on out with it."

Gesturing with her thumb toward Branch, she proclaimed, "This good-lookin' rascal didn't waste no time when he clapped eyes on Amanda. Any of you other young fellers who's got a mind to pay her a call is a mite too late." Her lips twitched with glee as she delivered, "Branch done married up with her already."

Ellie's announcement stunned the crowd into silence. Seconds later, the pall was broken by Opal's shriek. Graham turned to his wife just in time to catch her slumping figure and prevent her from falling to the floor. His face was ashen as he lifted her up and carried her from the room. "I . . . ah must see to my wife. All this excitement is too much for her in her delicate condition."

Billy was the first to react to the announcement. Upon reaching his eldest brother's side, he clapped him on the back and offered his congratulations. "No wonder you didn't want me or Reese to go on over to the Box H. Didn't want nobody to put in a claim 'til you got your brand on her."

He pumped his brother's hand, then scooped his new sister-in-law into his arms. He pressed a kiss on Amanda's stunned mouth. "That's to welcome my new cousin to Texas," he explained, then kissed her again. However, this time his mouth lingered a bit longer, and his arms held her more tightly. "That one was to welcome my new sister into the Colson family." Releasing her, he winked at his brother's glowering expression. "Don't look so riled. We *are* kissin' cousins."

Reese followed his younger brother's example, but with even more enthusiasm. "You're a right fine addition to the family, Amanda." He grinned at her startled expression as he set her back down on her feet. To his brother, he remarked, "She must really be somethin' special to get an experienced heartbreaker like you to tie the knot."

"She is," Branch responded, sliding his arm around his wife and settling her firmly at his side. "You just remember whose wife she is." The words were delivered to Reese, but Branch's dark eyes were on the man being wheeled through the parting crowd.

Amanda knew immediately that he could be none other than Big John Colson, Branch's father. Ellie had been right. Father and son were so alike, the similarity of character more significant than the superficial coloring and years that differentiated them. There was an unmistakable air of nobility about each of them. It was there in the way they held their noble heads, the set of their broad shoulders, the obvious power that went far beyond physical strength. Not even a wheelchair could detract from the overwhelming presence of the man occupying it.

It was no wonder Nita had named her son Juan. Amanda had picked up enough of the language by now to know that Juan was the Spanish name for John. Upon seeing Big John, she knew why her husband was called Branch. It was even more appropriate than his given name. They seemed to be extensions of each other, opposing limbs on the same tree. Others had obviously seen this resemblance, too, for Ellie had once explained that "folks started callin' the little shaver Branch almost from the beginnin'. You'll understand once you see Big John."

She could feel the tension in her husband as his arm tightened around her waist. His body was rigid, and Amanda found herself unconsciously leaning into him rather than shrinking away. Because of her knowledge concerning his childhood, she felt a need to protect him from the torment she knew resulted every time father and son were together. Images of a little dark-eyed boy came to her mind, a little boy who'd been so full of anger he'd come at this man with a knife.

Tall, fiery-haired, and green eyed, Big John must have seemed like a giant to a small boy. Had those piercing green eyes ever softened when they'd gazed upon his eldest? How could they not reflect the pride a man should feel in having a son like Branch? Wasn't it possible that Big John loved Branch but had never found the right way to tell him?

"Give me a minute alone with my son," John

announced autocratically, and the gathered guests drifted away to discuss the startling news they'd just been given. Big John waited until only Ellie, Lucía, Amanda, and Branch remained. "So, you've married Ben Hamilton's girl," he began, his words a statement rather than a question. "My congratulations, boy. You've moved fast and clever. All this time I thought you were shirking, you've been mighty busy."

Ellie stepped forward and glared at John. "I ain't said my full piece. I'm turnin' over the Box H to them as a weddin' present, Colson. This boy's going to get what you never did. What do you say to that?" she challenged, obvious glee in her voice.

Amanda froze, completely stunned by this latest disclosure. Unconsciously, she dug her fingers into Branch's arm. She was speechless, but her husband didn't appear to suffer from any such impediment.

"Amanda and I thank you, Ellie. That's mighty generous, and we certainly didn't expect it, did we, sweetheart?" he asked as he removed Amanda's painful grasp from his arm and kept her hand safely imprisoned within his own.

"Ah . . . we certainly did not. I don't know what to say."

"You don't have to say nothin', honey," Ellie supplied happily. "It's enough for me to know that I've put the Box H in such good hands. Now I can die happy."

Branch offered his assurance that they would do their best to live up to Ellie's faith in them, but Amanda wasn't listening. Her brain was a whirl of doubts, anger, and suspicion. That first night when Ellie had suggested Amanda and Branch get married, she had offered the Box H as part of the bribe, but Amanda had never thought she'd actually go through with it. Had Branch known all along that by marrying her he would get both the mineral rights and the ranch? If so, no wonder he'd been so anxious to get his ring on her finger. What a fool she had been to go along with him.

Accusation flared like a beacon in her gaze as she looked up at her husband. Her fingers clenched into fists when she saw that he felt none of the shock she was feeling. As if he could read her mind, Branch gave an almost imperceptible shake of his head. His eyes warned her to keep silent, that they would discuss this new turn of events when they were alone.

Big John's words interrupted the visual byplay going on between husband and wife. "I'll say it again. Damned clever of you, boy."

"Now, Big John," Branch drawled with seeming nonchalance. "Considerin' your eye for a thoroughbred, I thought you'd see right away why I moved so fast to rope this pretty little filly into my corral."

"The Colson stock could use some new blood," John responded sarcastically. A knowing grin split his features as he went on, "And if I know you, it won't be long before she's sprouting with your seed. I won't have to wait five years like I did with Graham to get me a grandchild. Maybe you're good for something after all."

"Oh!" Amanda gasped, incensed. She wished

she was the type of woman to fall victim to the vapors. Then, like Opal, she could escape from this outrage to her sensibilities. Both men had spoken of her as if she were a prime addition to their breeding stock. The only satisfaction she had was sensing that Branch was as angered by Big John's crude remarks as she.

"Like father like son," Branch decreed in a deadly quiet tone.

Before Amanda could utter a word, Branch quickly swept her into his arms. The musicians had begun playing when Big John had dispersed the crowd. "If you'll excuse us," he said coldly, "I'd like to have this dance with my wife."

He gave his father a frigid glare but smiled warmly at Lucía. "You're looking as beautiful as ever, Lucía. Glad to see you at this shindig. I know how you love to dance. After this waltz, I'll be happy to stand in for Big John and give you a whirl around the floor."

As Branch turned away, he was gratified to see the white-knuckled grip his father had on the arms of the wheelchair. He'd vowed long ago not to throw his father's impotence back in his face, but the man had gone too far tonight. It was all right for Big John to goad him. He could handle it, but he refused to let the man's bitterness spill over onto Amanda. He would not allow Amanda to be made a victim of the animosity that surged like a living thing between himself and his father.

With a firm grip that brooked no denial, Branch guided Amanda to a small clearing in the middle of the crowd. "We're going to dance,

Peaches. And we're going to look as if we're enjoying it."

Even though he was angry, his movements were as graceful as any partner she'd ever had. Amanda, however, had difficulty following his steps. "Your father is the crudest man I've ever met."

"That he is," Branch agreed as he spun her around in an intricate pattern. "Forget what he said. He wasn't trying to get at you but at me."

The waltz was being played with far more enthusiasm than expertise, and Amanda was grateful that none of the other couples appeared to be aware of her agitation. After a few moments, Branch commanded her to relax, and to her great amazement she was able to comply, at least up to a point. Her body moved as one with his, but her mind was in total contradiction with their loving appearance. She couldn't wait for the evening to be over so they could have it out.

Branch's smile was lazy and contented as he looked down at her, confirming her suspicions that he had known all along what Ellie was going to announce. If it wouldn't have caused another scene, Amanda would have given him a vicious kick in the shin. Her answering gaze was murderous, but Branch didn't seem to comprehend that he was the target of her anger.

"Is something wrong, Mrs. Colson?" Branch asked solicitously as he swirled her through the other couples on the floor.

"Having that as my name, for starters," Amanda answered through gritted teeth.

Branch stiffened for a moment, then relaxed.

"Marry in haste, repent at leisure," he tossed out glibly. "Be of good cheer, Amanda. Ellie's generosity has provided you with plenty of time to get used to that name."

Looking about her, Amanda was assured that no one else could hear her words. "You knew about this, didn't you?" she accused in a fierce whisper.

"What if I did?" he returned smoothly. "What difference would it make?"

"You know very well what difference it makes. You married me under false pretenses," she countered angrily. "Our agreement was to go our separate ways once we struck oil. She'll never get over it if we do that now. How can you be so complacent about it? We're in a horrible fix!"

Branch's chuckle infuriated her further. "Have a little patience, honey. Later tonight, I'll be happy to show you it's not nearly as horrible as you think." With that, he crushed her to his chest, staving off anything else she might say.

He twirled her around and around until she was so dizzy that she didn't have the presence of mind to admonish him any further. To ensure that she remained in that witless condition, he ended their dance with a kiss that left her in no doubt of what she could expect once they were back home and in bed. To Amanda's complete mortification, his possessive embrace was greeted by hearty applause from the other couples around them. Branch's laughter increased her humiliation as he acknowledged the crowd's approval.

As he assisted her unsteady form from the dance floor, he leaned over as if to whisper some sweet endearment in her ear. "My brothers are standing right over there, and I want them to think all is well. We'll deal with your reservations at a better time. For now, start acting like the happy, blushing bride."

Amanda had no problem with the blushing portion of that order. Images of what he might do to overcome her reservations were clear in her mind. Just as clear was the shameful knowledge that he could make her forget everything once he had her naked and writhing beneath him. It was almost more than she could do to bring some semblance of normalcy to her features.

Reese, Graham, and Billy were indeed waiting for them at the edge of the dance floor. She forced herself to concentrate on the present, willing to follow Branch's order. "Whatever you wish, my *love*," she bit out as they walked toward the three men standing by the parlor door.

Seeing the Colson brothers together, she was struck by how little they resembled Branch or their father. They were all of medium height, blond and slighter in build than Branch. Obviously, they took after their mother, Ida Hamilton. None had the regal bearing, the strength of body and character Big John had thrown down to his first born—or had that come through Nita, whose family had been Spanish aristocrats? Maybe Branch had inherited those traits from both his parents, and that was why all the other men in the room faded in comparison. He was magnificent, and despite her anger at him she felt a certain joy in the knowledge that she was the envy of every woman in the room.

"Mind if I dance with the bride?" Graham tapped Branch's shoulder.

"Amanda?" Branch questioned, his dark eyes warning her to keep their personal problems between themselves.

Amanda was more than happy to place her hand in Graham's waiting palm. When she was with Branch, she couldn't think, and she needed time to sort out her feelings. What if her marriage to this arrogant, virile, stubborn, beautiful man really was permanent? What if she was going to be tied to him for life?

Amanda missed a step and was grateful for Graham's support. Could she live with a man who didn't love her? Granted, life as Mrs. Branch Colson had its compensations, but how long would their desire for each other last? She had assumed that she would probably marry some day, but in none of her wildest dreams had she imagined being married to a man like Branch. On the other hand, forming a business partnership with him had been appealing to her. The traits that had convinced her to become his partner were the same ones that made a real marriage between them impossible.

He was strong, went after what he wanted, and was willing to work as hard as she was to bring in their oil well. He was an intelligent man with an ambition she respected. However, there was no doubt in her mind that he expected to run things his way. Because of his power over her in bed, she was afraid he would force her to accept a life style she abhorred.

She had spent years proving she had the right to take her place in a man's world, but now she was married to a man who believed her greatest asset was her body. She could discuss her business theories to her heart's content, and he'd still do what *he* thought best. Keeping her own identity was going to be a long uphill battle, and she didn't know if she was going to have the strength or the will to survive it.

# Chapter Twelve

GRAHAM SEEMED PREOCCUPIED AS HE GUIDED Amanda through the throng of dancing couples. His steps were mechanical, more like walking in a circle than keeping any time to the music. Though he held her very lightly, Amanda was able to detect the tension in his body. His complexion was also much paler than she remembered, and concern for him overshadowed her own problems. "Are you feeling well?"

"Oh . . . er . . . I'm fine. I . . . ah . . . I'm just worried about Opal. The preparations, the excitement, and the party itself have been a bit much for her, I'm afraid. What with her expecting a child and all . . ." His voice trailed off, and he gave her a peculiar look, then cleared his throat.

"I must say, Amanda, your marriage came as a bit of a surprise. I had no hint that anything like this was in the offing that day I was out at the Box H. My older brother does have a way with women, but I hadn't thought he would appeal to a lady like yourself. Branch is . . . shall we say, a bit rough around the edges in comparison to the men you must be used to."

Taken aback by Graham's condescending tone as well as his slur on Branch, Amanda retorted feelingly, "There are many sides to my husband, as you must know, Graham. His rough edges, as you call them, are mainly on the surface. Beneath, he's a very special man, and I'm proud to be his wife."

"My, my," Graham remarked sarcastically. "Perhaps I've misjudged this alliance—and you."

Amanda ignored the music and came to a halt, glaring up at her newfound cousin and brother-in-law. Though she might be furious with Branch at the moment, she wasn't about to involve anyone else in their differences, not even a member of the family. Maybe it was feminine pride that prevented her from apprising others of what lay behind their hasty marriage. And now that it appeared she might be trapped in the alliance for life, she had even less desire to admit that it had been a mutual greed for mineral rights that had brought them together.

"And just what do you mean by that?" she demanded.

Since their disagreement was drawing attention, Graham smiled and began dancing again. "I apologize, dear cousin. It would seem that rogue really has managed to win your heart."

Amanda was saved from any further discourse

with Graham when a middle-aged woman hailed them, bringing their attempts at dancing to an abrupt and welcome end. "Graham, I won't wait another minute to meet this lovely cousin of yours," the woman explained, pulling a decidedly uncomfortable-looking man along in her wake. The man's face was red and perspiring. He tugged self-consciously at the celluloid collar buttoned snugly around his thick neck.

Relieved to escape from Graham, Amanda turned her full attention on the couple. Amanda's hand was immediately caught up in the woman's grasp. "I'm Sarah Shelton, and this is my husband Neil. He's the owner and editor of the *Barrysville Times*. You've taken us all by surprise, my dear. Why, you could have knocked me over with a feather when Ellie announced your marriage.

"Tell me, honey," she entreated as she pulled Amanda to one side. "Did Branch sweep you off your feet, or had you met him before coming out here?"

"I suppose one could say he swept me off my feet," Amanda supplied. It was true, she thought as she hid a grin behind her hand. Branch had quite literally picked her up and tossed her back into her automobile the day they'd met, immediately after kissing her most thoroughly.

"Never thought that boy would marry unless he was dragged to the altar by somebody's papa totin' a shotgun, but that's sure not the case here, is it?"

Much like Ellie, the woman went on without giving Amanda's answer much notice or giving her a chance to interrupt her running commentary. The quiet Neil was left behind as Sarah swept Amanda toward a cluster of women gathered together in one corner.

"I declare, Opal's been so close-mouthed about you, none of us knew a thing except that you're from New York. Of course, we knew a pretty young lady arrived on the train and drove out of town in a shiny little horseless carriage. You caused quite a stir that day, but nothing like tonight.

"I declare, you could've heard a pin drop when Ellie announced your marriage. None of us ever expected a woman of quality to settle for someone like Branch Colson. Of course, he is a handsome devil. I'll give him that. I'm sure you'll be good for him. His mama's family were fine folks, even if they were Mexicans."

Amanda inwardly seethed at the woman's prejudice. She'd been happy to escape Graham's snide comments, but it looked like she was in for even worse with Sarah. Was this the kind of abuse Branch had had to deal with his whole life? If so, no wonder he had such a large chip on his shoulder.

Glancing at the woman's guileless face, however, Amanda decided that Sarah really meant no harm. Tactless people like Sarah Shelton merely talked without considering the ramifications of their statements. Even so, she'd be hard put not to say something nasty if she had to spend much more time in the woman's company.

Amanda looked around for Branch, hoping he would come and save her. Anticipation was written all over the other women's faces as Amanda approached, and she began to feel as if she were about to be interrogated by the Spanish Inquisition. Again, though less than an hour had passed since their arrival, she wondered if the evening was ever going to end.

Branch was nowhere to be seen, and Amanda soon found herself being introduced to the ladies of Barrysville and the surrounding countryside. She tried to remember their names, but with Sarah constantly firing questions at her between introductions, it was impossible. Though a majority of the women extended smiling congratulations and their best wishes, a few were barely civil as they acknowledged her, disapproval clear on their faces.

Amanda's initial irritation with Sarah's non-stop babbling was rapidly replaced with genuine gratitude for the woman's natural effervescence. It was probably for the best that no one else was able to offer a comment. Amanda had dealt with enough unsettling revelations this evening without having to respond to more, and she could tell that a few of these women would have loved to tell her everything they knew about her new husband.

"I want to hear all about the wedding so I can write it up in the paper," Sarah gushed. "I write the society column, you know. Now, what did you wear? Being from New York, I'm sure it was the latest thing."

"I suppose it was," Amanda replied airily, forcing herself to ignore the glowers directed at her. She concentrated on the smiling women who were eagerly anticipating her answer. A giggle threatened to erupt as she thought about the ensemble she had worn for her wedding.

It had been the "latest thing" all right—very fashionable, designed expressly for any athletic endeavor. She'd elected to wear her college gymnasium outfit that day in deference to the heat and the activity, never dreaming it would serve as her wedding gown. Cool, comfortable, and practical—that would best describe her bloomers and middy blouse.

Suddenly aware that all conversation had stopped and the women were eagerly waiting for her description of her wedding gown, she searched for the vaguest terms. "I wore a rather informal ensemble of white and navy linen," she began.

"You ladies will have to excuse Amanda," a male voice interrupted, and Reese Colson shouldered his way toward her. "Big John wants to spend a little time with his new daughter-in-law." Tucking her arm through his own, he began ushering Amanda away despite Sarah's protest. "Sorry, ma'am," he apologized. "But y'all know Big John."

Just as the crowd had bowed to Big John Colson's command earlier on, no one argued with this latest directive. "Don't let your daddy keep her all night, Reese," Delia Parker, the storekeeper's wife, called after them. Reese smiled back over his shoulder but offered no assurance.

Looking about the crowd, Amanda spied Branch's dark head amidst a small crowd of men standing near the punchbowl. His back was to her, and it was impossible to draw his attention. "Don't worry, little sister–cousin," Reese remarked. "Big John won't bite ya."

Glancing up at the congenial face of her new brother-in-law, Amanda returned his reassuring smile with a shaky one of her own. What was the matter with her? She'd been conversing with men in power since she was a small child. But never with someone like Big John Colson, she reminded herself. Like Branch, he was nothing at all like the men she was accustomed to. Little in her previous experience had prepared her for the uncivilized situations or the unconstrained personalities she'd encountered since she'd stepped off the train.

As she studied the young man walking beside her, the doubts she'd had about Ellie's suspicions concerning him and his brother were even stronger. Though she had trouble reading Branch and John, she trusted her first impressions of the other Colson men. She knew her husband was right when he said there was no way Reese or Billy could be involved in the incidents at the Box H.

Granted, mischief danced in Reese's green eyes, but she sensed a basic honesty in him. Recalling Billy, she dismissed him as a possible culprit as well. Young, good-looking, and full of themselves, yes, but neither of the younger Colson brothers appeared capable of plotting anything more devious than getting a young lady out from under her mother's watchful eye.

Then, who else would stand to gain from running Ellie off her land or from her death? Graham? Ridiculous, she deemed, as soon as his name floated into her thoughts. From the looks of this house, Graham was living a very good life, plus he had a successful law practice. Tonight, she had heard talk that confirmed Ellie's opinion that he was considering a career in politics. It was the consensus of those at the party that he would some day occupy the governor's mansion. He certainly didn't need Ellie's land to achieve that goal.

Branch had been erased from her list of suspects the day he'd been shot. Therefore, Amanda could think of only one other possibility—John Colson, the man she was about to face again. If Ellie's allegations about a feud were true, Big John could well be behind the attempts on Ellie's life. Maybe he'd finally decided to end the squabble over the boundary by eliminating the one obstacle that stood in his way. Before Amanda's arrival, it was quite possible everyone believed there were no other inheritors than the Colsons.

Reese ushered Amanda down the hallway and into the library. "You favor Ida in looks," were the first words Big John spoke to her as she was escorted to his side.

Subjected to his piercing once-over, Amanda met his gaze with a steady one of her own, refusing to allow him to disconcert her again. "That may be, but my mother was blond and small also. My father always said I was like her."

Big John continued his careful study, and Amanda returned the appraisal, surprised when she saw a smile lift the corners of his mouth.

"Not afraid of me, are you?" John asked, pleased with the flash of defiance he saw in her blue eyes. She might look like his late wife, but he was willing to bet a tidy sum that her character was more like Ellie's. Yet he sensed there was a good deal of her father in her as well.

He'd known Ben Hamilton when they were youths, and even then Ben had been known for his common sense and strength of conviction. Being his daughter, Amanda probably wasn't the kind to fall into a fit of the vapors at the first sign of adversity. He could tell she was a woman who faced things squarely and knew he wouldn't be able to intimidate her like he did Opal.

"Should I be?" Amanda countered, bracing herself for a barrage of insults.

He laughed. "No reason. No reason at all." He twisted slightly in the chair and addressed the black-haired woman behind him. "What do you think, Lucía?"

"I think Señor Branch has made a very wise choice," the woman responded softly, giving Amanda a warm smile. Coming around John, she offered, "I am Lucía Montez, and I have known Branch for many years. I hope you and he will be very happy together."

"Thank you," Amanda answered, feeling an instant rapport with the woman.

"Lucía practically raised us," Reese explained. "She's been Pa's . . . ah, housekeeper for years."

"More'n that, and everybody knows it," John admitted, watching for Amanda's reaction. Not seeing the distaste such a statement would have elicited if he'd misjudged her, John softened his tone and caught Lucía's hand. "Been my conscience, too, haven't you?"

Lucía smiled down at Big John. "Sometimes."

Amanda watched the exchange with interest. It appeared that John Colson did have a tender side, and it was Lucía Montez who brought it out. Considering the implications of his earlier remark about their relationship, Amanda wondered why the two had never married, for it was obvious that John held a great deal of affection for the woman. And, unless Amanda missed her guess, that affection was returned. Lucía's beautiful dark eyes sparkled when she looked at the large man who held her hand.

Ida had been dead for years, and Nita too. But then, Amanda reasoned, maybe his past relationships were the reason Big John hadn't married again. He'd lost two women he must have cared something about, and maybe he couldn't risk giving his heart again. It was a wildly romantic thought, she admitted to herself, but knowing the complexity of her husband, Amanda was sure his father could be every bit as multifaceted.

The blunt crudeness that had colored their earlier confrontation was gone or at least held at bay. Amanda began to believe Branch's comment that Big John's insults had been directed toward him. Some day she was going to find out if anything could be done to end the hostility that smoldered between the two men.

"You goin' to keep on livin' at the Box H, or is Branch plannin' on bringin' you over to the Circle C?" John's inquiry interrupted Amanda's philosophizing.

"The Box H is our home," Amanda stated firmly. "Even if the property hadn't been deeded over to us, I wouldn't want to leave my aunt all alone. Too many things have been happening there lately."

"I'd like to talk about some of those things, but that will have to wait for some other time," he declared without a flicker of underlying guilt, and for some reason Amanda immediately believed he was not behind any of the accidents that had occurred on the Box H.

Enhancing that feeling, John continued, "There's too many ears open around here, but now that my boy's been involved I can promise he'll get to the root of this thing. Ellie's too stubborn to move out to the Circle C, I suppose."

"I'm sure of it," Amanda affirmed sadly.

"She still thinks we're feudin', don't she?"

"I'm afraid so."

"It's a waste. Waste of a lifetime," he commented as much to himself as to Amanda. "Hers and . . ."

He didn't finish the statement, and Amanda's curiosity was piqued. She was about to ask for an explanation when a pair of large palms closed possessively over her shoulders. "Sorry to break this up," Branch said, but his tone conveyed no apology. "Ellie's finished her business and wants to go home."

Big John's friendly countenance disappeared as he looked past Amanda to his son. "None of this foolishness makes any difference, boy. Since you're all recovered, I expect you back over to the Circle C as my foreman. You might have gotten that land, but you're not gettin' nothin' from me to throw into this oil scheme of yours. You're no better off than you were before, except now you've got a pretty woman to spend your nights with after all the chores are done. 'Course, that's never really been a problem you've had in the past, has it?"

Amanda could feel Branch's anger as clearly as her own. She'd felt protective earlier, had wanted to do something to shield her husband from this man. She wasn't about to stand by and listen to Branch being taunted like this, even if before his arrival she had sensed that Big John truly loved his son. All the primal instincts of a lioness fighting beside her mate came to the fore.

"Branch got more than that land and a bed-warmer when he married me," she announced, her bluntness silencing the two men. "I'm a geologist, and what's more, I've got the money to drill for the oil that lies beneath *our* land. My husband and I don't need anything from you, Mr. Colson. I can support the both of us quite easily. And if I have anything to say about it, Branch won't be returning as your foreman. He'll have plenty to do at the Box H."

Having let loose with this volley, Amanda turned to leave, not caring that her husband's black expression matched his father's. She'd been pushed and manipulated enough by Branch during the past few days, and she refused to put up with more of the same from another Colson male.

"Just a minute, young woman," John's imperious command halted her escape. "Looks like Branch did get everything he wanted and a whole lot more. What I'm wonderin' is why you married him."

Amanda turned back and adopted the quick mood swing of her husband. With a feigned sweetness in her tone and expression, she stated, "For the same reason most women marry. I love him."

She didn't wait for a response from Big John and didn't want to see the expression she knew would be on her husband's face. Pushing her way through the crowd and out of the parlor, she spied Graham at the foot of the stairs. She thanked him for the party, asked him to extend her best wishes to Opal, who hadn't reappeared since the marriage announcement, and walked to the door where Ellie was waiting.

"Let's go, Aunt Ellie." She grasped her aunt's arm, pulling her down the hallway and out the front door without allowing the older woman to utter a word. Just as they arrived at the carriage, a man stepped out from the shadows of the veranda.

A drunken sneer twisted his weatherbeaten features. "Never thought I'd see the day when you'd fall in with the almighty Colsons, Ellie Hamilton. Now they've got the Box H, Baker's old place, and mine. If people don't start openin' their eyes pretty damned soon, Big John Colson'll own everybody. Tonight you went a long way toward makin' him king."

"Hold on there, Ezra Deets." Ellie stepped in front of Amanda. "You ain't got no call to make them accusations. I ain't turned nothin' over to Big John. I gave the land to my niece here and her husband. Branch is more son to me than he'll ever be to John. He's—"

The man was too full of hatred to listen, and

he interrupted with, "Yeah, you wish he was the pup you would've whelped if Anson Colson's seed had ever took."

Amanda felt Ellie stiffen beside her, heard her draw in a sharp breath. *I've only known one man, and he was as fine as Branch.* Amanda recalled the words Ellie had spoken the day Branch had been shot. Ellie had been in love with Branch's uncle!

"The day ol' Anson showed up with his new bride, I thought you'd learned your lesson, but you're still soft in the head where them Colsons are concerned, ain't ya?" the man prodded angrily. "Makes me think you might have kept sharin' his bed even after his marriage. Makes me think you're just as loose with your morals as they've always been."

Amanda stepped forward, ready to demand that the man apologize for his crude remarks, but Ellie pulled her back. "I'm goin' to forget you said them things on account of all the years we been friends, Ezra Deets. Now you skeedaddle home to Martha and let her talk some sense into you."

There was a flicker of something, maybe apology, in the man's eyes before he saw Branch striding across the lawn toward them. "I'll tell you this, Ellie. You mighta forgot that a Colson done you wrong, but I ain't never gonna forget what they done to me. Me and mine have been forced off our land, but we're not leavin' here 'til I see Big John and all his litter get what they deserve."

Deets gave a swaying semblance of a polite bow to Amanda. "Too bad a lady like you has to be sacrificed to the likes of Big John's bastard. I knew your daddy, and I'm sure glad ol' Ben ain't here to see his gal defiled like that."

"You're making a fool of yourself, Deets," Branch said as he reached them. "You're lucky I know it's liquor talking. I've called out men for less."

The older man seemed to shrivel, but he had enough will left to make one last warning. "Folks 'round here won't take kindly to your marryin' above yerself. I'd watch out if I was you, Mex."

It was Ellie who grabbed Branch's arm, preventing him from delivering a blow. "Let him go. T'ain't worth the trouble. He's lost everythin', and he's just lashin' out like any cornered varmint."

Amanda added her quieting influence. "There was no real harm done, Branch."

"Not tonight, at least." Branch shrugged off Ellie's hold but didn't relax his stance. He pushed his jacket aside to reveal a small revolver tucked beneath his arm. His hand hovered over the handle while they watched Deets weave down the drive. "But somebody's behind this thing, and by the sounds of it, it might be him."

"He don't have the backbone for that kind of thing. Besides, it's Big John he's wantin' ta kill, not me. Anyway, he'll probably pass out before he makes it home," Ellie said.

"I suppose you're right," Branch grumbled. "Still, I'll feel better once we're home. It's a long way between town and the Box H. I should've brought more men along."

"More men!" Amanda exclaimed, chilled that Branch thought they were in constant danger. It had been such a relief to leave the armed camp he'd made of the Box H. Seeing no outriders during the trip into town, she'd assumed Branch had given up on the idea that someone was intending to cause more harm to either Ellie or themselves. "You didn't bring any men when we came to the party. I didn't see anyone."

"That's only what you and everybody else were supposed to think," Branch explained as he handed Ellie up into the carriage. "They're out there. Wouldn't be doing any good if you could see 'em."

"Crazy as a peach-orchard boar, that's what you are, Branch," Ellie deemed from her perch on the carriage seat. "Nobody's goin' to take no more potshots at me or you. Iffen they was a mind, they would've tried it again right after they shot you. Ain't no reason fer a body to be travelin' around with a hosta bodyguards every place they goes."

"We'll see. For now, we'll keep the guards." Branch turned to Amanda but didn't offer to help her into the carriage. Instead, he towered over her, his eyes glowing. "We've got something to clear up before we head out."

Amanda knew what Branch wanted to clear up. Her bold statements to his father must have come as quite a shock to him. However, she was not about to withdraw any of them and had enough knowledge of military history to know when to take the offensive. Hands on hips, she returned her husband's glare.

"Don't give me that black-eyed devil look, Branch Colson. Somebody had to stand up to your father. He's rude, domineering, and ruthless. I won't allow him to speak to you like that in my presence. We don't need the scraps from his table. I wasn't lying when I said I've got the money to back us. I do, and I will."

Branch threw back his head and laughed, which was the last thing Amanda had expected. "Hold on, Peaches," he drawled lazily, amusement now coloring his tone. "You sure do get goin' when you get your feathers ruffled, don't you?"

"Don't you slip into that lazy cowboy routine either, Branch Colson," she warned, confused by his response. "You only do it to cover what you're really thinking."

"And what do you think I'm thinking right now?" he asked smoothly, his deep-timbered voice seducing her senses and reducing her reason.

"Whatever it is, it can wait," Ellie interrupted. "If you two are fixin' to start bellowin' at each other, you'd best wait 'til we get out of earshot. We set enough tongues to waggin' tonight. No need to give 'em anymore to jaw about."

Branch promptly picked up his still sputtering wife and tossed her onto the carriage seat beside Ellie. "Just want you to know, Ellie. Tonight your niece put Big John in his place better'n anybody ever has. He's probably still speechless with the shock."

Ellie's cackling laughter split the stillness of the night and made the horses stamp nervously.

"Told you she's worth her salt. Cain't wait to hear what she said to him."

Branch climbed into the carriage beside Amanda and flicked the reins over the team's back. "You'll hear about it, Ellie, I promise. She's worth a whole lot more than salt, I'm afraid. We'll have plenty to discuss on the way home."

# Chapter Thirteen

"WE'RE NOT USIN' YOUR MONEY, AND THAT'S THE end of it," Branch reiterated, never wavering from the stance he'd taken since the beginning of the argument that had filled the time traveling back to the Box H.

Amanda closed the bedroom door and lowered her voice. "I don't know why you have any qualms about using my money. You married me to get your hands on this land. Why not use my money too?"

"It might surprise you to know that even *I* have some honor." He shrugged out of his jacket and tossed it onto a chair.

"Indeed," Amanda snapped. "How honorable it was of you to marry me in order to get my land."

Branch looked across the room at his wife. She was still leaning against the door, her blue eyes fired with anger and her color high. This argument was going nowhere, and he saw no reason to extend it any further into the night. There were far more pleasurable ways to spend the next few hours than hurling insults back and forth.

As far as he was concerned, the matter was settled. She could do whatever she wanted with her money, but he wanted no part of it. All he wanted to do was strip off all those yards of silk and lace and see those beautiful eyes reflecting an altogether different emotion. They had enough disagreements during the day over their business partnership. Up here, in this room, they weren't business partners. Here, they were husband and wife, partners of an entirely different sort.

Unbelievably, she'd defended him tonight, and, what's more, she had declared in front of everyone that she loved him. As much as that had pleased him, he wasn't about to allow a woman to fight his battles for him, especially when that woman was his wife. It was unmanly to stand meekly behind her skirts, but at the same time her protective attitude had been more than flattering.

He hadn't known then or now what to do about this situation. It had been a pleasure to see Big John's slack-jawed expression as Amanda had whirled around in a rustle of perfumed skirts and stormed out of the room. Branch, like everyone else who'd heard her statements, had stood immobile for a moment. Finally, he'd found his voice and made a vague statement about women not always being rational.

He'd tried to follow Amanda but had been waylaid by Reese and Billy. Both had congratulated him again on his marriage, adding that he'd married a spitfire. "Even you might have a little trouble handling her, big brother," Billy had jibed.

Damn it! He could handle her. He wasn't going to let any woman think she could arrange his life for him. But Amanda wasn't just any woman. What if she really did love him? What if her anger had caused her to admit her real feelings?

"Is it possible that your explanation for marrying me might be true?"

Amanda clenched her hands around the doorknob behind her. For one fleeting moment, she considered bolting out of the room. But that would only postpone the inevitable. She'd known Branch wouldn't forget one word of that speech she'd given his father, especially that final declaration.

She could still hear herself proclaiming that she loved Branch. At the time she'd uttered those words, she'd been too angry to realize they were true. They'd just poured out, and she'd actually congratulated herself on her quick thinking. The remark had seemed the most logical explanation for her marriage, and one Big John wouldn't be able to refute.

It had only been later, in the carriage as she mulled over Ezra Deets's remarks to Ellie that she'd come to realize the veracity of her statement. Like Ellie, she had met a one-of-a-kind man, and now he was the irrevocable owner of her heart. When they parted, she would feel the same void Ellie had lived with for most of her life.

The drive home had taken hours. Some had been filled with their argument over the use of her money, but part of the time had been quiet, each occupant of the carriage lost in private thoughts. It had been during one of the quiet times that she'd looked over to Ellie and seen tears in the corners of the older woman's eyes.

"Aunt Ellie, are you all right?" Amanda had seen the slight tremor in the older woman's hands as she wiped away a tear.

"I'm fine, honey, just fine." She'd patted Amanda's knee. "Just bein' an old woman thinkin' about things best left in the past. I told you once before that I made a choice and I've lived by it. Too late for me to be feelin' sorry now. When Anson brought his bride home from the war, it was pretty hard to take, but I'd already chosen the land over him. He deserved some happiness, and I deserved what I got. Just you remember what else I told you so you never make the same mistake."

Ellie had looked around Amanda and nodded toward Branch. "You're not alone, girl. I'm glad fer that. It's no good bein' alone. Love's no good unless it's shared. It's a waste of livin'. I let my daddy convince me otherwise, but he was dead wrong."

Her words had been soft, and only Amanda had heard them. Branch had been intent on the shadowed landscape around them, his gaze continually sweeping from one side of the road to the other. He'd occasionally touched the brim of his hat, and Amanda had known that he was signaling to someone and hadn't been paying any attention to Ellie's conversation. Once or twice during the drive, she'd thought she'd seen a rider off in the distance, had seen a faint flash of light as if a match had been struck, then quickly extinguished.

*A waste.* Hadn't Big John said the same thing? Now that Amanda knew the name of the man Ellie had once loved, she could guess at what had kept them apart—two rivaling families, feuding over the boundaries of their connecting land. Ellie had chosen not to go against her parents' wishes and in so doing had lost the only man she would ever love.

*Love*—a simple word describing such a powerful emotion. Amanda's thoughts had taken a startling turn when Branch's arm had brushed against her as he guided the team of horses around a bend in the road. That physical reminder of his presence had forced her to recall the feelings she'd experienced when Ellie had announced the signing over of the Box H.

She'd been shocked by that but even more shocked by the sense of relief she'd felt. Even though she was sure Branch had used her to achieve his own ends, she still found herself glad that they would not be able to terminate their marriage so easily. Ellie was right. It was no good being alone, and after having been married to Branch, Amanda couldn't imagine spending her life with anyone else. Like her aunt, she'd have only one man in her life, one love. And, like her aunt, that man was a Colson. Hamilton women seemed to have a fatal attraction for them.

Now, looking across the bedroom at her husband, the man who sent her heart racing with just a look, who filled most of her thoughts, she was even more convinced that she'd spoken the truth. However, this revelation was too unsettling to discuss with anyone, least of all Branch. She needed time to sort out her feelings and consider the consequences.

Love was meant to be shared. Amanda doubted that Branch thought of her as any more than a pleasurable means to attain his dreams. He might claim there was no way out of their marriage, but love for her was certainly not his reason for taking her as his wife. If she admitted how she felt about him, knowing he didn't love her in return, she would be giving him a weapon that could destroy her.

He was waiting for an answer, and Amanda knew she'd have to come up with something. Hedging, she looked away. "I had to say something, and that seemed the easiest way to explain why I married you."

"Was it?" he asked, crossing the space between them. Pulling her away from the door and locking his hands at the back of her waist, he judged, "I doubt it was that easy for you to say unless there was some element of truth in it. I haven't known you long, honey, but I do know enough to realize you wouldn't out and out lie."

Breathing deeply of the light fragrance that always surrounded her, Branch waited for some response. He hadn't anticipated his reaction to hearing her say that she loved him. He wanted to hear her say it again, to make him believe it.

He wasn't exactly sure how to explain how he felt about her except that he'd never felt this way about any woman before. He did know that he thought of her as belonging to him. Knowing what pride she took in her independence, he doubted she'd appreciate that sentiment, but he couldn't think of a better way to describe it.

On the other hand, if she had fallen in love with him, it would make everything so much easier. He had wrapped her up in the legal bonds of marriage and the sensual bonds of pleasure, but she still could choose to leave him. Once their well came in, she might decide she didn't like being married to a man who embodied none of the sophisticated polish she was used to. She was already wealthy, and, with the additional profits from an oil strike to add to her fortune, she might elect to return to the fast-paced, cultured life style of the city. If she were determined to go back East, there was no way he could stop her, and that filled him with an emotion he hadn't experienced for a very long time—fear.

"Would you lie?" he pressed harshly.

Amanda's arms were caught up between them. She nervously toyed with his silk neck scarf, inadvertently loosening the knot at his throat in the process. Keeping her gaze anywhere but on his face, her mind raced for something convincing to say. She knew if she looked up she'd be lost. Those dark eyes of his had a way of forcing the truth out of her, especially when he was holding her, the heat of his body surrounding her, the scent of him intoxicating her.

"I would if the lie didn't hurt anyone," she finally injected carefully. "You and I know we went into this marriage as business partners, but the rest of the world doesn't need to know that. If people think we're in love, it'll stop a lot of embarrassing questions."

Her words angered him and did nothing to alleviate his anxiety over their future. "So you don't love me," he stated. "But this marriage is still based on something other than business. We both know that. You need me, Amanda. If it takes years, I'll prove that to you."

Amanda struggled to escape his arms, but he held her fast. She realized that he'd unknowingly supplied her with a far better explanation than the one she'd just given. "Of course I need you. I need your strength and experience in order to bring in a well. After tonight, that's not all. Ellie turned the ranch over to us and expects us to run it. I certainly can't do that alone. I consider myself a good businesswoman, and I'm wise enough to realize I'll need your help there, too."

"With all that money you bragged about, you could hire somebody to do all that."

Amanda was well aware of what he was trying to get her to say and refused to give him the satisfaction. "Yes, I could," she agreed. "But according to Ellie, you're the best man for the job."

Feeling that she was presenting an irrefutable

case, she looked up at him. She forced up her defensive barriers, which was much easier to do when she could see anger in his eyes. Fire from her blue eyes matched the blaze in his. "Would you have come to work for me if I, a mere woman, had tried to hire you?"

"Hell no." Branch's fingers curled around her shoulders.

Amanda flinched at the cruel grasp, welcoming the pain. It kept her senses alert and prevented her from backing down and succumbing to the magnetic pull he always had on her. "Then I did the only practical thing. I wanted the best, so I married it."

"Don't you think that's going a bit far to get a hired hand?" Branch inquired, his fury building to mammoth proportions.

As Branch's temper rose, Amanda's calmed. She felt in greater control the more his slipped. Very matter-of-factly, she stated, "Out here, men don't have the sophistication to handle business dealings with a woman. I wasn't going to let a chance like this slip through my fingers because of your immature male pride."

"That does it, Peaches." Hearing her confirm his suspicion that she did put him in a lower category than the men she knew in the city, Branch fell back on the only weapons he had. They might not be very sophisticated either, but where she was concerned he'd found them very effective. He would use them to keep his advantage for as long as he could.

Scooping her into his arms, he was across the room in three long strides. Instead of dumping her on the bed, he stood her beside it, turned her around, and started unhooking her dress.

"Branch, what are you doing?" Amanda's brief moment of calm control disappeared.

"I'm stripping away the sophisticated city lady," he replied heavily, his fingers continuing down the row of hooks. "Bringing her down to my level."

Grabbing the top of her bodice before it dropped to her waist, Amanda felt as if she were holding a flimsy shield against overwhelming odds. "My clothes don't have anything to do with the person I am, nor do they make me feel superior," she argued desperately, striving to maintain her grip on the silk as Branch started pressing light kisses on her back.

She tried to step away from the exciting torment of his lips on her flesh, but he curled his thumb under the strap of her corset cover and pulled her back. Twirling her around to face him, he tugged the silk from her grasp, lifted it over her head, and tossed it somewhere in the vicinity of the chair. He ignored her swatting hands as he dispensed with the ruffled corset cover and went to work on the laces of her corset.

"You wear too many clothes, and you certainly don't need this." The steel-wired garment joined the growing mound of feminine apparel on the floor.

Wrapping his large hands around her waist, he pulled her close. "You're not always practical, city lady. Your waist is already so tiny I can fit my hands around it, so why do you wear that thing?" He nuzzled her ear and ran moist lips across her bare shoulder.

"Stop that," Amanda managed, but there was no use fighting him—he was far too strong for her. "Ladies aren't considered properly dressed unless they wear one," she persisted doggedly, then gasped when he removed her petticoat and threw it across the room. Her drawers and chemise quickly followed.

"My point exactly," he murmured huskily as his palms covered her breasts. "Like this, you're a woman, my woman." His mouth sought hers.

Amanda melted beneath the onslaught of her husband's expertise. She was his. Denying herself the pleasure of his lovemaking would be as hopeless as trying to struggle out of his strong arms. His superior strength wasn't the only thing that kept her in his embrace.

Her lips parted to give him easy access to the secrets of her mouth while her own tongue sought his. Even knowing the control she was giving away, she couldn't get enough of him. His hands were working their magic on her, moving unerringly to all the places he knew excited her most.

His calloused fingertips toyed with her nipples until they were ripened peaks throbbing for more. He moved one of his hands around to cup her bottom while the other moved to the golden curls at the juncture of her thighs. At the first touch of his fingers on the moist center of her being, Amanda couldn't stand it any longer. She needed to return the pleasure, needed to feel the hard muscles of his body ripple and tense beneath her touch. Most of all, she needed to know she had some power over him.

Never breaking their kiss, Amanda unbuttoned his shirt and smoothed her palms across his bared chest, carefully avoiding the bandage that still covered his nearly healed wound. She ran her fingertips down through the crisp, curling hair that covered his heated skin until she encountered his trousers. While Branch's hands were occupied kneading and tantalizing her breasts, Amanda unbuckled his belt and unfastened his trousers and drawers.

She fitted her hand over his flat stomach, then deliberately let it slip lower. Her fingertips pushed through the warm thicket and closed around the hardened rod, freeing it from confinement. Not that long ago, she'd feared this symbol of her husband's virility. Now she felt a sweeping satisfaction as his manhood grew to its full magnificence within her loving clasp.

"Damn you, Amanda," Branch groaned as he involuntarily arched his hips toward her.

Heartened by his reaction, Amanda stroked him with greater fervor. Her touch did have the power to render him mindless, and she gave no quarter. Branch's body alternately tensed and trembled as she caressed him. He cursed her again, but even as he spoke the words he pulled her closer.

Finally, he knew he could stand no more without embarrassing himself and lending credence to her belief that she was his master. He reached down to grasp her hands, stilling their movement and guiding them away. With a quick shove to her shoulders, he toppled her backward onto the bed and shed his clothing with amazing speed.

Just as he was about to join her on the bed, he saw the look of triumph on her face. "Oh no," he negated softly, dangerously. "I won't be your hired stud, too. You won't be the boss here. When I finally take you, you'll be begging for something no other man can give you and you can't buy."

Alarmed by the threat, Amanda scrambled across the mattress, but he caught her before she could get away. His body pinned hers down on the bed. He poised above her, and Amanda cried out in agitation, "I'll never beg you for a single thing."

"Not yet, *querida*." His mouth feasted on one feverish breast and then the other before moving downward. He pressed kisses across her belly, down the silken length of her slender thighs, then back up the sensitive insides. He parted the delicate folds with his fingers, then took possession with his mouth.

Amanda couldn't prevent her cry of shocked pleasure as the sensations she had expected to come from his skilled hands were magnified a hundredfold by his knowing lips. She had never dreamed such total intimacy existed or could produce such unspeakable pleasure.

"Please, Branch," Amanda wailed, a flood of warmth spreading out from her feminine center and cascading over her body. She twisted and writhed, wanting to escape from the rapture she thought she could not survive. He covered her mound of gold with his palm, keeping her in place for the exquisite invasion of his tongue.

"Branch. Branch!" She moaned as she lifted her hips toward total fulfillment. He pushed her down, withdrawing his mouth, his touch. On the edge but kept from release, she involuntarily cried out her frustration.

He smiled at her frantic plea, then drew himself up and over her undulating body. He nudged her legs further apart and settled between them. Amanda felt her womanhood throbbing with desire as his heated manhood hovered at the entrance. Certain now that pleasure only led to more pleasure and that life and sanity were not threatened no matter how high she soared, Amanda arched toward him. At the same time, she grasped his muscled buttocks and urged his immediate possession. Without restraint, she opened herself fully to her husband.

"Tell me you want me, Amanda," Branch demanded. "If you can't say you love me, let me hear how much you need me."

"I need you," she whispered, closing her eyes as soon as the words were out, afraid she might see the mocking triumph in his.

"Then look at me and say it," he ordered thickly.

Amanda opened her eyes, seeing not the triumph she'd expected but something else. The strain of keeping his desire for her in check had darkened his eyes, deepened the grooves in his face. This battle of wills was as difficult for Branch as it was for her. "I need you."

"You need my strength and experience for other things besides business." He pushed into her but didn't give her all of himself, even though her hips began to rotate in the rhythm she expected him to set. "I'm mature enough to handle you, Peaches. Admit it."

Tantalized to the screaming point by his shallow forward thrusts, Amanda would have agreed to anything to assuage her desperate need. "Yes. Please, Branch. I want you so much."

She felt the heat coil deep within her as he filled her completely. Flames suffused through her body until she shook with the force of them. Holding each other tightly, they arrived as one at a brilliant pool of sensation that separated mind from body yet fused them together in ways that defied description.

Recovering first, Branch lifted his head from the hollow of her shoulder. Brushing the damp tendrils away from her forehead, he waited until she had opened her eyes. "Now, explain again why you married me."

The sweet contentment that filled her fled. "I . . . you know why. It was—"

"The truth, Amanda," he demanded, his voice soft but steeled with determination.

Moments passed. Silence. Amanda stared up at him, saw the naked need in his eyes, and she couldn't lie. "I love you," she breathed out in an agonized whisper.

Branch lowered his head, his lips a breath away from hers. The glow in his eyes was brighter than she'd ever seen it. Moisture glistened at the corners. When he spoke, his voice was roughened by emotion. "That's not what I expected you to say. I . . . I wanted you to admit that you desired me. No woman has ever loved me, Amanda. I don't quite know if I can give it in return. No one's ever taught me."

"I'll teach you, Branch," she said and gathered him into her arms. It might take years to accomplish it, but she knew the time wouldn't be wasted.

# Chapter Fourteen

As soon as Amanda saw Branch dismount his horse, she knew he'd been no more successful in obtaining a loan from the banks in Dallas than he'd been with the First Freedom Bank of Barrysville. His normally erect posture was subdued by fatigue as he tied the horse's reins to the paddock fence, but tension still radiated from every taut sinew and angular bone in his long-limbed body. Seemingly skittish from his master's state of mind, the chestnut stallion sidestepped away from him and got a sharp slap on the rump for the supposed slight.

As she watched Branch hoist his saddlebags over his shoulder, draw his rifle out of the scabbard, and tuck it under one arm, Amanda chewed on her lower lip. As he strode purposefully toward the house, his boots kicking up tiny clouds of dust, she drew in a long breath. He not only appeared dusty and tired but in an extremely foul mood. That boded ill for her chances of success in gaining his approval for what she had done while he was away. Amanda felt a chill of fear snake down her spine.

She pulled herself up short. Why should she be frightened to tell him what she'd done? She wasn't a child caught out in misbehavior, but a mature woman who had made a sound business decision. As far as she was concerned, it was one that should have been made weeks ago. Branch was her husband and her partner, but that didn't give him the right to make all the decisions.

Still, wariness kept her in place at the parlor window as she watched him take the veranda steps two at a time, his obvious exhaustion overridden by a maelstrom of frustrated energy. Once on the porch, he whipped off his hat and slapped it against his denim-clad thigh with far more force than was necessary to remove the trail dust. The bright morning sun glanced off the bronzed planes of his face, enhancing the ebony gleam in his eyes and highlighting the heavy growth of beard that darkened his jaw. He looked even more sinister and forbidding than the first time she'd seen him and had thought he resembled a feudal warlord.

Taking a deep breath, Amanda smoothed her skirt while at the same time donning invisible armor for the upcoming siege. Why hadn't she put on something more attractive today than a simple white blouse and dark skirt? If she were dressed in something a bit more alluring, she might have been able to win him over to her way of thinking before the worst happened. Unfortunately, he'd come home four days early, and she was totally unprepared.

She had less than a minute to rally herself for the next in a series of confrontations they'd had about money during the days before his departure. By the look of him, mention of that subject was going to set off the most vitriolic battle yet. Fighting with Branch while he was in such a highly combustible state was never wise, but it looked as if it was going to be unavoidable.

She'd tried to be patient, to show some regard for his feelings, but his stubborn refusal to accept money from her had seemed more ridiculous with each passing day. Finally, she'd decided the time had come when her half of the oil rig was going up and his had no choice but to go up with it. They could haggle over the financial end of things after their well came in.

Not long after Branch had left the Box H, Amanda had driven into Barrysville and ordered the necessary equipment. That would have been bad enough, but her impatience to get started had taken her a step further.

She'd wired a former classmate who had secured a position with the Texas Company. Upon his recommendation, she'd hired a driller. Both the driller and the equipment were scheduled to arrive today. If all had gone according to her plan, the derrick would have been well under construction before Branch returned. Surely even a man as stubborn and prideful as Branch would come around when presented with a fait accompli.

Some diversionary tactics were definitely in order. If she could keep Branch's mind on other things until he'd enjoyed a long, hot bath, eaten a meal, and had a few hours of rest, there might be only a minor explosion when she told him what she'd arranged without his permission or counsel. Perhaps tonight, if by some lucky twist of fate the wagons were delayed, she could be such a wildly passionate and generous partner in bed that he would willingly accept whatever she'd done. Women had used such wily stratagems for centuries. Why couldn't she?

Amanda shook her head. Even if she were lucky enough for the wagons to be delayed, she doubted Branch would notice any great change in their lovemaking. Each time they were in bed together, he aroused her to a wildly passionate state. He wouldn't notice any difference in her behavior, even if her responses were supposedly premeditated.

Pasting a serene expression on her face to cover her anxiety, she went to greet her husband. Their parting had been far from amiable. His suspicions would be instantly aroused if she were to throw herself into his arms.

"So you're back." She announced the obvious in what she hoped was a genial tone. "And four days early."

"Yup." Branch dropped his saddlebags onto the entryway floor and hung his hat on a wall peg. Seemingly ignoring her, he ran his fingers through his sweat-dampened hair, then untied the bandanna he wore around his neck and stuffed it into a back pocket. His gunbelt joined his hat on the wall pegs.

He placed a hand at the base of his spine and began working out the kinks in his stiff back and shoulders. Amanda noted the small wince of pain that furrowed his brows as he straightened to his full height. When he rotated the aching muscles in his arms, his jaw went tight.

Through half-closed eyes, Branch studied Amanda, drinking in the sight of her from the top of her golden head to the tips of her polished shoes. God, she was beautiful, and he'd missed her. He wanted to scoop her up, hold her soft, pliant body next to his, and make up for those long, lonely nights on the trail, the emptiness he'd felt staying alone in that cheap hotel room. It would have been nice to have been greeted with a pretty smile and a passionate kiss from the woman who professed to love him.

Recalling the harsh words they'd exchanged when he'd left, he knew that was probably wishful thinking. Amanda had almost as much pride as he did. He'd have to do a lot more than just turn up to put her in a loving mood.

Still, it wouldn't hurt her to show some sign that she'd thought about him as much as he had her. He studied her face, hoping to find some indication that she was glad he was back. Her blue eyes were guarded, as if harboring some secret. He immediately stopped all movement.

"What is it?" he demanded, his tone edged with steel. "Did something happen while I was gone? Where's Ellie? Is she okay?"

"Nothing's happened," she assured him with only a small twinge of guilt. Too hastily, she added, "Really. We're all fine. Ellie's gone to town to get some supplies, and, yes, she was adequately guarded."

"Then why do you look like you're festering over something so all-fired bad you're scared to tell me?" His eyes were red-rimmed with fatigue but still had enough power to probe intensely as he took a step toward her.

Amanda took a step back.

His next words were both a curious question and a deadly warning. "All right, Peaches. What have you been up to while I've been gone?"

"Nothing except trying to run this place. I hired a woman to clean and cook. She's gone into town with Ellie."

"Who?" he bellowed. "What do you know about her? How do you know she can be trusted?"

Amanda flinched. If he was going to get this angry over her hiring a housekeeper, she had no illusions about how he would react to the rest of her confessions. She strove for calm. "She's a cousin of Lucía's. Lucía sent Dorinda over after Billy told her I needed someone."

Branch relaxed only slightly. "Billy was here?"

Amanda nodded.

"I suppose she's all right then." He leaned one shoulder against the wall and studied his wife's expression, not liking the fretful furrow he saw between her brows. "You still look worried. Out with it."

"If I look worried, it's only out of concern for you," she evaded, searching for the means to sidetrack him until she'd paved the way for her announcement. "You look like you're in pain, Branch."

"It was a long ride."

"You could've taken the train most of the way if you weren't so stubborn." When he didn't respond to her firm reminder, she pounced on her suspicion like a dog on a bone. "You've reopened that wound, haven't you?"

Branch continued to stare at her, but now there was a tiny glint of sheepishness in his dark eyes. Taking advantage of this golden opportunity for distraction, Amanda rapidly closed the distance between them. "Let me see," she ordered imperiously as she undid the top button on his shirt.

"I told you that you weren't up to riding a horse any distance, but you wouldn't listen. A few weeks back you were just getting out of a sickbed. I don't know what you were trying to prove except that you're as stubborn as a mule and have nothing but molasses for brains!"

Coloring her lecture with a stream of forceful Texan adjectives and phrases, Amanda advised him of his folly. She ignored the incredulous expression on his face as she continued unfastening buttons. However, throughout the lecture, she was well aware of what she was doing to him. To her everlasting delight, she felt a muscle leap under his skin as she slowly drew her fingers down his chest on their way to the final fastening.

She fiddled with the last button, deliberately brushing the tops of her hands along the tight waistband of his denims. If she'd learned nothing else since becoming this man's wife, she knew that her touch had just as strong an effect on him as his had on her. Maybe she'd be able to lull him into a good humor with her womanly wiles after all.

"If you've undone all Ellie's and my good work, I'm going to be very upset," she chided, praying he would think that the agitated flutter of her fingers on his skin was not done with any ulterior motive in mind. Reaching around him, she pulled his shirt tails out of his pants, making sure he felt the press of her full breasts against his chest for a long moment before she stood back.

"There now. Let's see how that shoulder looks." Hoping to lay a bit of groundwork for future discussion while he was attempting to calm his erratic heartbeat, she tacked on, "This trip was totally unnecessary, and you know it. I've got all the funds we need, and, unlike a bank, I don't charge interest."

"Don't you? I wonder," he managed.

Though puzzled by his question, Amanda was gratified by the strangled tone of its delivery. So far, things were going along just fine. At least, it appeared as if his ill temper was winding down to a more manageable level, and his desire was escalating at an even faster rate.

He couldn't quite hide his gasp when she tugged his shirtfront apart and leaned into him as she went up on tiptoe. Carefully, she pushed the shirt over his shoulders and down his arms. She didn't undo the cuffs, and the shirt hung behind him, dangling from his wrists. He might not realize it, but he was now very nicely restrained in case matters abruptly deteriorated before she had a chance to state her case.

"Damn your stubborn pride, Branch Colson!" she swore, forgetting all else as she saw the reddened bandage. "You're bleeding again!"

"I'll be fine, Peaches," Branch asserted softly,

but he didn't back away as Amanda probed the edges of the small bandage with gentle fingers.

"Hmmph." She dismissed his claim and commanded, "Turn around and let me see the back." When he made no move to comply, Amanda took hold of his belt buckle and jerked hard.

"Yes, ma'am." Branch's tone was amused as he allowed her to maneuver him until she could get a clear view of the condition of the second bandage.

"Well, at least you're not bleeding here, but the bandage is filthy." She took hold of his wrist, her slender fingers gripping tightly although they weren't long enough to form a secure manacle. "Come out to the kitchen so I can change your dressings and see what other damage you've managed to do to yourself. Honestly, Branch, you'd think a grown man would have more sense."

She continued scolding him, sounding like some ruffled banty hen, as she dragged his speechless form behind her all the way down the long hall to the back of the house. "There's no reason for this to have happened. You shouldn't have even been on a horse in the first place. If you had used the brains you were born with, you would've taken the Oldsmobile to Barrysville and then boarded a train."

Branch emitted a snort of derision at the mention of Amanda's automobile. "That machine of yours is the last thing I'd depend on to get me anywhere. I'd have been better off on foot."

Bustling ahead of him, Amanda tossed over her shoulder, "For a man who's so interested in the oil business, you have absolutely no respect for the very thing that has caused the boom. If it weren't for the automobile, there would be no real market for oil."

"If people want to make fools of themselves drivin' around in those noisy, smelly things, that's their business," he grumbled. "I just want to take advantage of the market while there still is one. The automobile will never replace the horse out here. Lord knows how long city folks will put up with the crazy things."

While Amanda gathered the supplies she needed, Branch lowered himself into a chair. When he tried to lean his arms on the table, he discovered the restraint of his shirt. Leaning back, he sighed wearily and closed his eyes, letting his arms dangle at his sides. He admitted this small bit of helplessness just as he'd been forced to admit defeat in the battle he'd been fighting ever since Amanda had divulged the full extent of her wealth.

He had no other recourse. He would have to use her money, but only with the understanding that it would be paid back in full with his share of their profits. At the first opportunity, he'd have Graham draw up a legal note to that effect. He stopped. No, not Graham.

Branch recalled his thunderstruck surprise when his brother's name was brought up as a possible backer. Somehow, unbeknownst to his family, Graham had managed to accumulate a fortune. Indeed, the Third National Trust Bank in Dallas had revealed that Graham was one of their major depositors. Until he knew how a small-town lawyer had managed to attain such wealth, Branch wouldn't trust any further business dealings to the man.

In the meantime, he would concentrate on building his own fortune. Then, as soon as they struck oil, he would buy out Amanda's share of the Box H. Nobody was going to accuse him of marrying her for her money or her land.

As soon as he'd been able, he'd gone back to work at the Circle C, driving himself to exhaustion by running two ranches, and all to prove he was no woman's kept man. He wondered if managing a ranch was his only viable skill. His experience in the Beaumont oil fields surely hadn't impressed anybody in Dallas.

Hell, maybe he really was the slow-witted cowboy she'd originally dubbed him. It had certainly taken him long enough to come up with a means to go ahead with the drilling and still salvage most of his pride. It was such an obvious solution, one he should have arrived at weeks ago. If he'd had the brains of a horny toad, he would've saved himself a lot of time, trouble, and humiliation.

Sure that he'd secure financial backing without touching his wealthy wife's money, he'd ranted and raved his way through every bank in Dallas. The Colson name had opened doors, but those doors had firmly closed again as soon as it had been determined that Big John wasn't behind him. Without collateral, no personal property except for his share of the Box H, he wasn't considered a good risk without his father's backing.

The initial rush to capitalize on oil drilling had waned in the months since Spindletop. Too many wells had come up dry. Not even a description of the surface pools had brought about any more than casual interest. Surface pools were all too often just that—shallow pools of black sludge.

Every potential backer he'd approached had offered the same excuses. Each had ended the interview with the same rejoinder. Branch had heard it so many times, he could now recite it to himself. "If you or your father were willing to put up some of the funds for this wildcatting operation, we might see our way clear to make up the difference, but without that there's no way we can turn over such a large sum with no guarantee of return."

Hell! He might be foreman of one of the biggest spreads in Texas, but the pittance Big John threw his way each month hadn't resulted in any great savings. He shook his head in self-disgust. He'd wasted one hell of a lot of time. While he'd been chasing pipe dreams in Dallas, he could have been demonstrating that though he might need her money to buy a rig, she needed his know-how to run it. All the while he'd been increasing the size of the chunk of pride he'd be forced to swallow, they could have been drilling.

But that wasn't all they could have been doing. Instead of sleeping alone in a rented room, he could have been making love to his wife upstairs in that big fourposter bed every night. He could have been teaching her the myriad of delightful things she still didn't know could happen between a man and a woman. He could have been proving that she was a creature of passion who needed all he could give her.

During his absence, she might have forgotten the lessons he'd taught her thus far. He'd forgotten nothing. Moments ago, the touch of her soft fingers on his skin, the pleasure that came from having her start to undress him, had been enough to make him feel as if he'd been running at break-neck speed for miles. To his chagrin, she seemed completely oblivious to his very evident arousal. Her concern for him was no different from what she'd feel for anyone she thought was hurting. Loving him had nothing to do with it.

Branch tried to will down his growing urgency, but his body refused to respond to the dictates of his weary mind. Amanda looked very much the prim and proper lady today in a crisply starched, high-necked white linen blouse and straight black skirt. Not an inch of her silken skin showed, but that only made him ache for her all the more.

He knew she'd be upset if she ever discovered that he found her demure outfits more provocative than anything else she could wear. He could always tell when she was trying to keep him at bay by putting on what he'd come to think of as her armor. She still hadn't figured out that, for him, the harder the battle, the sweeter the victory.

Her glorious golden hair was firmly constrained in a tight, pristine bun. Branch knew she styled it that way for two reasons. One, it was probably far cooler and more practical, and two, she probably thought it gave her a more businesslike appearance. However, to his way of thinking, it only gave his lips better access to the lovely curve of her slender neck. What she didn't know was that the errant wisp curling at her nape beckoned to him like a flame. He wanted to pull the pins out of her hair one by one. He wanted to . . .

"Good, you're sitting down." Amanda broke into his lustful reverie with a tart comment.

"Aren't you the least bit interested in hearing what they told me in Dallas?" he asked, pulling himself under control as she leaned over him. "Ouch!"

"Sorry." Amanda purposely avoided answering his question as she slowly continued peeling off the bandage that was stuck to his skin with dried blood. "But it's your own fault I have to do this. You could have changed these bandages occasionally along the way. You'll be sorry you didn't if this has gotten infected and you end up back in bed."

"I'm already sorry I didn't," he shot back, irritated by her continued harping on the precarious state of his health. She was treating him like a naughty boy. He was a man, damn it, and the last thing he wanted from her was mothering.

"It's a good thing you're a geologist and not a nurse. You haven't the touch for it."

Amanda refused to rise to the bait. She'd already sabotaged her plan to get on his good side by being much too critical, but she might do irreparable damage if she exchanged insults with him. Besides, he'd made far worse comments to her during his initial recuperation from the shooting. If she lost her temper now, she'd ruin everything.

"I'm sorry if I'm hurting you. I'll try to be as gentle as I can." Progress was slow, as Branch complained more vehemently each time Amanda was forced to pull on the bandage in order to lift the edges free. When she was finally finished, she was grateful to see that the recently healed wound was bleeding from only a small patch that had been rubbed raw. She thoroughly cleansed the area, applied a layer of soothing salve, then replaced the soiled bandage with a clean one.

With tight-lipped patience, Branch leaned over the table so she could repeat the process on his back. "Will you get on with it?"

She was able to change the second bandage with no complaints from her patient, although he did mutter some comment under his breath as he tried to straighten up before she was finished and she firmly pushed him back down.

"There now. All done," she announced. She stepped around to face him as he straightened.

"Satisfied?" he asked with a familiar and highly dangerous look in his eyes.

"I—I—yes."

"Well, I'm not." Branch brought up his arms. The shirt ripped in two as he reached around Amanda and abruptly hauled her down upon his lap. "I'm not satisfied. Not by a long shot," he muttered against her astonished lips.

His kiss was deep and purposeful. His tongue demanded a response, and Amanda gave it willingly. She wound her arms around his neck, threading her fingers through the hair at his nape. Her plan had worked. This was where she had wanted to be since he'd first walked in the door. Mixed with her feelings of triumph and confidence was the heady enjoyment of being held in her husband's arms.

Branch buried his hands in her hair, scattering pins across the floor as he kissed her again and again. His lips skimmed across her cheek, feathered against her eyes, then moved to her earlobe. His beard rasped harshly against her tender skin, but Amanda didn't feel the pain. Her body was atingle with much more pleasant sensations.

"You don't expect Ellie any time soon, do you?" he drawled thickly.

"No."

"Good."

He made far shorter work of unfastening her blouse than she had unbuttoning his shirt. The ribbon of her chemise came untied with a single pull, and the tiny buttons down the front of the frilly undergarment were rapidly slipped from their holes. His large palms covered her bared breasts, and he buried his face in the curve of her shoulder.

"Sure glad you quit being such a lady," he murmured against her skin.

"What do you mean?" Amanda asked, experiencing a twinge of disappointment that he would choose such a time to insult her.

"You're not wearing that wired cage." He slid his mouth down her neck to the tops of her breasts. "I can find the real woman so much sooner."

"Branch . . ."

The pronouncement of his name had started as a protest but ended in a breathless moan when his lips circled and pulled at a rose-pink nipple. Her back arched, and her fingers pressed into his scalp, urging his possession of her breast. Each opalescent mound was treated to equal torment until Branch's name was a continual sigh on Amanda's lips.

*"Mi bella flor. Mi amante.* How I want you." Branch pressed his words of adoration and need into the fragrant column of her throat.

*My beautiful flower. My sweetheart.* She'd come to understand and know those Spanish phrases so well. He pronounced them softly each time he made love to her. She knew just how much he wanted her, and she wanted him just as much. If her plan had been to be the seducer, she was just as much the seduced.

Amanda rose shakily from his lap and started toward the hallway on wobbly legs. Expecting Branch to follow her upstairs to the bedroom, she was surprised when her hand was grasped within one of his and she was gently pulled back. "Where do you think you're going?" he growled lazily.

"Up—upstairs."

"No need. Come back here."

"But—"

"There's much you have yet to learn, *mi chiquitita encantadora.*" He reached up and pulled her head down. While his lips tantalized hers, his tongue tasted her, and his free hand slipped up beneath her skirt and untied the waist string of her drawers. Swallowing her gasp, he continued the kiss as the thin cotton garment slithered soundlessly to the floor.

With a firm grasp of her waist and one smooth motion, he settled her astride his lap, chuckling softly at her shocked bewilderment. "We don't need a bed." His knuckles grazed her trembling belly as he unfastened his pants.

Amanda curled her palms around his shoulders to steady herself, feeling deliciously wanton as she realized his intent. The heated length of his manhood pressed against her flesh and the familiar liquid warmth of readiness radiated throughout her body. He joined them, filling her deeply. His palms cupping her buttocks, he guided her movements upon him.

Their separation, this new position, and the utter dissoluteness of making love in the middle of the kitchen in broad daylight all combined to heighten Amanda's pleasure to such a peak that she was hurtled rapidly into fulfillment. Her urgent little cries escalated Branch's response, and he quickly followed her into release, arching violently and spilling hotly into her.

They clung tightly to each other in that final moment. Their breaths caught and held before escaping in a single sigh of repletion. Amanda sagged against Branch, her head pillowed against his muscle-padded shoulder. Branch stroked her back in absentminded configurations.

Branch grazed her forehead with his lips. "Say it, Amanda. Tell me you love me."

"I love you."

"I didn't get the loan," he divulged quietly.

Amanda knew how difficult that must have

been for him to admit. Not moving a muscle she said softly, "I know."

Long moments passed in complete silence. Finally, Branch asked, "Is that all you're going to say?"

Amanda smiled, her lips soft upon his neck. "Yup."

Branch's chest rumbled with the low chuckle that rose from deep inside him. "You're soundin' like a Texan, city lady."

"'Spect it's the company ah been keepin'," Amanda drawled. "Ah seem ta be takin' to your ways, cowboy."

"Then I reckon I can take to some of yours, city lady. We'll use your money, but under one condition." He outlined his solution, and Amanda sent up her thanks to the Almighty. When he'd finished, she decided there would never be a better time to confess what she'd done, especially since the arrival of the evidence was imminent.

"Branch, I've got something to tell you . . ."

# Chapter Fifteen

Silence followed Amanda's confession, a silence broken only by the sound of her pounding heart. Why hadn't she waited until Ellie had come home before telling Branch what she had done? Now she was alone, all alone, to face the wrath of the man who towered over her.

The ebony eyes that had been filled with flames of desire now burned with a different light. His gaze no longer warmed but seared. The lips that had taken possession of her mouth and her breasts, that had tantalized the sensitive skin of her throat, were now set in a grim line. Every muscle of Branch's body was tensed, ready to spring into action. Amanda moved a little closer to the door.

"Get me another shirt," Branch ordered from between clenched teeth. When she didn't move immediately, he growled, "Get moving, woman. I don't have much time."

"Time?" Amanda asked dumbly, her blue eyes wide.

"To meet those wagons and whoever you hired," he supplied, his slowly pronounced words in direct contrast with the rapid movement of his fingers on his cuffs. He yanked the remnants of his shirt down his arms and tossed them aside. Seeing that she was still standing at the doorway, he bellowed, "Move!"

The roar and black glare that had reduced many a man to quivering acquiescence had an entirely different effect on Amanda. Moments before, she'd been quaking in fear, but suddenly her own ire rose to meet her husband's. "Don't you order me around!" she returned as she advanced on him. "I made a sound judgment, and, by God, nobody is going to cancel it. I know I probably should have waited for you, but it's done now. I'm not going to let you send that equipment back or fire my driller."

Slack-jawed, Branch gaped at Amanda. Then humor began to lift the corners of his mouth until a full white-toothed grin was revealed. "And just how are you going to stop me?"

"I'll get there first and tell him to ignore you, that's how!" She brushed past him, intent on getting out the back door and to her automobile while he was still occupied in the house getting a shirt for himself.

"Peaches . . ." He caught her shoulder and stopped her. Dangling her drawers from one finger, he inquired, "Wouldn't you like to put these back on before you go out there?"

Cheeks flushed scarlet, Amanda snatched the

lace and ribbon-trimmed undergarment away from him. Not looking at him, she stepped into them.

"If you'll wait long enough for me to get another shirt, we can go together," Branch added calmly. "I'll even ride in your automobile."

Not mollified by his sudden congeniality, Amanda demanded, "Why should I provide the transportation for you to go out and countermand everything I did?"

"Who said I was going to countermand anything?" was his surprising response.

"But—you—I thought," Amanda sputtered.

"Wrong," he finished for her. Tilting her chin up with the tip of his finger, he grinned down at her. "Do you think you could be a good little wife and go get me another shirt? After all, you're the reason I tore this one to shreds." Seeing the doubt etched on her features, he promised, "I'll wait right here for you. Trust me."

"What are you going to do about the equipment and the driller?"

"I'm going to make sure you bought the right equipment, check out the men, and probably let them on through."

"That's all?" she asked, still unsure.

"That's all," he confirmed, then turned her toward the stairs and delivered a soft swat to her behind to urge her on her way. "Humor me, Peaches. Let me think I'm the master of the house, at least."

Amanda stopped. Branch's statement, issued in such a tired voice, implied far more than he'd probably intended. Realization of how utterly defeated he must be feeling hit her. Underneath that cocksure exterior lay a fragile male ego. Had going ahead without consulting him, shoring up her own professional ego at the expense of his, been worth the price? Did she really want to strip away every shred of his pride? Hadn't the bankers and his father done enough of that? She didn't know a lot about marriage, but she did think it was each partner's duty to comfort and support the other whenever necessary.

"Oh, Branch," she uttered in a broken voice as she rushed back across the room and closed her arms around him. "I didn't mean to unman you. I only wanted to get started. I'm not a very good wife and an even worse business partner," she wailed against his chest.

"Hey, *querida*," he pronounced softly against the top of her head. He folded her into his arms, enjoying the new experience of consoling her. "I'll see how good a business partner you are after I look over the equipment and meet the crew. As for how good a wife you are . . ." He leaned back, forcing her to gaze up at him. "Get me a shirt, and then later tonight, up in that big bed, you can give me some more proof."

Amanda's cheeks flushed again as she stepped out of his arms. "Is that the only place I can prove my wifely worth to you?" she asked sternly, but the twinkle in her eyes gave her away.

"Maybe not, but you're awfully good there," he drawled with a grin.

His lazy smile and sensually roughened tone emboldened her to ask, "Am I really?"

"The best," was his simple reply, and Amanda

proceeded up the stairs with a smile of supreme satisfaction on her face.

"Needed a new gate anyway," Branch growled as the Oldsmobile sputtered, wheezed, then gave one last backfire before coming to a stop.

"The old one was a disgrace," Amanda deemed, keeping her gaze straight ahead and her features serious.

"Uh . . . you want me to crank it up again, boss?" ventured Bob, who had accompanied them to the entrance of the Box H.

"No, damn it," Branch swore impatiently. "This is as good a place to wait as any." He hopped down from behind the driving tiller and reached beneath the dash for his rifle.

Amanda hopped down from the Oldsmobile as well. After Branch's break-neck operation of the automobile over the twisting, hilly road, she relished the security of having firm ground under her feet. He'd surprised her by demanding to drive, saying that he'd give one of her city ways a try, and he had waited for only the most rudimentary instruction before setting off. By the time he'd stalled the little engine for the fourth time, Bob had ordered Jock to get down from his horse and crank it up again, saving them all from suffering through the vehement curses Branch emitted whenever he manned the crank.

"Damned thing'll never replace the horse," Branch reiterated for what seemed the tenth time as he kicked away a piece of splintered gate. "See anything?" he shouted at his elderly foreman.

"Not yet, boss," Bob volunteered, rising up in his stirrups to peer toward the horizon. "You want me and Jock to ride over yonder and take a look-see?"

Branch lifted his hat, then resettled it on his head as he gazed up the empty road. "I reckon we'll hear 'em. That's enough warning." With his rifle held loosely in one hand, he bent and picked up a piece of wood from the grass. "Banny," he called. "Ride on back and tell Sam to start building a new gate." He studied the wood in his hand for another moment, then tossed it away. "Tell him to make up a new sign while he's at it."

Issuing more orders, he positioned the remaining two men and then turned his attention on Amanda. "Mrs. Colson," he pronounced with authority.

She stepped carefully over some of the debris, mindful of the loose barbed wire, and came to stand beside Branch. She'd bearded the lion once today and miraculously escaped the encounter unscathed. Considering his frustration with driving her automobile, the numerous stallouts, and the final ignominy of crashing through a gate, she wasn't about to test the hand of providence again. Therefore, she answered her husband's imperious summons and waited meekly for whatever orders he chose to deliver. It wasn't that she'd suddenly become the epitome of docility, but rather that she was particular about the choice of battlefields and what issues they fought over.

"Since it looks like we've got some time, why don't you tell me about this driller you've hired?"

Amanda let out a sigh of relief. The words tumbled out in a torrent as she strove to convince Branch of the soundness of her action. "I'm sure that if John Davenport recommends him, he's all right. John graduated at the top of my class and was very highly thought of by the faculty. I'm sure the Texas Company must be impressed by him because he's already been promoted to senior geologist. He said this driller, a Karl Molinski, was very experienced. He's brought in a lot of the wells that supply the company."

"Hold on, Peaches." Branch stopped her before she could continue. "No need to keep runnin' on." He leaned against a fencepost and crossed his ankles. "I think I might know this Molinski fella."

"Then we have nothing to worry about, and this . . ." She paused and gestured toward the men. "This kind of reception is unnecessary. Call them off, Branch. Put your gun away and let's go back home." Without waiting for an answer, she started back for the automobile.

Not moving away from the fencepost, Branch watched her retreat, enjoying the very feminine sway of her hips as she walked. "Didn't say I liked him," he stated quietly but loudly enough for Amanda to hear.

She stopped midstride, nearly losing her balance before whirling around and retracing her steps. The light of battle shone in her eyes, and her resolve to prevent Branch from dismissing the crew was stronger than ever. "John Davenport would never recommend someone who wasn't trustworthy."

"Molinski's all right," Branch returned, again very quietly.

"Then why—why didn't you say so right off?" Amanda demanded, hands on hips, her vexation clear by the flames fairly leaping from her blue eyes.

"Sorry, Peaches." A maddening grin gave lie to his words. The grin grew wider, and a mischievous light sparkled in his dark eyes as he took in every nuance of his fuming wife. Tapping the tip of her nose with one finger, he chuckled. "You're such a fetchin' figure of a woman when you get your dander up. I purely enjoy settin' you off just for the pleasure of lookin' at you."

Would this man never stop rendering her speechless? Amanda could not believe he'd staged this whole thing just to see her in a fit of anger. "Don't try to soothe me with that cowboy talk," she berated him, adding force to the scolding by shaking her finger at him. "You've got more on your mind than just wanting to see me get angry."

"Sure do," he admitted, the grin growing even wider. "But with witnesses around, I reckon I oughta wait 'til we're alone tonight. I do like my privacy."

"Oh! You hedonist!"

"Is that another one of them fifty-cent words like *expeditious*, Peaches?" Branch teased.

Remembering how it had come back to haunt her when she'd impatiently defined *expeditious*, Amanda refused to define *hedonist*. If he didn't know the meaning, she was certainly not going to enlighten him. On the other hand, the thought occurred to her that she would be the recipient of his singleminded pursuit of pleasure, and it might well be worth defining this latest fifty-cent word.

*You're as bad as he is*, she reprimanded herself and turned on her heel, intent on putting some distance between them. She was already flushed and breathless in expectation of the coming night. It certainly wouldn't do to meet the drilling crew in this state.

The derrick took form within the first week. The skeleton of raw timber rose more than thirty feet above the rig floor. With each passing day, a sea of mud grew larger and larger around the platform as water was cycled down through the rotating pipe and flushed back up again, bringing with it the soil and rock carved out by the rotary bit. A steam engine puttered and chugged continuously, powering the walking beam as the bit pounded deeper, hundreds of feet below the surface.

"Still so sure this was the right spot?" Branch growled, not looking at Amanda but glaring at the assortment of onlookers gathered on the ridge beyond the site.

"More than ever," Amanda confirmed, looking away from her microscope only long enough to jot down some figures on a piece of paper. "It's a salt dome, just like I thought." She returned her attention to the study of the scraping she'd taken from the bailer. "It's got to be down there. Everything confirms my theory."

"Got a theory on how to get rid of all those nosy fools up there?"

"You're in charge of security," she reminded him gently. "Can't the men stop them at the gate?"

"They try, but the damned busybodies keep findin' other ways to get through. We've got so many knocked-down fences, the men can't keep up with the repairs. All they do is chase cows all day. I don't have enough men to patrol the borders. If this keeps up much longer, we'll be back to open-range ranchin'."

"How many head do you estimate we've lost?" Amanda cleaned off the glass slide and replaced it in the case. She began to pack up her microscope and other equipment.

Branch rested a booted foot on the support rung of her work table and propped his elbow on his knee. Continuing to stare at the ridge, he divulged, "Most of them were scrub cattle, but we lost at least a dozen of the new blood stock."

Amanda blotted beads of perspiration from her forehead and lip. Even though a corrugated tin roof shielded them from the sun, it was hot this close to the engine. The temperature beyond the "doghouse" wasn't much cooler, and Amanda wondered if she'd ever be able to adjust to the Texas weather.

September had proved to be just as sultry as August. The heat sapped her strength and dulled her mind. She felt tired, light-headed, and slightly nauseated. At that moment, she would have given anything to be walking along the Atlantic shoreline, feeling the ocean breeze blowing through her hair and against her skin.

She couldn't seem to concentrate on anything for very long. A few moments before, the magnified images had blurred, and she'd had to force herself to continue identifying the shapes. The salt crystals were there as they had been since almost the first sample, but this time she thought she saw tiny fossils. She'd ask for another core sample and have it brought back to the house. She could study it later when it was cooler and she'd had a short rest. For now, she tried to concentrate on what Branch had just said.

"Blood stock? What blood stock?" she asked listlessly. She pushed away from the table and started to stand.

Branch lifted his hat, wiped his forehead with his sleeve, and replaced the stained Stetson on his head. "I figured the Box H herd could stand a little improvement, and I bought a couple dozen Hereford calves and a bull. I thought my savings should be good for something. In case the well doesn't work out, we'll have the ranch to fall back on."

Glaring up at the spectators who lined the ridge, he growled, "Nobody's been fool enough to break down the fence we built around the new bull . . . at least not yet. I guess I can understand why Big John is so against this whole business. The Circle C has some broken fences, too. This rig's hardly a thing of beauty, and all those damned sightseers are—*Amanda?*"

She crumpled into Branch's arms. "Amanda!" He called her name repeatedly, but there was no response beyond a slight fluttering of her lashes. She was too pale, and her skin was clammy to the touch.

"My God! What happened to the little missus?" Karl Molinski was the first on the scene.

"She's fainted. Must be the heat. Get me some drinking water." Branch's eyes never left Amanda's white face as he fanned her gently with his hat.

A crowd of anxious men gathered around but were soon scurrying to follow the driller's orders. "Go on back to what you're supposed to be doing. She don't need to see your ugly faces when she wakes up. Turnbull, bring me that canteen, then get back to the hole and see that the casings fit in right. Branch, get your lady away from that engine and out where's she can breathe."

On the rig platform, Karl Molinski was the unquestioned authority. Even Branch bowed to the man's greater expertise. The operations resumed, and the canteen was delivered. Hank Turnbull lingered for a few minutes until Branch gestured him away. "I'll see to my wife, Turnbull. You've got your orders."

An immaculate white handkerchief miraculously appeared from Molinski's pocket. After soaking it with the water, he handed it to Branch. "This oughta help," he said, his normally booming voice gentle.

Amanda could hear Branch calling her name, but the sound seemed to come from far away. She tried to open her eyes, but it took too much effort. Ah, the ocean. The breeze was cool and the spray cooler yet as it blew against her face. If she could only stay a little longer along the shore, then she could . . .

She opened her eyes to see Branch peering over her, his expression grim, worry grooving the lines of his face. "What's wrong?" she questioned weakly. "Did something happen to the rig?"

"The rig's fine. You're what's wrong, Peaches," Branch told her, his eyes soft with concern. To her look of puzzlement, he gently teased, "You had a fit of the vapors."

"That's ridiculous," Amanda negated. She tried to sit up, but the world started spinning and she quickly lay back upon the grass where Branch had placed her. "I don't faint."

He chuckled low in his throat. "Then maybe you just took a short nap." He lifted her head carefully and brought the canteen to her lips. "Here, drink a little of this."

When her thirst was satisfied, Branch scooped her up and carried her to the Oldsmobile. After settling her on the seat and firmly ordering her to stay there, he went back to the derrick. Amanda used the short time he was gone to try to recollect what had happened. The last thing she remembered was Branch talking about calves.

"Send somebody up there and clear those people out." Branch's deep voice rose above the steam engine. "This isn't a sideshow! Tell them they're trespassing and we'll start shooting beginning tomorrow!"

Looking over her shoulder, Amanda saw him coming back toward her, leading his horse behind him. By the length of his stride and the set of his shoulders, she knew he was angry. Still feeling shaky, she crossed her fingers and hoped that none of his anger was directed at her. She was too tired to withstand it right now. What she really wanted to do was rest her head on his shoulder and open the floodgates of tears she could feel welling inside her. For the first time in her life, Amanda Hamilton Colson felt like weeping for no good reason at all.

Branch tied the chestnut stallion to the back of the auto, cranked the engine to life, then climbed behind the driver's seat. "I'm taking you back to the house where you belong," he announced as he threw the Oldsmobile into gear.

"My equipment case," Amanda wailed, struggling with her tears.

He gave her a quelling glare, then called for Molinski. He drummed his fingers restlessly against the tiller while they waited for the equipment case to be strapped against the running board. Despite his obvious impatience, Branch eased the vehicle forward and drove slowly and cautiously away from the drilling site.

"You feeling any better?" he inquired over the noise of the machine.

Amanda nodded but kept her lips pressed tightly together. She feared her voice would break and those silly tears, totally without foundation, would flow. More for a shield to prevent his seeing her face than to protect her from the dust, she reached for her motoring hat and adjusted it over her head.

The drive back to the house was, for Amanda, blessedly devoid of further conversation. However, once they'd arrived, Branch refused to allow her to walk and again scooped her up, entering the house in a few long strides. "Dorinda!" he shouted as he strode down the hallway, Amanda firmly nestled in his arms. They were halfway up the stairs before the housekeeper appeared in the hallway.

"Señor Branch?" Dorinda inquired softly from the base of the stairs. "Señora!" The plump woman mounted the steps and was immediately at Branch's heels. Also having heard Branch's roar, Ellie wasn't far behind.

Branch laid Amanda down upon the bed and started unbuttoning her shirtwaist. "There's absolutely nothing wrong with me," she declared, swatting at Branch's hands and trying to rise.

He gently pushed her back down on the mattress. "You'll stay put until I say you can get up," he informed her in a tone that brooked no denial. "As you said out at the site, you don't normally faint, so there's obviously something wrong with you."

"Land sakes, child." Ellie jostled past Branch. "You're white as them sheets. What happened to you?"

"Nothing."

"She fainted."

Branch and Amanda both spoke at once, but it was Branch Ellie turned to for confirmation. He gave all the details and ended with a declaration that a doctor must be sent for immediately. "Hold your horses, young fella," Ellie ordered, grabbing for his arm as Branch turned toward the doorway. "No need to bother the sawbones. Probably just a case of the heat. She ain't used to these hot, dry spells. You don't look so good yourself. Go on down to the kitchen and get somethin' cold and wet in your gullet. Me and Dorinda will see to Amanda."

Branch hesitated and received a steely-eyed glare from Ellie, accompanied by a colorful admonishment. More tactfully, Dorinda took him by the arm and led him away from the doorway, assuring him that Amanda would be fine. "I will go with you and then bring up something for the señora."

Ellie finished undressing Amanda, poured water into a basin, and sponged her face. Tucking the sheet around her, she leaned over, a bright smile on her face. "You gonna be just fine, Amanda, honey. We're all gonna be just fine now. You rest fer a spell. You got to take good care of yourself from now on." Wearing a supreme look of satisfaction, Ellie patted Amanda's hand and left the room.

Amanda discovered she wanted to do nothing more than nestle down into the bed and close her eyes. She'd been so tired the last few days. A good long rest would probably put everything to rights. She drifted off to sleep, awakening only slightly when hours later she felt the sag of the mattress and knew that Branch had joined her in the bed.

Instinctively, she rolled toward him, loving the gentle way he held her in his arms. That night, unlike all the others they had shared, he made no demands. He simply held her, murmuring something unintelligible against the top of her head, accompanying the softly spoken words with even softer kisses.

# Chapter Sixteen

"THIS IS RIDICULOUS! I CAN'T SPEND ANY MORE time in bed." Amanda threw back the covers and shifted her legs over the side. Her head spun when she attempted to stand, and she clutched the bedside table until the room stopped spinning. "It's from sleeping so late," she assured herself aloud, then took a step. Waves of nausea washed over her, and she barely made it across the room to the chamberpot before her stomach gave up its contents.

"Aiyee! Señora!" Dorinda set a covered tray down upon the table and hurried to Amanda's side. "You should not be up."

Feeling utterly miserable, Amanda made no protest when Dorinda settled her back into bed. "It is like this sometimes, Señora," the amply bosomed woman consoled her as she smoothed the sheets. "But it will pass."

"Whatever I've contracted can't last forever," Amanda mumbled, relaxing against the pillows.

"This will not last too long. It is worst with the first," Dorinda told her, reaching for the tray and whisking the linen napkin away.

Amanda stared at the pot of tea and the plate of lightly buttered toast, her stomach recoiling at the thought of putting anything in it. "It isn't the first time I've been sick. I had something like this once when I was in college."

Dorinda poured tea into a cup and handed it to Amanda. A smile revealed her straight white teeth, a twinkling light in her warm brown eyes. "I think this is something different, Señora."

"What do you mean, different?" Amanda sipped hesitantly at the tea, testing her stomach. "I'm dizzy and nauseated. I don't have a fever, but—"

"*Cielos!*" Dorinda interrupted, exasperation clouding her countenance. Her eyes rolled heavenward as she explained, "Of course you have no fever. If you did, then we would have something to worry about. Instead, you and Señor Branch should rejoice and give thanks that you are so blessed."

Blessed? What merciful God would bless her with such misery? Amanda stared at her new housekeeper as if the woman were talking in riddles. A spate of rapid Spanish and exaggerated gestures quickly followed, ending with what Amanda could only judge was hysterical laughter. "A *bebé*. A *bebé*," Dorinda finally said, cradling her arms and rocking. "You are expecting a *bebé!*"

"Oh my God," Amanda breathed, clattering her cup onto the saucer. She'd been too busy to pay any attention to the obvious signs. Pregnancy was the most logical explanation for every symptom of this strange illness she was suffering. "Does Branch know?" she asked, her mind making some fast calculations. She hadn't had her monthlies since . . . since before she and Branch had married.

"Men. Bah!" Dorinda dismissed. "What do they know of such things except how to cause the little ones to grow in a woman? You will have to tell him—and soon."

"I—I can't tell him we're going to have a baby. He thinks we—" Amanda stopped herself. She couldn't tell this dear woman that her marriage was really a business partnership which might very likely end after their well came in. Dorinda lived in the house and knew she and Branch shared this room, and for all outward appearances theirs was a perfectly normal marriage. Not just outwardly, Amanda admitted with a silent groan. The only thing abnormal about this marriage was the way it had come about.

"Please, Señora, take pity on your husband. Tell him. He is half out of his mind with worry over you. Your aunt had much trouble keeping him from sending for a doctor straight away."

"Ellie knows?" Amanda asked, her shaking fingers closing around her cup. Dorinda nodded, smiling broadly.

"Ah, sí, that one is so happy."

Amanda could imagine her aunt's joy. Wasn't that exactly what the woman had wanted right from the beginning? Another generation? Amanda could also imagine how difficult it must be for Ellie to keep the news to herself. She'd have to tell Branch before someone else did. "Where is Branch?"

"He is gone since before the dawn. Out to the well, I think, but he will be back soon. He say you are not to be allowed out of bed until he sees for himself that you are fine. It is like that with some men. They have no fear of anything except when the woman they love is sick."

All the while Dorinda talked, she bustled about the room, straightening anything that seemed out of order, swiping at imaginary dust on gleaming surfaces, and then coming back to gently urge Amanda to drink the tea and eat all of the toast. She refused to allow Amanda to do anything for herself. She pampered her thoroughly, giving her a sponge bath and, dressing her in a fresh, frilly nightgown.

Dorinda Montez was truly a marvel, Amanda mused as she gave herself up to the woman's care. In the short time she'd been at the Box H, she'd put the house in perfect order, managed somehow to clear away the years of debris without insulting Ellie, and each day performed culinary miracles in the kitchen. She had the energy of three women.

No corner of the house had escaped her discerning eye. Floors and furniture shone with a layer of wax, and windows sparkled. She'd enlisted Sam and Thurman to do repairs and apply fresh paint to many of the walls and ceilings. The graceful old house was sparkling with renewed life.

"You must look extra pretty for your husband, Señora," Dorinda instructed as she finished brushing Amanda's hair into a shiny golden mass. "But I think the señor thinks you are always beautiful. He sees you through the eyes of love."

After she'd gone, Amanda burrowed into the plump pillows, breathing in the clean scent of the linen covering. *The women they love* and *the eyes of love*. Those were conveniently romantic explanations for Branch's behavior, but Amanda knew better. Love for her couldn't be what had prompted his near panic at her collapse, could it? It was far more likely that his reaction was the result of, for once, not really knowing what to do.

Amanda rested her palm across her stomach. Just like the renewed life permeating the house, a new life she and Branch had created rested inside her. They hadn't talked about children or anything about the future beyond bringing in their first oil well. The only reference to children had been made by Branch's father the night of Opal's soiree. Big John had certainly been right in his estimation of Branch's virility. Branch had immediately made their marriage a very real one, introduced her to pleasures she hadn't known were possible, and given her what Amanda had thought would become the memories she would treasure for the rest of her life. However, it would seem that his vigorous and repeated lovemaking had left her with far more than memories.

Whenever Amanda thought of the future, all she really expected to have of Branch was half ownership of a thriving oil business and sweet memories of the nights she'd spent in his arms.

She'd thought joint ownership of the Box H would make it difficult to terminate the marriage without hurting Ellie. Now there was far more to think about than her aunt's feelings.

A baby. A baby conceived because of the desire she and Branch had for each other. A simple biological result of their passion. No, not so simple, Amanda amended. She loved the father of her child and would cherish this baby, but what of Branch? How would he react to this news?

Considering his background, Amanda knew that Branch would not desert the baby. He'd want this child, but what about its mother? She knew he cared something for her, but she didn't know how deeply his feelings went. He'd told her he didn't know how to love but continually demanded she declare her love as if he needed the repeated declaration in order to believe it. His emotions were so tied up by his bitterness toward his father that she wondered if he would ever believe in her and allow himself to trust in her love, return it.

The tears that had been close to the surface for the past week spilled from the corners of her eyes. Amanda dabbed at them, berating herself all the while as they continued to fall. *Tears never solve anything!*

Once again, she threw back the covers, intent on getting up and dressed. She absolutely could not lie in bed weeping. Just as her feet touched the floor, the bedroom door opened. "Get back in that bed!" Branch entered the room, no trace of the tender concern he'd shown the night before evident in his dark scowl.

His sharp tone acted like a lock opening a canal. Amanda's tears fell faster but didn't stop her from declaring, "I'm absolutely fine, perfectly healthy, and I refuse to spend the day in bed." She started toward the wardrobe, gratified that she experienced no dizziness and could walk steadily. The only impediment to her progress was the moisture blurring her vision.

Branch was immediately across the room. He folded her into his arms. "*Querida*, forgive me. You're in pain, and I'm snarling at you. Please, tell me what I can do for you." He held her close, smoothing his large hands over her small frame, the caresses emphasizing his strength and her fragility.

*You can tell me you love me*, Amanda wanted to say as she buried her face against his chest and wound her arms around his lean waist. He sounded so desperate, so miserable. Dorinda was right. She had to tell him about the baby. If only she could stop this ridiculous weeping. Why on earth did his tenderness and the comfort of his arms only make her cry harder?

"I'm not in pain," Amanda managed between swallows. "There's nothing you can do . . . it's already done . . . I'm going to have a baby . . ." It wasn't at all the way she had wanted to tell him. The words had formed and been pronounced without thought, but now that they had been said she felt almost relieved.

Branch's hands stilled. Minutes passed like hours until he asked, "Is it so horrible for you?"

"No. I told you I really am perfectly fine, disgustingly healthy."

"You're not the kind to shed a bucket of tears

over nothing. I'm sorry the thought of my child growing inside you is so distasteful," he told her in a tight, cold voice. "You don't have to keep the child. The child will have a home with me, will be safe and well taken care of. You can go back East after it's born if that's what you want."

"Is that what *you* want?" Amanda retorted, leaning away from him and searching his expression for some sign of his true feelings. As far as she was concerned, it was now or never. She had to know exactly where she stood.

He swallowed hard, once, twice, before answering, "No, that's not what I want."

Hope seeped through Amanda's soul. She smiled up at her husband, loving him more than ever before, more than she thought it possible to love another living person. But she needed to hear all the words. "What do you want, Branch?" Her voice was soft.

"You. I want you *and* this child."

He was so close, but Amanda wanted it all, even though she knew what the admittance was going to cost him. "Why?"

"Because . . ." He paused. He closed his eyes. His jaw clenched repeatedly.

"Say it, Branch," Amanda urged gently. "You do know how. I've told you so many times, and now I need to hear it."

"I love you." The words were wrenched from him as he swept her back into his arms, and buried his face against her throat. *"Yo te quiero, mi vida.* I love you. You hold my heart, my life, my very breath."

He trembled in her arms, and it was Amanda's turn to offer solace. Her small hands ran gently up and down his broad back. "It's not horrible carrying your child. It's wonderful."

Her tears began to flow again and with them a fountain of words. "I don't know why I'm crying about it. Dorinda says that pregnant women often cry for no reason at all. I never thought I was a woman with uncontrollable emotions until I met you. I love you, you big, wonderful man. I was so afraid you'd never love me back. That you'd feel caught in this marriage because of the baby."

"You're not the only one with uncontrollable emotions, Peaches. Every time I'm near you, I'm out of control." He proved his words by pulling her hips into the cove of his taut thighs. His desire for her was evident even through the rough, stiff fabric of his denim pants. "It's you who've been caught in this marriage. I never had any intention of letting you go without a fight. I couldn't put a name on how I felt about you. All I knew was that I couldn't lose you."

He bent his head and tenderly covered her mouth with his own. Amanda felt her softer body tighten in reaction to his lean, hard one pressed so intimately to hers. Now it was she who trembled, his hands and his lips that soothed. He cradled her face in his large palms, kissed her eyelids closed, the tip of her nose, then returned to her lips. Sweetly and tenderly, he made love to her mouth. "My Amanda. How I love you."

"*Yo te quiero*," Amanda returned. "Love me, Branch, please . . . now," she whispered against his lips.

He looked down at her, his dark eyes warm,

but the eagerness she hoped to see was banked. "Now? Are you sure?" he asked, his deep, husky voice filled with awe.

"Yes, now." Amanda slid her palms down his chest, fumbling with the buttons of his shirt until she encountered the heavy buckle at his waist. When she tugged his shirt free and spread it open, his chest was rising and falling rapidly to accommodate his ragged breathing. More sure of wanting him than she'd ever been, Amanda untied the ribbons of her gown, then let it fall away from her body.

She went to him without reservation, hungry for the feel of her breasts pressed against his hard chest. "Branch," she whispered achingly, her lips sliding across his muscled flesh.

"Amanda," he ground out, his hands skimming over her waist, her buttocks, and her thighs before he lifted her into his arms. He carried her to the bed and laid her down upon the mattress. His eyes never left hers as he dropped his gun belt to the floor and then removed the remainder of his clothing.

He came to her slowly, carefully lowering himself to cover her as if any minute he feared she might break. Amanda arched beneath him, wrapping her arms around his shoulders to bring his full weight down upon her. Her thighs parted, her hips lifted, initiating their union.

The gentle taking Branch had intended was undermined by the ferocity of Amanda's demands. In a turbulence of searing need, they took and gave to each other, flesh onto flesh, man onto woman. Shaking and trembling in the aftermath, words of love tumbled freely from lips that caressed and were caressed.

"*Por Dios*," Branch muttered when reason returned. He rose above her, balancing the bulk of his weight on his forearms. "I should be whipped. You are with child, my child, and I took you like a wildman."

Amanda brushed her fingertips along the lines of remorse that defined his expression. "No, my love. I wanted you and wanted to prove to you that I'm no invalid. I'm a woman who needs her husband's love very much."

Not convinced, Branch rolled to his side and rested his palm lightly over her smooth belly. "But . . . the child?"

Amanda covered his hand with hers, a smile more radiant than ever before brightening her eyes. "Safe. Safe and loved as he will always be."

His smile matched hers, but a twinkle of mischief glittered brightly from his black-fringed eyes. "He? I'm hoping for a golden-haired daughter."

"Sorry." She giggled. "Colsons have only boys, don't they? And you are most definitely a Colson."

A shutter came down over Branch's face. "I carry the Colson name—now," he bit out. "But I was born a Villanueva, and I *am* a Villanueva!" He was off the bed in one smooth motion and reaching for his clothing.

"Oh, Branch," Amanda pleaded. "Will you never stop hating him?"

He sat down on the edge of the bed to pull on

his boots. "How can I? At least our child will not have to cower in a corner and watch his mother sell herself to support him. He won't watch her die a little each time she passes a church her shame keeps her from entering. He won't hear her cry each night . . ."

Amanda took him into her arms and held him as he continued to pour out the sordid details of his first years of life. She wanted to cry for that frightened little boy who had loved his mother so very much, but she knew Branch didn't want her pity, wouldn't want her tears. He needed her strength, and she gave it, continuing to hold him cradled against her bosom long after the vehement outpouring had stopped. "How could he do it?" Branch asked agonizingly.

"Perhaps he didn't know. Have you ever talked about your mother with him?" Amanda felt him throw his defenses back into place.

He moved out of her arms and finished dressing, never meeting her eyes. Once finished, he crossed to the window and gazed out as if the rolling countryside might provide him with answers. Amanda slipped from the bed, extracted a fresh set of undergarments from the bureau, and began dressing. She was reaching for a dress in the wardrobe when he turned and noticed what she was doing. "Oh no you don't."

"Oh yes I do," she countered and pulled a soft muslin daydress out.

Branch took it out of her hands and tossed it back into the wardrobe. "Pretend, just for today, that you're a weak female," he coaxed, placing his hands on her shoulders to prevent her from going after the dress.

"I'll go crazy up here all day with nothing to do," she insisted, then reached up to fiddle idly with the shirt he'd just put back on. Coyly, she suggested, "Of course, you could stay up here and keep me company. Then I might have a good reason for staying in bed."

He grabbed her hands and shook his head. "Tempting, Peaches, mighty tempting, but I have work to do and—"

"So do I. I should study the cuttings. I want to see what's happening out at the well."

"Slow down. Nothing's happening out there. When I got back from seeing you home, there was a breakdown. The mud tank level dropped way down, and the man watching it didn't say anything. I knew Turnbull wasn't as experienced as he'd claimed. I gave him a week's pay and told him to clear out. Until I have another sample for you to look at . . ." He turned her toward the bed. "There's nothing for you to do. Now back in bed with you."

"Not alone."

"Amanda!" Branch warned, hands on his hips and a stern scowl on his face. "You've had enough excitement today. You need to take care of yourself—please."

"All right. I won't go out there today, but I'm not staying up here either." She started back to the open wardrobe, but Branch barred her way. "If I give you my word that I won't leave the house, may I have my dress?"

His dark gaze told her what he thought of that idea, but she met it with a determined blue blaze. Realizing he wasn't going to win this battle, for the minute his back was turned she'd probably do as she pleased, Branch gave in. At least he had her word that she'd stay at the house. He'd have a talk with Dorinda and Ellie before he left and leave orders that Amanda not be allowed to do anything more strenuous than lift a teacup.

He muttered in exasperation beneath his breath and reached to the bottom of the wardrobe for the dress. When he handed the creamy garment to her, an envelope fell to the floor. They both bent to pick it up, and Branch reached it first. As he started to hand it to her, he froze. The handwriting, a very feminine script, caught his attention. "*Madre de Dios*," he breathed as he stared at the envelope. "Where did you get this?" he demanded as he held the fragile stationery.

"It was here when I came." Amanda's response was muffled beneath folds of delicate fabric as she pulled the dress over her head. "I found a stack of letters and a beautiful inlaid jewelry box in the bottom of the wardrobe when I put my clothes away. My Aunt Ida had this room years ago, and I assumed the letters and the box belonged to her." She finished fastening her dress, then looked up curiously at her husband. "Why?"

Branch didn't answer. With trembling hands, he slipped the letter from the envelope and quickly read the contents. When he had finished, his face was whiter than it had been after he'd been shot. Wordlessly, he handed the letter to Amanda.

She took it, saw the signature and understood. It was from Nita and addressed to Big John.

Written shortly after Branch was born, it informed him of his son's birth and went on to valiantly wish John well in his marriage. Nita bravely claimed that she was safely situated and then apologetically requested a small sum of money to be used for her child.

"Why is this here?" Amanda asked, her question barely audible.

"That's what I'm going to find out." Branch reached for his gunbelt and buckled it around his hips, his fury evident in his quick, jerky movements as he secured the holster to his thigh.

"Wait," Amanda commanded, playing for time to cool her husband's temper before he confronted his father. "Maybe there's more." She bent down and started digging around in the bottom of the wardrobe. The ribbon that had held the packet of letters together had evidently broken, and they were scattered. She pulled them out, then reached for the box.

"I didn't go through these before, except for one that I recognized had been written by my father," she explained as she brought the letters and the box to a table by the window. "I assumed they were some of Ida's things that she either left here before she married or were returned to Ellie after Ida's death. I hadn't thought they were any of my business before, but maybe we'll find some answers."

They sorted through the letters, discovering two others from Branch's mother. Each had been addressed to Big John, and they had become progressively more desperate in nature. "Still think he didn't know?" Branch demanded, crumpling one of his mother's letters in his hand, his fury higher than she'd ever seen. He threw himself down in a chair.

"Maybe he never got the letters." Amanda tried to open the box but found it locked. Using one of her hatpins, she attempted to pry it open, having no idea what she might find but driven to discover the contents. If what Branch believed turned out to be true, she wouldn't be able to keep him from going to his father, and she shuddered to think of the outcome of that confrontation. It didn't make sense that Nita's letters would be among Ida's things.

The rusty lock finally gave, and Amanda flipped the top open. A small leather-bound book lay inside, plus a few pieces of jewelry. It was the book Amanda took out, seeing that it was her aunt's diary. Leafing through the pages, she found an entry matching the date on Nita's first letter. She felt sick when she read it and sicker yet when she read some of the following entries.

Handing it to Branch, she said, "I'm so sorry." She felt ashamed, ashamed that a Hamilton, her father's beloved little sister, Ellie's treasure, could have caused such misery. She was sure her aunt didn't know of Ida's duplicity, and Amanda didn't know if she had the heart to tell her.

"My father didn't know. He never got the letters. He told the truth. All these years I've hated him. I've hated him for . . ." Branch leaned forward in his chair. Elbows on his knees, he covered his face with his hands.

It was all there in the diary. Ida had gloated as she wrote of how she'd gotten rid of her rival, how she'd convinced Nita that John would never marry a Mexican. Ida knew John didn't love her, but she had been determined that she, not Nita, would become mistress of the great house at the Circle C. She'd intercepted the letters, writing delightedly of what a miserable life Nita was leading, going so far as to hope that both Nita and her child would perish.

While Branch sat in the chair, alone with his thoughts and anguish, Amanda read through the diary. Ida had been a spoiled young woman who had been guided by her own selfish needs. However, though loneliness and heartbreak at the loss of Nita may have prompted John to marry Ida, he did not turn to her in love or desire. The diary revealed that it had been Ida who had sought John's bed, in the hope that if she produced several children she'd secure her marriage. However, it had been Nita's name John had cried out in their marriage bed, Nita he'd wanted to hold in his arms.

At first, Ida had viewed sending Nita away, her marriage, and her conception of her children as a game, and herself as the winner with each deceptive move, but as the years had gone on she'd been as much a victim as John or Nita. The final entries were less legible and full of terror that her actions would be found out. They were sometimes bitter and vindictive but more often the meandering thoughts of one bordering perilously close to insanity. It was clear that, at the end, Ida welcomed death as an escape from the hell she had created.

It was late afternoon when Amanda closed the diary and placed it nestled among the pieces of jewelry in the box. Laying a hand on Branch's arm, she called his name softly. "Go to your father."

Branch turned to her, his eyes so vacant that Amanda wasn't sure he recognized her or even heard her words. Fear clutched at Amanda's heart, fear that the love he felt for her was too new, too fragile to survive the knowledge that it had been her aunt who had caused all the misery his mother had suffered. She waited, standing beside him, praying that the hatred he had to be feeling for Ida wouldn't extend to her.

He wrapped his arm around her waist and gently brought her down onto his lap. Seeing the worry in her eyes, Branch guessed at her thoughts and assured her, "It happened a long time ago, and you're not responsible. I love you, Peaches. Nothing will ever change that."

# Chapter Seventeen

TEARS RAN UNABASHEDLY DOWN BIG JOHN's worn cheeks as he finished reading the letters Branch had laid down on his desk. "God help me, but I'm glad Ida suffered for this," he said gruffly as he tucked the time-yellowed sheets back into their envelopes. "What she did must have eaten away at her for years, because when she knew she was about to die she told me about Nita and you."

He turned red-rimmed eyes toward his son. Branch stood with his back to the room, one foot propped against the raised stone hearth and his arms resting on the heavy oak mantel. It was an idle pose, but the tension that threatened to erupt at any moment was evident in every line of his long, lean body.

Amanda sat on the edge of a wide overstuffed chair near the large desk that dominated the study. Under other circumstances, she would have described the room as comfortable. The polished wood floor was dotted with colorful Indian rugs. Two of the soft ivory walls were adorned with a varied collection of paintings and wall hangings. Long windows flanked the stone fireplace that encompassed most of the south wall. A map of the Circle C hung over the mantel. The remaining wall was completely covered by floor-to-ceiling bookshelves.

This evening, though, as the shadows lengthened across the floor, the room was anything but comfortable. The atmosphere was heavily laden with emotions too long suppressed. Amanda's knuckles were white as she gripped her hands tightly in her lap. She wanted to go to her husband, to wipe away all the pain he was suffering, but she knew she couldn't. This confrontation was between Branch and his father. She could only sit quietly and wait, praying that the strength of her love would help Branch get through this ordeal.

"Does Ellie know about these?" John directed the question toward Amanda.

"I don't think so, and if it's all right with you, no one will tell her," Amanda returned softly.

Big John nodded his agreement. "It'd serve no purpose. Ida was Ellie's blind spot. If anything, she loved her too much. She's had enough heartbreak and disappointments in her life. No use adding another one."

Big John closed his eyes. His shoulders slumped weakly against the back of his chair, but his fingers never left the small stack of letters. "I loved Nita more than my life. I barely waited for my wife's body to be lowered into the grave before I lit out for Mexico to bring you and your mother back to the Circle C where you belonged, where you should have been born. In the end, though she confessed how she'd scared Nita into leaving, Ida didn't really think I'd find either of you. I almost didn't, and when I did it was too late for Nita, but at least I still had you. Bringing you back helped, even if you were a constant reminder of what a fool I'd been."

Branch pushed away from the fireplace, his dark eyes blazing as he turned the full force of his gaze on Big John. "You could have told me that you loved her," he said bitterly. "All these years, I've hated you for not loving her, for deserting her to marry someone more acceptable."

John's green eyes were dull with pain and regret. "It was easier to let you hate me," he confessed. "I deserved that and more for ruining your mother's life. She was so beautiful, so fine and gentle. I loved her so much. I knew I never should have touched her until I had the right, but I was selfish. I wanted her and never thought that I'd lose her."

A haunted expression came over his face. "Everyone knew that Alban Ricaud had been old Gregorio's choice for his daughter. When Nita disappeared, it was easy for Ida to convince me that the two of them had run off together to fulfill Gregorio's wish. I knew Nita and knew how important her family had been to her. I was feeling too sorry for myself to really think, to trust in the love Nita had professed for me. I was . . ." He shook his head, too choked with memories to continue.

"You were afraid," Branch supplied gruffly,

crossing the room to clasp Amanda's hand. "Afraid to believe that the woman you loved really loved you in return. There's no greater fear."

He held Amanda's gaze with his own, his dark eyes softer in their intensity than they had been since their arrival at the Circle C. "I should know," he said softly. The words were meant as much for Amanda as they were for Big John.

The jealousy over Big John's name being the last one on Nita's dying lips had ebbed away. Looking at his wife, knowing she carried his child, made him understand the depth of love his mother must have shared with his father. Branch knew that no matter how much he would love his child, it would never replace the feelings he had for its mother, no more than he could fill the space Big John had held in his mother's heart. Yet that jealousy was only part of it. He had to deal with it all—today.

He kissed Amanda's palm and gently replaced it in her lap before turning his attention back on his father. In a softer, less accusing tone, he began, "You brought me here and made me a Colson, but until today I've always thought of myself as a Villanueva."

"You're the best of both families," John asserted, his grave expression lightening just a little as he acknowledged Branch's oblique acceptance of the name that had been forced upon him. "Colson men and Villanueva men share two things. They love the land, and they love one woman for life. However, there's one big difference. Colsons fight for the land first, and Villanuevas put their woman first. I think Nita hoped that both would be there in her son, and that's why she named you after me and Rafalgo."

"Rafalgo?" Branch asked, one dark brow raised in puzzlement.

John's whimsical tone had effectively lightened the atmosphere, but Amanda had no doubt it was a temporary respite. No matter how brief, she welcomed it and settled back more comfortably in the chair, relaxing for the first time since she and Branch had left the Box H.

"Surprised you never heard of him," John said, his smile a little broader. "He was a real Spanish grandee somewhere way back in the Villanueva clan. According to the legend, he stole his wife right out from under her daddy's nose, then ran off to the New World. He left a title and land behind, but he had the woman he loved."

"I pulled a few tricks to get Amanda," Branch confessed, a touch of humor softening his mouth.

"What of his wife?" Amanda felt compelled to ask, though she doubted the lady had protested overmuch. She could easily imagine her husband as that long-ago romantic hero. Would any woman protest being kidnapped by him for very long?

"Had eight children and lived to a ripe old age," John supplied with a twinkle in his eyes. He and Branch shared a knowing chuckle that brought a bright blush to Amanda's cheeks. Big John pushed his chair away from the desk, finally moving his fingers away from Nita's letters.

His expression once again serious, he fixed a

steady gaze on Branch. "You've got more to say, son. Out with it now, so we can put it behind us once and for all."

Though his softer tone continued, Branch held back nothing. Big John was right. He needed to purge himself of the deep-seated hatred that had motivated him for the better part of his life. "I found a certain satisfaction in being your acknowledged bastard, thinking that every insult thrown at me went double for you."

Holding his father's gaze, he admitted, "Almost everything I did, I did to bring shame down on the Colson name, the way I thought a Colson had shamed a Villanueva."

John nodded. "I know. Like I said, Villanuevas fight for their women, all their women. Mothers, sisters, and most of all their wives." He shuddered visibly. "You came at me with a knife that first day, and you've been after me ever since."

"I lived for the day a Villanueva would take back everything that rightfully belonged to us, avenge our name." Branch stopped before one of the long windows, staring through the panes to the purple-shadowed land beyond. "The only thing I could never do, even though I knew it would hurt you the most, was attempt to destroy this land. You knew that, and I hated you for the control that knowledge gave you."

"You didn't hate me as much as I hated myself," John vowed heavily. "Every time I looked at you, I was reminded of the coward I'd been, but that wasn't all. I had three other sons by the time I found out about you, but from the first I loved you more. Your hatred seemed a fitting punishment for favoring you above the others."

"Favoring me?" Branch queried with an incredulous snicker. "Being worked like a plow horse and ridiculed at every turn was your idea of special treatment?"

Amanda knew that all was going to be well between these two strong, stubborn men when she saw Big John's answering grin and heard the honest affection in his voice as he retorted, "It earned you the respect of every man on this place, didn't it? On my land, Branch Colson is the king's son and treated as such. They've done that from the day I rode up with you perched in front of me in the saddle. Why do you think they called you Branch? Everyone knows the nickname stuck, cuz when this old oak falls you'll be there to live up to your roots."

"Everyone except me," Branch clarified. "I earned my place with my bare fists, and it galled me to know that you could yank the rug out from under me any time you chose."

"Never have, though, have I?" John questioned dryly. "Like I said, a pure case of favoritism." He reached across the desk and offered his hand, a gesture that had never been given before for fear it would be rebuffed.

John was shocked when the conciliatory gesture was ignored. He tried to cover the pain by dropping his hand to the desk, averting his eyes as Branch walked around the desk.

Branch leaned down and grasped his father's shoulders. *"Esta demonio, mi padre."*

"And I've lived for many years in my own

private hell," John murmured thickly, his relief almost palatable as his arms came up and tightened around his son. "But no more, son. No more."

"How very touching!"

"Graham?" Branch straightened away from his father and faced the man who had intruded on their reconciliation. "What are you doing here?"

"Protecting my interests," Graham announced, his lips curled in a sneer. "By the sound of things, that crippled old man has not only gone soft between the legs but soft in the head."

At Amanda's shocked gasp, Branch took a threatening step toward his half-brother, but Big John's staying hand gripped his thigh. "Let him talk," John ordered, seemingly unaffected by Graham's cruel insult. "To my recollection, this is the first time he's ever had the gumption to state his true feelings about me. Been pussy-footin' around me for years."

Big John's green eyes bored into Graham's face. "I 'spect folks have figured I might've lost my manhood three years back, but yours has been in doubt since you left the cradle."

Graham flushed at his father's damning verbal reprisal but, with uncustomary fortitude, held his ground. "You won't have cause to doubt it much longer, old man."

"Is that so?" John queried sarcastically as he loosened his grip on Branch's thigh and slipped his hand beneath his desk. "You've developed some backbone all of a sudden?"

Branch remained standing in front of his father, a self-derisive glitter in his dark eyes. "Big John, I've made a helluva mistake and gave you the wrong news first. I've got some very interesting facts to relay about Graham that I discovered on my trip to Dallas."

With a gaze as intense as his sire's, Branch focused on Graham. "I know you've been skimmin' off Circle C profits to line your own pockets, but your scheming goes even further than that, doesn't it?"

"I'm astounded, Mex." Graham showed no fear as he continued, "You must be smarter than you look. 'Course it wasn't too bright on your part to keep those suspicions to yourself."

His blue eyes slid to Amanda, and his smile was insolent as he went on, "I'm sure I've got you to thank for that lapse, dear cousin. You must be quite something in bed. Ever since you came, my bastard brother's hot Mexican blood drained out of his head and into his crotch. He's been too busy pleasuring you to put two and two together."

"Keep Amanda out of this." Branch lunged toward Graham but pulled back when an armed man appeared in the doorway. With lightning speed, Branch's hand was filled by his weapon, but no bullet was released from the chamber. Hank Turnbull's gun was aimed at Amanda's head. "Whatever you're after, Graham, my wife has nothing to do with it. Tell your man to point that gun somewhere else, or I'll blow his brains out."

"Not before Amanda sports a few new holes in that pretty face of hers," Graham advised coldly. "Drop your gun, Mex, and do it quick."

Branch had already sized up Turnbull as a professional killer and begrudgingly complied with Graham's order. He dropped his revolver onto the floor. He might have been able to get off a shot before Graham's hired gun, but the man could very well have killed Amanda before taking his last breath. He couldn't take the risk. "You'll never get away with this, Graham."

"Oh, won't I?" Graham jeered. "We're all alone. Lucía's off on her annual trip to San Antonio, and the boys are in town. I can finish my business with you, and no one will ever know I've even been here. All the hands are guarding the wrong place."

Turnbull stepped forward and kicked Branch's gun across the floor, well out of reach. "Got you real good in my sights this time, Colson," he taunted. "Last time my aim was off an inch or two, but up this close I ain't likely to miss."

Branch's eyes narrowed with hatred and self-condemnation. If he'd followed through with his investigation as soon as he'd arrived home from Dallas, nothing like this would have happened. He'd had a mistrust of Turnbull from the first day the man had set foot on the drilling site but had ignored his instincts. Now, not only himself but Amanda and his father would pay the price for his procrastination. On that score, Graham was right, and so was Big John. He was a Villanueva and had put his woman over his land. Now it appeared he was about to lose them both.

"From now on, Mex, you'll take orders from me, not Big John," Graham pronounced gleefully. "I suggest you follow them very carefully. Do exactly what I say, and I'll get rid of you before I get rid of her. She's still going to die, but at least you won't have to watch Turnbull with her first."

Amanda cringed back in her chair. She could sense Turnbull was already mentally stripping off her clothes, and bile rose in her throat. She looked to her husband, telling him with her eyes that she loved him and that no matter what happened, he was not to blame. She knew that nothing Turnbull could do to her would be worse than seeing her husband die.

Amanda tried to close out the scene around her, to prepare herself for an oblivion without thought so that she could withstand what was to come. But then, something deep within her urged her to fight back, not sit helplessly by doing nothing. The will to live, to protect the tiny life within her, was too strong.

Trying not to arouse suspicion, she glanced around the room, hoping to find some sort of weapon within range of her grasp. Branch's gun lay only a few feet away from her chair but still too far out of reach for her to get before Turnbull killed her. From beneath her lashes, she studied the armed man, hoping to see some sign of weakness, something she could use to her advantage.

"That's the only favor you're ever likely to get from me," Graham tormented, reveling in the fact that he'd rendered both Branch and Big John impotent. "You can take it or leave it." He had dreamed of this victory all his life and was going to savor every minute of it.

His blue eyes glowed with pleasure as he read

the rage on Branch's face. "I've finally bested you at something, haven't I? I've waited a long time to get back the place you stole from me. The Circle C, the Box H, and every last barrel of oil underneath them will belong to me. As Big John's lawyer, I've made sure your name won't even be mentioned in his will. Reese and Billy might question the circumstances surrounding your deaths, but not for long."

Like the successful lawyer he was, Graham completely outlined the defense he would use when Big John, Branch, and Amanda were found dead. "It's no secret that there's been bad blood between you, but I will be as shocked as anyone when it's discovered that your hatred led you to kill one another. I will be deeply aggrieved that Amanda had to be the innocent victim caught in your crossfire."

"Don't be a damned fool," Branch warned, but he could see that his words did nothing to diminish Graham's malice. "Up 'til now, no real harm's been done. But if you murder us, you'll be found out. Reese and Billy are a lot smarter than anybody gives them credit for. They know about all the accidents that have gone on at the Box H, and they'll figure out who was at the bottom of them."

"I've managed to keep the wool over everyone's eyes this long. I reckon I can a while longer," Graham bragged. "As soon as I occupy the governor's mansion, no one will have the guts to question anything I may have done in my past. After all, I've been a fine, upstanding citizen, a credit to the community, and all my father and his bastard have ever done is take advantage of their neighbors' misfortunes. After your funeral, Big John, it'll come out how you cheated Ezra Deets and old Seth Baker out of their land. They got paid half of your offer, and I pocketed the rest. As for you, Branch, not a soul in this town will mourn your passing."

"That's enough," John said before Branch could respond. "If it's more of my money you want, Graham, I'll see that you get it," he inserted quickly, reading the bloodlust in Graham's eyes, the anticipation on the face of the hired gun. There was no way on earth he was going to let this happen now that things had been put right between himself and Branch. Money meant nothing when compared to what he'd lose if Graham killed the only son of his conceived out of love.

"It took a fair amount of brains to embezzle money from me," John complimented him. "I'm impressed. I never suspected that I couldn't trust you. Keep on using those brains, Graham, and there's no reason we can't make an equitable arrangement for the future. You want to occupy the governor's mansion? I've got the power to see that you get there, and there won't be a noose looming over your head when you take office."

Graham laughed his dismissal of that idea, then directed Turnbull, "Tie and gag the woman until I've settled up with the beloved Colson heir."

He drew a derringer from his pocket and kept it focused on Branch as Turnbull holstered his gun and pulled a length of rope out of his hip pocket. "In the next few minutes, we'll determine who will die first. It'll be up to you, Mex. I want to see you on your knees and hear you beg. It doesn't matter much to me if you plead for his life or your own, but I'll promise to abide by your wishes."

"For God's sakes, Graham," John shouted, afraid Branch might soon be provoked beyond all reason and do something that would end any hope they had of escaping Graham's vengeance. "If you require beggin', it should come from me. By rights, I'm the one who fostered all this jealousy and hate by giving Branch what you thought was your due. Don't punish him for what's my fault."

*Now*, Amanda ordered herself as Turnbull stepped in front of her and Graham's attention was turned toward Big John. She leaped out of her chair and launched herself at Turnbull, catching him completely off-guard. One hand reached for the gun in his holster while the other clawed at his face.

Just as Amanda had hoped, Branch's reflexes were much faster than either Turnbull's or Graham's. In seconds, he had retrieved his own fallen gun, pulled Amanda to safety behind him, and taken aim on his half-brother. "That peashooter is no match for a forty-five, Graham, and we both know it."

"Nor would I put it up against this here ol' piece," John put in as he leaned backward in his chair, giving Branch a glimpse of the weapon he'd pulled out of his desk and was currently pointing at Turnbull. "Blink and you're a dead man," he admonished the paid killer as he watched the man struggle to regain his balance.

Turnbull's gun was heavy and unwieldy in Amanda's inexperienced hand, but she gamely aimed it at the killer. Standing next to her husband, she had the courage to point out, "I've got you covered, too, Turnbull."

Tongue in cheek, Branch proclaimed, "And I've been told she's pretty fast on the draw." He smiled down at his wife, enjoying his private joke even though the circumstances were without humor. When this was over, he'd make sure she was able to live up to her reputation.

It was clear to everyone in the room that the odds had been reversed, and John growled stonily, "Give it up, Graham, before I forget that you're still my son and shoot you where you stand."

Graham didn't move for several seconds, his hate-filled gaze locked on his father. It was apparent to everyone that he had a choice to make and had yet to make it. Even if Branch and Big John discharged their weapons, Graham might still be able to squeeze the trigger on the derringer. At such close range, the little weapon would put a sizable hole in Big John.

The moments ticked by, the suspense mounting as they all held their breath.

"It's all over, anyway," Graham muttered fatalistically.

Before anyone could make a move in his direction, to act on their horror, Graham turned his gun upon himself and fired. He fell backward onto the floor. His eyes locked with his father's as he mouthed his last words through a pink

bubble of blood. "I couldn't . . . kill you . . . no
. . . guts."

All eyes were on the derrick as the ominous
rumbling from far beneath the ground grew
louder. From his seat in the Oldsmobile, Big
John winked at his driver. "Think you'd better
move this contraption back a few feet, Ellie, or
we're goin' to get doused."

"Reckon so." Ellie frowned at the tiller and
fumbled with the gears. "I promised Amanda I'd
give this here buggy a try, but I don't mind
tellin' you, Big John, it's a whole lot easier just to
yank on some reins."

She struggled to find reverse while Thurman
hastened to crank up the stalled engine. "Looky
there. Them horses have got some sense and are
movin' back by they own selves." She pointed to
the nervous animals rearing away from the
hitching post. "They can outrun this blamed
machine, too."

Big John grinned. "I agree with you, Ellie, but
you and I have to change with the times. We've
been able to put aside the past."

"It was a right nice thing you did for Opal,
settling all that money on her and sending her
back to her Pa like you did. That poor gal never
did take to this country, and with Graham
gone . . . I sure am sorry about Graham, John."
Ellie reached across the seat and patted his
knee. "Never understand it. That boy had a
bright future, and he tossed it all away, grabbin'
out for what weren't his. I'm glad Ida didn't live
to see it."

Big John accepted Ellie's condolences in the

spirit in which they were given. "I have to take most of the blame for Graham. He was eaten up by jealousy, and I never saw it. Now all I can do is make sure his wife and child are well taken care of. With Turnbull and his gang locked up, we can all get on with the future."

"They's the future." Ellie pointed to the derrick where Branch and Amanda stood with their arms about each other. "That is, if they don't get blown up."

A loud grinding noise preceded the reverse motion of the Oldsmobile as Ellie finally managed to find the right gear. Both occupants breathed a sigh of relief when they were safely moved back from the drilling rig. Their escape had been just in time, for a geyser of mud spurted up from the well.

"It's gonna blow!" Karl Molinski shouted as he jumped off the vibrating platform. "Everybody back!"

Amanda stood spellbound, staring at a dream about to come true.

"This is it, Peaches," Branch yelled as he picked her up and started running. Before they were more than thirty yards away, a high-velocity jet of water shot up from the hole. Drenched by the muddy rain, Branch paused and set Amanda back on her feet. His fingers squeezed her hands tightly as they both turned back to watch.

Two hearts rose and sank in time with the brown gush of water that spurted upward toward the sky, then back down again. Seconds later, the vibrating stopped, and the waterspout fizzled to nothing. Despairing tears welled up in

Amanda's eyes as the dirty water spilled off the derrick and pooled on the ground. "We've come up dry," she wailed as a collective groan of disappointment rose up from the crowd of people watching from the ridge.

"Maybe not, maybe not, Peaches," Branch encouraged, his eyes riveted on the hole. "Have a little faith. You convinced me we were drillin' in the right place, and I've heard of this happenin' before. There's gotta be oil down there. You're a damned fine geologist."

Amanda could feel the trembling in his fingers and knew he wasn't half as confident as he sounded. She loved him even more for declaring his respect for her ability when it might very well turn out to be unfounded. A current of conciliation passed through their clasped fingers, and both knew that even if the well failed they would still be wealthy. As Ellie had said months before, "A body could be in a lot worse straits than to have a spread like this to call home." They had the Box H, each other, the love of their families, and a new baby to look forward to.

Suddenly, the ground shook beneath their feet. Amanda reached for her husband as a new sound, a much more powerful one, gathered force around them. The drilling crew started shouting with glee before the first spurt of thick black oil bubbled out of the pipe. In the next instant, the bubble burst into a gushing ebony tower.

As slick, smelly oil cascaded down from the skies, Branch scooped Amanda off her feet, spun her around, and let out a whoop. "We did it,

Mrs. Colson! We've just struck enough oil to keep your Oldsmobile going 'til the day we die! A hundred of them damned machines! A thousand!"

Amanda's laugh was filled with jubilation. Her face was black, her hair hung in oily strands, and her clothes were covered with muck, but she had never felt better. "I love you, cowboy!" she shouted. "The best day of my life was the day I rammed through your fence."

"And my heart, Peaches," Branch shouted back. "This dumb old cowpoke has never been the same. With you as my wife, I get smarter every day."

His mouth came down on hers in an exuberant kiss. Cheers resounded from the ridge at their embrace as everyone around them applauded their success. Within the security of her husband's arms, Amanda applauded, too, but for another reason. She knew that today was a perfect reflection of her future with Branch. Their love would always be as free-flowing, explosive, and bountiful as the black gold gushing up from their well, as rich and lasting as the fathomless treasure they had discovered beneath their land.

# Tapestry

## HISTORICAL ROMANCES

## POCKET BOOKS

# If you've enjoyed the love, passion and adventure of this Tapestry™ historical romance...be sure to enjoy them all, FREE for 15 days with convenient home delivery!

Now that you've read a Tapestry™ historical romance, we're sure you'll want to enjoy more of them. Because in each book you'll find love, intrigue and historical touches that really make the stories come alive!

You'll meet Aric of Holmsbu, a daring Viking nobleman...courageous Jeremiah Fox, an American undercover agent in Paris...Clint McCarren, an Australian adventurer of a century ago...and more. And on each journey back in time, you'll experience tender romance and searing passion...and learn about the way people lived and loved in earlier times.

Now that you're acquainted with Tapestry romances, you won't want to miss a single one! We'd like to send you 2 books each month as soon as they are published, through our Tapestry Home Subscription Service℠ Look them over for 15 days, free. If not delighted, simply return them and owe nothing. But if you enjoy them as much as we think you will, pay the invoice enclosed.

There's never any additional charge for this convenient service— we pay all postage and handling costs.

To begin your subscription to Tapestry historical romances, fill out the coupon below and mail it to us today. You're on your way to all the love, passion and adventure of times gone by!

HISTORICAL *Tapestry* ROMANCES

Tapestry™ is a trademark of Simon & Schuster, Inc.          T103P5